FIRST CONTACT . . .

The quake shook the facility so hard that parts of the ceiling tumbled down and filled the corridor with dust. Huge support beams thrust through the cast plastic walls and ceiling, letting in debris and dirt from above.

Walden took Anita's arm and turned her around. There was no time to spare: the entire Sov-Lat complex was disintegrating from the Frinn attack.

"I need to look around!" Anita protested. "We need information!"

"We're leaving alive and to hell with what the Soviets were doing here." Walden guided her to the entrance. A quick check of his displays showed elevated radiation levels; the Frinn had melted the doors off with their microwave cannon.

"We got big problems, Doc," said Hecht. "Take a gander at the reports I'm getting."

Walden didn't have to ask for an interpretation of what flashed across the displays. The Frinn had circled them and now concentrated all their fire on a small area.

And they were standing squarely in the middle of that target . . .

BIOWARRIORS
Book One

THE
INFINITY PLAGUE

Robert E. Vardeman

ACE BOOKS, NEW YORK

This book is an Ace original
edition, and has never been
previously published.

THE INFINITY PLAGUE

An Ace Book/published by arrangement with
the author

PRINTING HISTORY
Ace edition/August 1989

ISBN: 0-441-06266-0

Ace Books are published by The Berkley Publishing Group,
200 Madison Avenue, New York, New York 10016.
The name ''ACE'' and the ''A'' logo
are trademarks belonging to Charter Communications, Inc.

PRINTED IN THE UNITED STATES OF AMERICA

10 9 8 7 6 5 4 3 2 1

*After a long time, this one is for
Lois Duncan*

CHAPTER
1

"This will not work," whispered a shadow-cloaked man. "It is too primitive. We cannot know it will give us the death required for our statement!"

The woman sighed softly and shook her head, even though the man could not see her response in the darkness. She knew the loutish terrorist accompanying her preferred the complex, the intricately overwrought to the elegant. Her orders were simple; her methods reflected this.

And became even deadlier because of it.

"Trust me. They are capable and can detect electronic timers. Acid fuses emit vapors their sniffers pick up easily. Even passive radio or laser pulse detonators will not work for this mission. Their security is too tight."

"But a mechanical timer! It is madness! It will never work."

She ignored him. What did he know of terrorism, of mass killing and striking fear into the hearts of the enemy? She had conducted four successful campaigns in the very stronghold of the North American Alliance. Those had been direct, quick strikes reducing launch ports and busy passenger terminals to rubble. She smiled in memory of her *real* accomplishments. She had penetrated the Emperor's Palace in Tokyo and assassinated their foreign minister. *That* had been a masterful piece of work.

1

She had received the Order of Lenin for it in secret ceremonies presided over by the Premier and the entire Politburo. And she had deserved it. The intricate, diabolical Japanese security had been difficult to circumvent.

That they had retaliated by scuttling the Premier's pleasure yacht on the Black Sea and killing fourteen people did not concern her. The Premier had been rescued before the Japanese aquatic killer robots had finished gnawing off his legs.

"The real problem," she said, "is constructing the bomb so that they cannot detect the presence of explosives. Surface acoustic wave detectors can find a milligram of our bomb amid thousands of kilos of inert mass."

"Their sniffers are worthless. We can use more accurate timers and detonators."

The man's scorn for her ability and that of the NAA security specialists began to irritate her. Centuries of inborn Latino machismo and contempt for women, even highly trained and well-placed field representatives of the Sov-Lat Pact, could not be erased quickly.

"They will die. Confusion will dog their steps. What more do you want?"

She tensed when she heard the muffled whine of a charging laserifle.

"I will kill them and *know* that they die!"

She moved away from him. There would be violent death on this night of celebration. The dawning of the year A.D. 2101 would find many fewer inhabitants of the world—and her companion would be among the dead.

Dr. Jerome Walden lounged back in the chair. The softly moving electric currents inside the fabric found the tensed muscles of his back and applied just the amount of voltage required to relax him. When the subtle heat began welling up through the cushions, he fought to keep from drifting off to sleep.

"Do we have to go, Anita?" he asked.

"You know we do," the tall, flame-haired woman said as she came from the bedroom. "It's our last New Year's on Earth." Anita Tarleton motioned and mirrored a wall. She spun around, studying herself critically for the smallest of flaws. If she found any, she didn't comment. Walden saw only perfection in every line of her body, tantalizingly revealed—then mysteriously hidden—by the ever-shifting transparent patches in the dress.

"You've never shown much sentiment about the planet before. Why now?" Walden rolled over and let the chair conform to his body. New tingles danced along his chest and thigh and hints of coolness kept him from perspiring. "You're not upset over lifting for Schwann, are you?"

"I'd rather work here. I know it's silly, but being so far from home bothers me." She settled onto the chair beside him, the electrically clinging cobalt-blue fabric of her evening gown shimmering as it interacted with the chair's field. Tiny flashes of lightning raced around her trim body and left the clear spots that tantalized Walden.

He reached up and gently touched her cheek. The woman's makeup sizzled and popped, causing him to jerk back.

"Why do you wear that stuff?"

Anita smiled and bent to kiss him. The light brush of her lips on his sent his heart racing. The lipstick carried a gengineered pheromone.

"What is that?" he asked, startled. He had been relaxed. The scent, the touch, the notion that he *heard* her makeup, excited him. "You didn't put drugs in it, did you?"

"Not this time, not exactly. I know I shouldn't have done it, but I mixed this batch up specially for tonight."

"It's part of your project?" Walden tried to calm himself and couldn't. The fleeting kiss had aroused him completely. "You shouldn't risk exposure like that of a classified discovery."

Anita sighed and ran her fingers through the soft pile of brilliant hair. Tiny diamond sparkles appeared wherever her nails touched. "Everything's classified," she said in disgust. "I hope we don't have to be so tight-mouthed on Schwann. I want to talk over my work, especially with you."

"Just because we're forty zillion light-years from Earth doesn't mean security will be lax." Walden took deep breaths to quiet his accelerated pulse; it didn't work. The bio-engineered protein in Anita's lipstick kept him aroused. His thoughts turned to what it might do for him during lovemaking.

"I know what you want. You'd prefer leaving behind the security force, too, but you go along with them," she said. "Jerome, you can be such a fool at times. But I love you."

"I've got nothing against your project. Hell, I know mine will probably be turned into some sort of weapon, too, but I've got confidence we'll never use it that way."

He rolled onto his back and looked at her, still wondering what genetically engineered miracle she had worked into the lipstick. His own field of signal transmission in the human nervous system had only peripheral impact on the biowar research being done by the NAA. Anita's mutated viruses and aerosol delivery systems were funded heavily and had great attention focused on them. Walden didn't care that she was the shining star for the military. His work was important and might make life less painful for those afflicted with degenerative nerve diseases. He might even be able to repair those damaged by Anita's researches.

He smiled more broadly. Besides any humanitarian concerns, they needed him. He was one of the few scientists able to effectively administer large projects. He was the bureaucrat-scientist, a new breed that hadn't come out of the gengineering test tube.

"I could lie here staring at you all night," he said. The chemical effects lingered, but that wasn't what he referred to. The gamboling dress teased and tormented. Patches of seductively perfumed white skin would show for a millisecond, then be hidden. No part of Anita's body seemed immune from the flashing glimpse, yet certain spots never—quite—were fully revealed. How the designer had wrought such a gown was beyond Walden's imagination. He often thought more time and effort went into designing women's clothing than into any other field.

"We ought to go. I don't want to miss the New Year displays."

"We can create some of our own here," he said.

"We can do that anytime. This is our last party on Earth. Please, Jerome. For me."

He heaved himself to his feet. "For you, my dear, anything. To the party! Our chariot awaits!" He touched a stud on his wristwatch. A reply signal flashed twice showing that the cab had been summoned and would be waiting for them by the time they reached ground level. They left the apartment arm in arm, pausing only to be sure the locking mechanisms secured the door against intruders. The elevator dropped them forty stories to the street. As elegantly as he could, Walden escorted Anita to the front door. His watch pulsed once and keyed open the defense door. Two quick steps through the dangerous night got them to the armored cab.

It accelerated away smoothly as they settled into the cushioned rear seats.

Walden sat holding Anita's hand in silence. Neither spoke. Rumors always circulated in their social circles about how the cabs were festooned with spy devices—and not all were of NAA origin. Walden had lived under extreme security conditions long enough to appreciate the need for caution. Besides, he had little need to speak. He sat staring at the enchanting woman next to him, wondering how he had ever been lucky enough to attract her.

Anita Tarleton might not have had the beauty of the vidnews reporters or the stunning elegance of a Thespian, but Anita was not computer-enhanced and carefully remodeled to fit the current ideas of attractiveness. Walden knew she had never had cosmetic surgery, even if she did indulge in the gengineered lipsticks and makeup.

Their eyes met. Anita started to speak, then stopped. She knew the value of security better than he did. Her projects were dangerous. Anita's eyes flickered from purple to a deep blue as her emotions changed.

"Dye?" he mouthed. She nodded. Walden smiled and lightly kissed her, again experiencing the surge of primal lust for her. She almost laughed at him; she knew the effect her lipstick had—and enjoyed every instant of his discomfort.

The cab beeped to indicate that they approached their destination. The armored window plates lowered to give him a view unhindered by protective devices. He glanced around and saw several marines in full battle gear at curbside. By the door leading into the Japanese ambassador's home four more marines in formal uniform stood stiffly at attention. Behind them a few paces and just inside the security doors milled the ambassador's own guards.

Walden touched the ACCEPT stud on his watch and the appropriate fare was debited from his account and paid to the autocab company. The door slid open. He and Anita hurried out. The tiny warmth at his wrist betrayed the spy beams searching him and Anita as they walked briskly to the security door. The guards inside were already opening up for them; they didn't have to break stride as they entered.

"Made it again," he said, letting out breath he hadn't even known he was holding. Going out unescorted at night always bothered him. Both he and Anita rated two bodyguards from the military science's guard pool, but New Year's Eve had drained all available personnel. More important personages were out and about Los Angeles, and minor scientists had to fend for themselves.

"Dr. Walden, Dr. Tarleton, a true honor. Thank you for joining us this evening."

"Mr. Ambassador," Anita spoke up, bowing the proper amount in response to his greeting. "It is a true distinction in our group to be invited to such a ceremonious occasion at your home. The honor is ours. We will never be able to repay you." Anita bowed even more deeply to show that they were truly appreciative of the invitation to the second most important New Year's party in the capital. Only the NAA President's Gala exceeded this one in prestige.

Walden swung around when he heard scuffling behind him. Two officers in the Japanese Army tugged at each other's lapels in a manner showing true disrespect. This startled him. The Japanese never betrayed such gaucheness in front of NAA personnel.

"What is it, Major Nagura?"

"Sir!" The nearest officer bowed deeply. From this position he began speaking rapidly in Japanese. Both Walden and Anita understood the language enough to get by; the officer rattled off code phrases meaningless without the proper key. Walden and Anita exchanged glances. Such rudeness on the officer's part meant trouble.

Walden took Anita's arm and pulled her back a pace. "Should we leave?" he asked in a whisper.

"No," she said. "It might not be anything."

Both knew she was wrong. The second officer stepped forward. Walden saw that the man was only a captain—and he had physically assaulted a superior officer. Major Nagura, the captain, and the ambassador exchanged a dozen code phrases. The ambassador shut off further discussion with a chopping motion of his left hand.

"Is there anything we can do, sir?" Walden asked.

Walden knew the matter was far more serious than he had thought when an insincere smile crossed the ambassador's face. Ambassador Honda-ko negotiated with the NAA and the Soviet-Latino Pact countries and never showed a flicker of emotion. Now he worked desperately to conceal his true feelings.

"Please enjoy yourselves. Excuse me. I must greet other guests. Doctors." Honda-ko bowed perfunctorily and hurried off toward a concealed command post instead of greeting the New Zealand prime minister and his wife.

"Something has him rattled."

Anita nodded. They stood together near one wall, studying the revelers in the huge ballroom. Most danced to the synthesized music with abandon. A few huddled near the bar and worked their way through scores of new and enticingly different inebriants concocted for the festivities by Japan's finest psychochemists. Still others refused to leave behind their duties and stood in small groups, discussing business matters trivial and significant.

"They're bug-sweeping. See?" Walden pointed to a half dozen inconspicuously dressed men and women walking around the periphery of the room. Most carried small devices in their hands, which they consulted constantly. Major Nagura stood near the command post, a com-link pressed to his left ear. If any of the guards' detectors found anything amiss, he would know immediately.

"Something's not going right. That junior officer is still making a nuisance of himself." Walden watched in fascination as the captain argued with Nagura.

"He—" Anita's comment was cut off by the surge in activity among the guards. The party-goers on the dance floor never noticed. One or two at the bar might have. Only Jerome Walden and Anita Tarleton saw the frantic grabbing for weapons. Whatever the guards had found, they had discovered it simultaneously. Eight turned their small but potent pistols on a spot high above the floor.

Walden started to cry out. His incoherent yelp was drowned out by the buzzing of the pistols firing and eight explosive shells finding their target in the sniper's body.

The assassin rose and teetered precariously on the decorative ledge. He tried to touch the gaping hole in his chest; his hand had been blown off. Words refused to form. Part of his jaw was gone. The only sound came when his laserifle clattered to the floor two stories below. Major Nagura scooped it up and backed off in time to avoid the falling corpse.

"Efficient sons of bitches, aren't they?" observed Anita. Nagura's guards removed the body so quickly only a few nearby revelers noticed any disturbance.

Walden nodded, but his attention remained on the captain. The man's agitation had grown. Killing the sniper had done nothing to soothe him.

"Let's dance," said Anita.

Walden and Anita melted into each other's arms and drifted across the dance floor in perfect step, but Walden couldn't get the captain's protest out of his mind. The old year, 2100, had seen thousands of similar scenes. NAA and Japanese security forces had been especially effective against Sov-Lat-backed terrorists. One classified document he had seen reported over fourteen hundred killed, most caught at gatherings like this one. Walden had no doubt that the NAA had sent an equal number of killers against Soviet-Latino targets.

But for all his outward calm, he shared the captain's uneasiness. Why would an assassin clever enough to penetrate the considerable perimeter security stupidly expose himself—and with a laserifle whose power source was quickly detected?

"Cat's-paw," he said.

"What?"

He gazed down into Anita's eyes. They had changed to a sea green. "There's something more planned."

"Of course. It's a few minutes until midnight." Anita sighed and rested her head against his shoulder. Tiny blue and green sparks flew wherever her hair touched his metallic-thread dinner jacket.

He glanced toward the end of the room. A replica of the ancient Times Square red ball poised at the top of a twenty-meter-tall shaft. Below it a pendulum clock ticked off the minutes until the new year.

"I wish I could have seen the original," Anita said softly next to his ear. "The city must have been special."

"It's gone," he said, more bitterly than he intended. New York—what was left of it—lay fifty meters underwater.

"Jerome, please, let's enjoy ourselves. I want this to be fun." She raised her lips. He kissed her and the surge of animal lust passed through his loins once more.

"With you, I don't need anything artificial," he said, kissing her with increasing passion.

He broke off and stared at the mechanical clock. Anita started to protest.

"Wait," he said. "Something is wrong."

"Jerome," she said in exasperation. "Can't you *ever* relax, even for a few minutes? This is a party. The guards removed the terrorist."

He spun from her arms and motioned to the captain. The man came over.

"How may I help you, sir?"

"I saw your argument with Major Nagura."

"I am shamed." The officer hid his face in both hands. Walden grabbed the man's wrists and pulled his hands away.

"You might be right." He outlined his suspicion about the ease with which the sniper had been detected.

"Hai, I understand this," the captain said. "I have a premonition of something more. They are cunning."

"Jerome, it's almost midnight."

"Sorry, dear." Walden's eyes flashed once more to the mechanical clock. "Why did you choose such an old-fashioned timepiece? It's out of place, even with the New York Times Square theme."

"The original timer malfunctioned," said the captain. "We replaced it this afternoon with that relic. It has been checked thoroughly."

"How?" asked Anita, interested in spite of her desire to partake fully of the festival mood and ignore everything else. "That isn't a wood cabinet. The grain is wrong."

"Is it? I have seldom seen real wood," said the captain.

Walden went cold inside. He had worked on explosives projects during graduate school. A few early attempts had produced explosives looking suspiciously like the mock-wood clock case. "The entire case might be a bomb," he said in a choked voice. He grabbed Anita's arm and began pulling her away from the ticking clock.

"They've checked it," she protested. "There can't be an electronic detonator in it." Even as she spoke, her face paled.

"Mechanical detonation!" The captain pushed them aside and ran toward the clock. The hands pointed upward and the clock began striking midnight. The illuminated red sphere began to slowly descend.

The final chime of the clock, the ball's fall, and the eye-searing, deafening detonation came simultaneously.

CHAPTER

"That's all?" asked Jerome Walden, still shaken. He knew he shouted because of the deafening ringing in his ears, but he couldn't stop himself.

"This is most unfortunate," said Major Nagura, hands clasped behind his back. The security officer looked as if he would start pacing at any instant.

Walden glanced around the ballroom. The captain had thrown himself on top of the clock cabinet just as it exploded. The officer had been vaporized; only a thin red mist on walls and party-goers remained of him. But his action had saved most of those in the room. Nagura claimed that only six others were injured.

"No one else died," the major declared. "Shinji died in a fitting manner. His name will be honored at the Kyoto cherry blossom festival this spring." He bowed abruptly, spun, and went about the disagreeable task of cleaning the room.

"When can we lift for Delta Cygnus 4?"

"What?" Walden's mind had been on the havoc wrought all around. Anita's question took him by surprise.

"This isn't home anymore," she said. "I don't want to live on a world where death is this easy."

Walden said nothing. Pointing out that they contributed to

such terrorism through their work wasn't what she needed to hear. He put his arm around her shaking shoulders and held her. A tiny trickle of blood ran across his hand. Gently touching the wound on her arm, he saw that it had been caused by a thin white sliver. He swallowed hard. It was a piece of bone from the heroic Captain Shinji. Walden delicately plucked the sharp-edged piece from Anita's arm. She never noticed.

"May I be of assistance?" The voice slid out soft, sibilant, and threatening in spite of the offer.

Walden looked up and saw a small, sallow-complected woman. From her nondescript evening dress he knew she belonged to the ambassador's security force.

"We'd like to be escorted home."

"I will see to it. Until starlift next Tuesday we will assign you protection." Her tone indicated that she found such trivial duty beneath her station.

"How do you know that?" Anita jerked erect and stared down at the woman. "Launch schedules are secret."

"This unpleasant . . . occurrence has robbed me of my manners. Permit me to introduce myself properly. I am Miko Nakamura, civilian advisor to your EPCT." She pronounced the acronym for Extra-Planetary Combat Team like a veteran, turning it into ee-pee-cee-tee.

"Civilian?" questioned Walden.

Anita smiled without humor. "Your leaders feel that too much contact between the Japanese Hegemony and the NAA is unwise. I do not hold rank; I merely *advise*."

Her emphasis told him that her position was one of command, no matter what the title proclaimed officially. Japanese advisors had proven invaluable in the forty years of guerrilla wars in Central and South America before the NAA had withdrawn and built the Amity Wall across the Isthmus of Panama. Since then, their influence had grown as the NAA's power declined in the world.

"We'll appreciate getting home."

"It will be my great pleasure to accompany you to the *Hippocrates* next Tuesday," Nakamura said. She folded her hands and bowed slightly. Walden noticed the edges of her hands had unusual calluses. Seeing his interest, she said in her softly menacing tone, "Your laboratories have produced many remarkable gengineered cells."

Nakamura held out her hand. "The cells where a knife-edge blow would be delivered have been replaced with artificial ones enjoying iron consistency."

"You need bone reinforcement for that," Anita said, obviously horrified at the idea of such genetic enhancement.

"Of course." Nakamura smiled nastily. She turned, moving with lightning speed. Her hand smashed down onto a table. The pseudo-wood top exploded under the force of her blow. Nakamura held out her hand to show that it had survived uninjured. She gestured and two of the full-dress NAA marines came up.

"Escort the doctors home," Nakamura commanded. She bowed formally, then walked briskly to where the ambassador and Major Nagura exchanged heated words. Walden saw from the two men's stiffening who held the superior rank. The ambassador's bow was significantly deeper than Nakamura's. Nagura held back, saying nothing as Nakamura and the ambassador talked.

"She's going to accompany us to Schwann?"

"From the way she uses her hand, she can go anywhere she wants."

"I'm glad she's on our side," said Anita.

"She," said Walden, "is on her own side. If it suits her purpose to help us, she will. Otherwise, we'd better plan on covering our own asses."

"Promises, promises," Anita said. She pressed closer to him, her hand slipping across his stomach, then hinting at a journey lower. "This is 2101, a new year. Let's celebrate it the way you wanted in the first place."

"Alone? Just the two of us?"

"Just us," Anita promised, "and our two faithful guards."

They went to get an autocab, arms around each other, ignoring the clicking boots of the marines following them.

"What took so long?" Walden asked, irritated.

"Sorry. Dr. Greene changed my research assignment for when we get to Schwann. I had to approve new equipment and two new team members." Anita Tarleton sat next to Walden, her mind already light-years away from Earth. She hardly noticed him.

"This is a bit late to be starting a new project, isn't it?"

"Definitely."

"If it's similar to what you were doing before, it won't be too hard, I suppose."

"I can't talk about it, Jerome. This isn't just classified, it's super top secret. I'm supposed to cut out my tongue before going to bed every night, if I talk in my sleep."

"This is ridiculous," he said. "I'm project director. I have to know what every member's doing if anything goes wrong. You know all the containment problems that might occur."

"Sorry. Dr. Greene specifically said I wasn't to discuss this with you."

"What!"

Anita looked apologetic. "He said it is part of a new push by NAA to dry up security leaks—not that he thinks you are one. You wouldn't be director, if he did. Anyway, the reason we're going to Delta Cygnus 4 is to avoid contamination hazards. Who cares if we trash a planet with only rudimentary lifeforms on it?"

"This is carrying 'need to know' too far. Someone's got to be accountable. While we're working on Delta Cygnus 4, it's *me*."

"Jerome, you know I agree. But these are direct orders. I don't think Greene likes them any better than we do. I had the impression that they came down from *very* high in the chain of command."

Walden heaved a deep, shuddery sigh and walked off. Anita called after him, but he was too angry to accept anything less than complete disclosure—and that was as likely to happen as the Sov-Lats and the NAA calling off their sniping terrorist warfare.

Everyone distrusted everyone else. They had to. The bio-weapons Walden turned out of his laboratories could obliterate all life on Earth. Walden knew what the change had been in Anita's assignment, in general terms if not specifically. She had worked on defensive bio-guards. New orders meant they had given her offensive bioweapons work.

"Just what we need," Walden grumbled as he pushed into his deserted lab. "More ways of infecting each other."

"Distemper?" asked a whining, high-pitched voice. Walden turned to a rough, wet tongue intent on licking his face.

"Get down. Go on, oh, hell, go on." He hunkered down and let the large dog sniff and lick to its heart's content. The animal's heredity was obviously confused. The coloration marked it as a German shepherd, but the whipcord body suggested a greyhound and the legs were too short by half—a dachshund might have entered the genetic mix at some point. Making the animal even stranger looking was the massive head. A hologram of only the creature's head might have caused misidentification as a St. Bernard.

"Taste . . . sexy." The dog continued to lick across Walden's face, occasionally touching his lips.

Walden pushed the dog away. "Must be residue left over from Anita's lipstick." The New Year's party at the Japanese ambassador's had been almost a week ago but the insidiously powerful aphrodisiac Anita had used in her lipstick still lingered. He found himself getting excited at odd times until he stopped chewing nervously on his bottom lip.

"She's a sexy bitch." The dog sat on his haunches and tipped his massive head to one side. "Can I have her?"

"No!" Walden laughed at his own vehemence. Egad's intelligence was unsurpassed—for a canine. Egad—Enhanced intelligence, Genetically Altered Dog—could too easily be mistaken for a human in his logical reactions. His emotional responses and his physical drives were only slightly less restrained than the average dog's, however.

Egad dropped flat on the floor and put his paws on either side of his head. His long, ratlike black tail slithered under his back legs. He showed obeisance to the alpha animal: Jerome Walden.

"Sorry," Egad said.

"That's all right. Anita's to blame. She shouldn't use that lipstick."

The dog laid his head against Walden's thigh, one huge brown eye and a smaller blue one on the left staring up. Walden tried to judge what thoughts ran through the animal's brain. As always, he failed. For all his friendliness, Egad was an alien creature produced through a bastard combination of Nature and human fiddling. A mechanical, slightly tinny voice was produced by a transducer placed against the dog's throat muscles and translated by a small computer embedded in the bulky collar.

Sometimes, Walden wished that he had never embarked on the research that had developed Egad. He had been experimenting with improved neuron transmission in animal brains, hoping to learn enough to repair neurological damage in humans. The data he had obtained were barely satisfactory; Egad was a rare find.

"You are sorry you hide me," the dog said suddenly.

"What?" Walden looked away, a guilty flush burning his cheeks. The dog had the uncanny knack of knowing what *he* thought, even if the process didn't work the other way. "Nonsense. I'm happy you're here, alive, with me."

"Gets lonely."

"I know. For that, I'm sorry." He hugged Egad.

"Never be more like me." The dog spoke without emotion. Walden knew that the poor creature had long ago become resigned to the fact. Only a few even knew of Egad's abilities. The NAA Research Council might have brought criminal charges against him if they had learned of his work.

Now it hardly mattered. Egad was coming along with him to Delta Cygnus 4.

"Have you policed the lab?"

"Nothing left," the dog said. "All equipment gone. Bad-smelling men took it this morning."

"Good. Come on. We've got to get to the launch site. The *Hippocrates* is waiting in orbit for us. Once we're aboard, it's off for the stars!"

The dog clacked his teeth together and rocked his head to and fro. This was all the response he gave. Walden wasn't sure if Egad even understood the concept of stars and space and other solar systems. He patted the dog's huge head and got a broad wink of the brown eye as his reward.

"There you are," called Anita, sticking her head into the nearly empty lab. "Miko Nakamura sent a cab to take us to the launch port."

"We're ready to go," said Walden.

"Are you ready, Egad?"

The dog turned from the woman and peered up questioningly at Walden.

"No!" Walden said firmly.

"What's that about?" asked Anita.

"Never mind. You don't want to know."

"Are you so sure?" Anita bent and patted Egad, then gave the top of his head a quick kiss.

"Let's get out of here. The old labs have too many memories for me," said Walden. He had come here immediately out of college. His first fumbling research in nerve transmission had been done here, as well as his more important work that had brought him a modicum of fame and the position of project leader.

In spite of leaving behind equipment too heavy to transport across forty-seven light-years, Walden felt good about the move. The research his bio-team conducted was dangerous, possibly too hazardous for an Earth teeming with eleven billion humans. Delta Cygnus 4 was a perfect site for many reasons, not the least of which being the lack of spying and authorities continually interrupting him. He preferred privacy when he worked, and he seldom got it around the national labs.

"Hurry, Jerome. There's the autocab."

Anita quickly scanned the area for danger. Seeing nothing, she sprinted for the autocab and slid in. Walden and Egad followed closely. The cab accelerated smoothly, and the combat shutters rose to block any possible attack. A small vidscreen gave a 360-degree scan of the area to put any passenger fears to rest.

Walden knew better than to trust electronic imaging. A good tech could jam the vid and provide any picture desired. He always demanded full lowering of the shutters before getting out. What he saw with his own eyes had to be more reliable than the pictures relayed by a CCD camera.

Egad nuzzled his ear and took the opportunity to ask, "Talk?"

Walden and Anita both shook their heads. Autocabs were notorious security leaks. The dog accepted this and curled up at their feet.

"Not much longer. Nakamura said we'd be met at the port by the NAA security force leader."

"An EPCT officer?" Walden had dealings with military administrators in his position as research director. The off-planet soldiers were the hardest to cope with. They were more inclined to ask for weapons to destroy a world than bio-products to surgically remove a tiny impediment to official policy enforcement.

"She seems to have a considerable amount of power over this expedition," said Walden.

"You know how it is." Anita shrugged and stared at the vidscreen. "We're almost at the launch site. See?"

The vidscreen shimmered as the onboard computer magnified the forward picture. A stubby, pock-mocked cargo shuttle stood in the center of the launch field. Plumes of liquid nitrogen vapor rose all around from cooling the superconducting coils immediately under the tarmac. In a few minutes, the cargo shuttle would be lowered through the magnetic launch rings, then mass-driven skyward with the flip of a switch.

"There's Nakamura. I'd recognize her a light-year off." The woman stood with feet planted in a fighting stance. Her arms were crossed and she was rocking forward slightly onto the balls of her feet. She looked as if she would explode violently at any instant.

"The man she's talking to is in full-dress uniform. He must be an honor guard."

"For us?" Walden was skeptical. He reached down and patted Egad, keeping the dog silent. Egad reacted violently to the organic dyes used in NAA dress uniforms.

"Why not? We're important. You're the head of the bio-research team—and I'm with you." She squeezed his arm. The autocab doors popped open, taking them both by surprise. The usual security measures had been dispensed with.

"Glad you're on time," the brilliantly uniformed officer said sarcastically. "I'd hate to leave you behind."

"Nakamura," greeted Walden, ignoring the NAA major. "It is a pleasure to see you again."

"I'm Major Edouard Zacharias." The man turned slightly to be certain both of them saw his row of medals. "I'm the one who rescued the battle team on Persephone. Operation Pomegranate.''

Neither Walden nor Anita said anything. Walden wondered if Zacharias would babble on. He had heard of the rescue but remembered little of the details. A Sov-Lat combat unit had attacked a small garrison on a remote world used for testing spy equipment. A fully equipped frigate had orbited the world, a miserable hunk of rock and bad air, and landed a marine detachment. From the way he paraded around, thrusting out his chest and drawing himself up, Zacharias must have been the officer in charge of the mission.

''Pleased that you're here to see us off,'' said Walden, prepared to ignore any further puffery from the officer.

''You misunderstand,'' cut in Nakamura. She bowed the barest amount in the major's direction. ''He is military commander for the expedition.''

''He's going with us? All the way to Delta Cygnus 4?'' Walden sighed. Again he had to deal with hardheaded military officers. He had hoped to limit his diplomacy to hardheaded scientists.

''Hai.'' The woman bowed more deeply. ''Come. It is time for us to prepare. We will launch in the next shuttle.''

They entered the small glass-walled building which was little more than a waiting room for an elevator. Walden turned to watch the shuttle already on the field being lowered into the launch tube. The plumes of dense vapor rose in a thick fog. The superconducting coils hummed with energy and sent vibrations through the soles of his shoes.

''There she goes!'' cried Anita. She pressed against the window in rapt fascination, watching the dull-skinned cargo craft erupt from the Earth and shoot upward.

The blast when the cargo shuttle exploded blew out even the shatterproof safety glass in the small building.

CHAPTER

They stood, staring at the fiery debris raining down on the launch port. Major Zacharias was the first to recover. He touched his lapel com-link and barked, "Seal the area. Bring in troops. We have a terrorist situation. Repeat, we have a terrorist attack in progress."

"No!" Miko Nakamura held up her hand. The hardened edge gleamed dully in the light from the burning pieces of cargo shuttle still falling. "There is no need."

"This was *sabotage*!"

"I do not think so, Major. Accidents happen." Nakamura glanced over at Anita Tarleton and Walden.

Walden rocked back and forth, feeling as if someone had ripped the ligaments from his knees. He wiped sweat off his forehead and looked at Anita. Her face had turned as white and shocked as he felt.

"It blew up." Her voice was cracked and shaking with emotion. "That could have been us."

"Was it a robot shuttle?" Walden asked. He was instantly sorry for asking. He read the answer in Zacharias' expression. Men and women had died. The only consolation lay in the abruptness of their deaths. They couldn't have had an inkling of anything wrong.

"There is no need to cordon the area. It is more important that the launchings continue according to schedule," said Nakamura. The way her words snapped out—crisp, clean, and forceful—robbed Zacharias of his certainty.

"Why not?" the major asked. "The port has an unblemished launch record—except for terrorist activity."

"My forces finished a sweep of the field less than an hour before launch."

"That's enough time for a trained group to infiltrate and sabotage." Some of Zacharias' confidence returned.

"We left behind sensors. We are not fools." Nakamura ran her fingers along the decorative fringe on her left sleeve. Walden wondered what signals were being sent. He did not see the woman as the type to have nervous habits. With the proper electronics woven into the fabric, light touches on each fringe strip could send coded messages—and probably did.

"The Sov-Lats are behind this." Medals jingling, Zacharias rushed into the elevator cage when it opened. Walden and Anita hung back. To their surprise, Miko Nakamura did not join the major. She let the cage sink quickly into the depths of the launch complex.

"Major Zacharias jumps to unwarranted conclusions," Nakamura said in her soft, deadly voice. "I assure you that this was not terrorist activity."

Walden jumped when Egad pressed his head against the man's hand. Mismatched eyes stared up. The dog wanted to speak but had been well trained. He wouldn't show his abilities in front of the Japanese advisor.

"Why not? They tried to assassinate your ambassador and a roomful of people at the New Year's party last week," said Anita.

"There was much about that attempt I find confusing," Nakamura said in a confident voice belying the words. She gave the impression of finding nothing strange; she had everything under strict control. "The sniper was killed too easily. He was used as a diversion to keep us from finding the mechanically timed bomb." She paused, two fingers resting lightly on her cheek as she thought. "*He* was the victim. A falling out occurred in the terrorist ranks. From our work, we believe we have located the Sov-Lat agent responsible. She is nullified."

"So why couldn't another group have been responsible for this?" demanded Anita. Her temper replaced the numbing shock she had experienced watching the shuttle be destroyed.

"No reason, except that I tell you it is so. You and the major are far too apprehensive. A Western failing, I am sure." Nakamura bowed slightly and turned to the elevator cage, which had returned from delivering Zacharias to his destination in the buried launch control center.

Egad nipped lightly at Walden's hand. The scientist waited until the elevator doors closed and the soft sighing and static crackling of the superconducting elements inside marked the descent of the cage.

"What?" Walden said softly. He knelt, holding the dog's massive head in his hands.

"She doesn't smell."

"What?"

"No odor. She is . . . a no one."

Walden frowned. Anita spoke up. "She might have blanked out her pheromones to prevent anyone using a surface acoustic wave detector to track her."

"Possible," mused Walden. "And she accused us of being paranoid." He looked across the launch field. Mech crews worked to pick up the still smoldering debris from the destroyed shuttle.

"Jerome." Anita held up her wrist to show the balefully blinking red light on her watch. "It's time to go."

"We don't have to go on the next launch," he said. "What do you think, Egad?"

The dog shook his furry head. "Don't like being around women with no odor. Love Anita." The dog pulled free of Walden and went to thrust his head against the woman's hand. Egad sniffed loudly.

"I like you, too." Anita gave the dog a quick kiss and then stood. "What are we going to do? Go on the next one or wait?"

Walden heaved a deep, steadying breath. "This one," he decided. "If Nakamura is on it, so are we."

Anita cocked her head to one side and looked at him quizzically. "You trust her that much? Even Japanese Hegemony military advisors make mistakes."

Walden smiled suddenly. "Who do you want to go with? Zacharias or her?"

"Good point. Let's lift for the *Hippocrates*. I'm getting tired of Earth."

Walden said nothing to this. A single glance at the destruction wrought by two factions too terrified of nuclear weapons to ever use them convinced him Schwann might be a better place. No matter that they went there to further the madness on Earth. It would be better not thinking of the viral destruction he and Anita and the others in his research team might unleash.

He took a deep breath before entering the awaiting elevator cage. Anita clutched at his hand and Egad pressed between them. Then the elevator plummeted to the port loading facility six hundred meters underground.

"Always takes my breath away when it drops like that," he said, staggering slightly as he got out of the cage. All around soldiers hurried. Some carried laserifles. Other guided huge crates resting on the backs of loading robots.

"There're the others," said Walden. His entire team had assembled early. Without their labs, most had nothing to do but anxiously—or impatiently—await launch. Too many were socially inept, devoted more to their work than anything else.

Walden shook his head. Social cripples they might be, unable to get along even with each other, but they were the best the NAA and Earth had to offer. He was a good researcher; he damned most of them for being better. A few had to be classed as geniuses, making genes jump at their command, splicing insane and ingenious ribbons of DNA, twisting Nature to their whim.

"When do we launch, Walden?" demanded a short, pudgy man. "I simply *must* get back to work. The incubation times for my T-odd bacteriophages are critical."

"Willie, you didn't set your incubator on automatic before packing it, did you?" Walden was horrified at the notion of another shuttle exploding and raining down a mutated phage that would destroy the gut flora of everyone within a thousand square kilometers. The digestive tracts would rebel and people would starve to death within a month, no matter how they were treated.

Willie Klugel thrust out his chest and pulled himself up to his full height. The top of his balding head barely came to Anita's shoulder.

"I cannot be interrupted. This move is unnecessary. You interfere, Walden!"

"Willie, tell me you aren't shipping equipment put on automatic. Tell me there won't be any problem if the shuttle has to abort or jettison your equipment in the cargo bay."

"There will be no problem."

Walden knew the scientist lied through his crooked teeth. The watery blue eyes flashed with impertinence, and the set of his rounded shoulders radiated defiance. Walden patted Klugel on the shoulder and went on. He had others in the team to soothe. Few liked the idea of starring to Delta Cygnus 4 and even fewer wanted their experiments interfered with for any reason.

What bothered Walden most was that Dr. Willie Klugel was one of the least obnoxious and defiant.

"You will not all go on the same shuttle," came Edouard Zacharias' strident voice. The officer bustled around, two armed guards trailing behind him like captive satellites. "Choose. Stay or go."

"Wait!" cried Walden. He knew that most, if not all, his team would immediately volunteer to stay. Some might never get onto a shuttle and reach the orbiting *Hippocrates*. "We all go together."

"Sir," Zacharias said coldly. "There is suspicion that sabotage might have occurred in more than one shuttle. I cannot take the risk of losing your entire team."

Walden grabbed the officer's arm and pulled him to one side. "Don't *ever* do anything to upset my staff again," Walden said in a low, cold voice. At his side Egad growled and showed savage fangs. The way Walden felt, he might let Egad rip out Zacharias' throat—or he might do it himself.

"Dr. Walden, I am in charge."

"You are *not*. I am. We are not under your command. The matter is closed. My team lifts on the next shuttle."

He spun angrily, Egad beside him. The dog butted his head against Walden's leg. Miko Nakamura stood by the entry tube, arms crossed and a slight smile on her sallow face. Her ebony-dark eyes did not blink when Walden tried to stare her down.

He had the feeling she had engineered the confrontation with Zacharias to observe his response.

He hoped she had learned not to cross him.

"Jerome, the transporter is ready." Anita waited for him. The others had already entered the first bullet-shaped car and were on their way to the shuttle through the underground tube.

Walden dropped into a seat, patted the one next to him and got Egad into it, then checked to be sure safety belts were fastened. Only then did he signal that they were ready.

"You're getting to be worse than a mother hen," chided Anita. "But you did have to put the major in his place."

"For all his medals, he seems incompetent, hardly more than a bureaucrat." The words burned his tongue. *He* was hardly more than that himself. His best research lay behind him and he knew it. Even worse, so did the others in the team. Having Anita know it, though, hurt worst of all.

The acceleration crushed him into the firmly padded seats. Before he could utter a sound, the deceleration threw him forward against the safety straps.

"End of the line," Anita said. "Next stop, the *Hippocrates*. Then the stars!"

Walden accepted a small pill from the flight doctor making the last visual inspection of the passengers before launch. He popped it into his mouth and within seconds could barely stand. Collapsing into a formfitting couch seemed the most reasonable thing in the world.

The cargo shuttle launched, and Jerome Walden was out of this world and into orbit.

"We're there?" he asked, groggy from the tranquilizing drug. "It didn't take any time at all."

"You slept," accused Egad. "Man nasty to me. I tried to bite him."

"What?"

"Don't worry about it, Jerome. He's just being feisty."

"Never left lab before," said Egad. The concept of a starlift ship and other worlds lay far beyond Egad's intellectual ability. For a dog, he was a genius. Compared with many humans, he was superior, but he still lacked basic information and the facility to process it.

"I need to check the equipment. Willie's experiment. Check it." Walden shook his head, fearing that something had come loose inside. Although the tranquilizer's grip on his senses faded, he wobbled a bit and clear thinking was impossible.

"I'll find our quarters," said Anita. "Egad can come with me." She lightly brushed her fingertips along his cheek. "Don't be too long. We're supposed to star out soon."

"Willie's experiment," he repeated. "Can't let it get loose on the ship."

"Be sure to run a full scan," Anita advised. "There's no way to know if the others did anything as stupid as Willie."

The flame-tressed woman reached down and locked her fingers around Egad's collar. The dog protested when she refused to let him explore, but he knew better than to object vocally. Walden had taught him well to conceal his talents.

Walden took a few seconds to gather his wits. The drug dulled his vision and turned colors into muted greens and browns. He sought a crew member to direct him to the cargo hold but couldn't get anyone to stop. The activity around him increased until he gave up and tried to figure out directions on his own.

The *Hippocrates* had been designed to serve as a hospital ship for the feeble empire Earth had established among the stars. The need for such a vessel had never been justified. The well-equipped wards were never filled, except when the ship orbited Earth. Many in the NAA Congress argued that its engines should be stripped out and the hulk put into permanent orbit to serve the needy of the planet.

Economics prevailed. Building a starlift ship capable of spanning the distances to other star systems was too expensive for such gutting. The need for a hospital ship was small; the need for faster-than-light transport was immense and growing every year.

The *Hippocrates* might never serve as its designers intended, but it could ferry researchers to their quarantine worlds and deal with any mistakes that might occur there.

"Starlift in one hour," came a rumbling voice. Startled, Walden jumped and looked around. A small transducer had been attached high up on the wall and acted as a public address system. Immediately below it a small display digitally read out the minutes until launch. If the corridor lost pressure, the sonic warnings would be useless and the readout would be the only way of learning what had happened.

Walden touched his nose. If the corridor decompressed, he'd need more than a few encouraging words. Walden stopped, sought out emergency air systems, and failed to find them. He shrugged off his uneasiness as an aftereffect of the tranquilizer. Starlift ships didn't have doors opening to space that accidentally unlocked.

Robot cargo handlers rolled along their powerstrip tracks set in the floor, magnetic grapples thrust in front of them like groping silver hands. Walden followed the tracks to a triple door airlock system. He took several minutes to read the posted operating instructions, then ran through the sequence.

The first door opened. He stepped into the chamber, two robots detaching from their tracks and rolling independently to join him. The inward door closed, air hissed, and the central door irised open. Walden stepped quickly into the new chamber and waited again. The full cycle took almost a minute. He chafed at the delay. Leaving Anita and Egad to fend for themselves didn't seem like such a good idea now that he was thinking more clearly.

"Come on, come on," he muttered impatiently. Finding Klugel's cases and examining them would be the work of a few minutes. Then he could return to the ship's core, find his quarters, and settle in. The drug had left his system, but a lethargy lingered that he had trouble fighting.

The heavy steel door opened. Walden pushed past it, not waiting for the robots. They had their jobs to do. He had his. Cursing constantly, Walden made his way through the tunnels constructed of cargo cases. The markings on most of them were hidden.

He retraced his steps, found the small computer beside the inner airlock, and punched out his request. A glowing yellow trail burst into being on the floor. Walden followed it through the maze of carefully stowed crates until he got to a stack he recognized. The robots had already secured them, but Walden opened a small inspection hatch and attached his command probe to the connector revealed.

The tiny computer inside the probe analyzed activity within the crates. The third packing box showed what he had feared. Klugel brewed his phages, oblivious to the danger of shipping untended equipment. Walden considered his choices. He made his decision, knowing Klugel would castigate him endlessly for it.

"Probe, power down the incubators. All safety devices *on*." He checked the progress until he was satisfied that there could be no accidental leakage. Even with double airlocks protecting the crew and passengers of the *Hippocrates*, a spill would be dangerous.

Every crate in the cargo hold might be contaminated. He'd hate to jettison everything because of Klugel's impatience and need to work constantly.

Walden pulled his probe free and randomly inspected a half dozen other crates. None had functioning equipment. The equipment that startled him the most belonged to Doris Yerrow. The packing had been done with uncustomary sloppiness. He expected more from the mousy, quiet woman with her dogged determination. Walden made a note to tell her to repack. He still worried that some of his staff had experiments breeding.

"There's no way to check. During the trip. Then." His head began to ache. He held it between his hands. The dull ache turned to a painful throbbing. Walden sucked in his breath and began to wheeze and gasp. He sat down on a crate and tried not to panic.

"Air," he choked out. "Oxygen. There's no pressure!"

Sharp pain lanced into his head from the side. Blood began trickling from his ear. Realizing what happened, he tried to get back to the airlock. He fell to hands and knees. Crawling took more and more energy. Strength flagging, his lungs burning as if filled with acid, Walden fell facedown on the deck.

Slowly, inexorably, the atmosphere in the cargo hold leaked into space. Within minutes Jerome Walden would be dead.

CHAPTER

4

First his vision blurred, then he began to see silver streaks darting in front of him. Walden tried to suck in enough air for his straining lungs and failed. Stainless steel bands fastened around his chest and tightened—and then they were set on fire. Worst of all was the aggravating roar in his ears. He screamed at the deafening noise, wanting it to go away. Only small, strangled animal noises came from his lips.

He rolled to his side and tried to signal a cargo loader robot. The mech rolled past, oblivious to his plight. It had been designed to do specific and demanding work. The only algorithms concerning humans in its programming were avoidance routines.

Walden needed more than that, and he could not verbally order it to help. The air had become too thin. The silver streaks began to turn black.

He struggled to crawl in the direction of the interior airlock. His only chance for survival lay there. If he couldn't cycle open the lock, he could signal for help.

The smooth decking made it difficult for him to gain traction. He slipped and fell to his face repeatedly. With dogged determination, Walden kept on. Even as he struggled, he knew he was making less and less progress and was moving closer to dying.

His fingers feebly clutched at the boron-fiber composite deck. He made no progress at all now. The silver streaks vanished totally, leaving only deathly, impenetrable black, and the roaring transformed into the hammering of his runaway pulse.

New pain exploded in his out-thrust hand. The sensation spurred him to lift his head. One blurry eye tried to bring into focus what gave so much agony. Red waves burned their way up his arm and collided with the fire in his lungs.

Walden tried to scream again when he began to slide along the floor. Small protrusions he hadn't noticed before cut into his belly and shredded his clothing.

"Wha—?" His question caught in his throat. But for a brief instant he saw the cargo loader that had seized his wrist and dragged him toward the inner airlock. Then he passed out.

Walden thought he would never be free of torment. His wrist hurt like hell, his lungs filled with superheated plasma, and now he hallucinated. Death was supposed to be peaceful. He felt too confused to die properly.

". . . some rupturing in the alveoli. A small amount of hemorrhaging, but nothing dangerous. I checked his eardrums and found no permanent damage, but he will have one nova of a headache." A tiny chuckle followed. "Can't give him anything for that since the painkillers are antagonistic to the theraminocen I gave him to repair the lung capillary damage."

Walden opened his eyes to bright light. It took several seconds for him to realize he had not died. He forced himself erect.

"How did I get out of the hold? The air. I couldn't . . ."

"Relax, Jerome." Anita pushed him back into the bed. "Leo's patched you up."

Leo Burch snapped his medical case shut. "I figured someone would be needing me. I would never have guessed you'd be the first patient. Hell, Jerome, we're not even out of Earth orbit yet. Even the marines are behaving themselves. Not so much as a mashed thumb in their ranks yet."

Burch dropped his case into the carrying compartment on a small medical analysis robot. "Albert here's going to be very useful. His computer comes up with a diagnosis faster than I can."

"And better?" teased Anita.

"Never. Albert's only a mech. You rest up, now, Jerome. I'll keep an eye on your readouts for a while. If you're feeling good and the reading's still in the green, take off those damned things. They must be as uncomfortable as an asteroid up your ass." Burch tapped his medbot and motioned for it to follow. The obedient mech silently trailed him from the room.

Walden looked around, trying to get his bearings. The room was small and bare of any but the most utilitarian furnishings. When he saw his personal cases he knew this was his assigned room.

He leaned back. "Is Leo gone?"

"Long gone," said Anita. "And I've checked the room for spy-eyes and everything else I could think of. It's clean."

Walden sighed. He doubted that. Microphones could be painted on the walls. The boron-whisker composite walls might be filled with listening equipment. A fiber optic camera lens was smaller than a grain of dust. And these were only a few of the devices he understood. The real professionals—and he thought Miko Nakamura was in this rank—could listen to his thoughts from halfway across the universe using nothing more than a spoon and a piece of string.

"What happened?"

"You got locked into the hold and the exterior loading bay opened. The secondary airlock jammed open, the primary released unexpectedly and spilled the air."

"It happened gradually. It took me by surprise. I hardly noticed the pressure drop until I couldn't even catch my breath."

"Something went wrong with the alarms, too," said Anita. "No warning sounded to get repair or rescue mechs down there."

"One pulled me out."

"You are welcome." Egad shoved his head onto Walden's bed and laid it next to the man's hand.

"You? No, Egad, it was a robot that pulled me out of the hold."

"Who sent it?" asked Anita. She pointed at the dog. "He trotted down to see what you were doing and came to the closed locks."

"Used vidcom into hold," the dog explained. "Saw you in trouble."

"You ordered the robot inside?"

The dog's head bobbed up and down. "Hard. Trash can would not obey. Had to change collar." Egad rolled his head to one side and showed Walden the scratches on the computerized speech circuit.

"He altered the frequency until he could subvocalize and directly command the robot."

"I didn't know that was possible," said Walden.

"Neither did I, but Egad's clever."

The dog looked from Walden to Anita and back. He barked twice to show his acceptance of their praise.

"I'll see about getting a transmitter you can switch whenever you want," Walden promised. He examined the collar and the way Egad had reset the computer device. He shook his head in wonder. The synaptic enhancement experiments he had run that produced Egad had been done secretly. Not even the NAA agency funding his research had been given full information. Walden was glad. Egad had been as much an accident as a deliberate result. The military would have demanded thousands of genetically enhanced and altered animals to do their bidding.

It was bad enough humans killed each other in the never-ending guerrilla wars. Breeding enhanced intelligence animals to carry on the fight struck Walden as morally wrong.

He jumped when a chime sounded. Anita looked toward the door. "We've got company. Do you want to see anyone?"

Walden touched a button on the control panel built into the wall and turned the door transparent. Major Zacharias waited impatiently for him to acknowledge. Behind the officer stood two armed guards.

"Is he really the military mission commander?"

"I checked. He's in charge," said Anita.

"Find out what you can about his record. For all the medals jangling on his chest I can't believe he's the hero he makes himself out to be."

Walden touched another button and opened the door. "Come in, Major. You can leave your assistants outside. It's crowded enough in here."

Zacharias glared at Egad, who growled deep in his throat.

"They shouldn't have allowed personal pets," the major said with ill-disguised contempt.

"The same thing can be said of your entire military contingent. When the mission was organized we were told we were a replacement research team. The scientists on Schwann were due to be rotated home after a two-year stint."

"Why do you call it Schwann? The proper designation is Delta Cygnus 4."

Walden leaned back and heaved a deep sigh. The drugs Leo Burch had given him caused his insides to radiate a mild, soothing warmth. It wouldn't take any effort on his part to drift off to sleep and not deal with this prancing peacock.

"It's something of a joke," explained Anita. "Delta Cygnus—the swan. And there was a German scientist named Theodore Schwann who did work in the early nineteenth century on the putrefaction of meats. Louis Pasteur stole his work and never gave him any credit."

"How interesting," Zacharias said, obviously irritated at the delay in finishing his business. He straightened nonexistent wrinkles in his black and silver uniform, quickly brushed over the row of medals, and said, "The investigation is under way. We hope to have some indication of the cause of your . . . misfortune soon."

"It was only an equipment malfunction. In a way it's my fault," Walden said. He was just as eager for this to end as the officer was.

"Why is that?"

"I should have informed the purser I wanted to examine the equipment crates."

Zacharias said nothing. He stared at Walden in the same way a researcher stared at a bug under a microscope.

"Is there something wrong?" asked Anita. Egad growled until she motioned him to silence. "It *was* an accident?"

"I believe it was sabotage. In addition, it might have been aimed at you specifically, Dr. Walden."

At this he had to laugh. "Why me?"

"You are the team leader. You are a respected gengineer. Your loss would significantly hinder the performance of this mission.''

Walden laughed heartily. "You overestimate my importance. I do some research, but my primary function is coordinator. The men and women who do the real work would get along just fine without me.''

"You are the *coordinator*," Zacharias said. "A good leader is worth a thousand willing followers.''

"There is a school of personnel management espousing that," Walden said carefully. He tried not to laugh at the earnest Zacharias. The major's beliefs had come to the forefront with that single statement. He thought his role in the mission was far more important than any of his soldiers.

Walden sobered as the implications occurred to him. Edouard Zacharias was a man who would sacrifice others to save himself. *He* was important. The rest were simply along to do his bidding.

"What is the mission?" asked Walden.

"You have your orders. You will perform research on various classified offensive and defensive biological systems to further the security and safety of the North American Alliance. My orders are to support you fully in this endeavor.''

"I saw a marine with the burst planet and lightning bolt patch on his sleeve," said Anita. "Isn't that the insignia of an elite unit?''

"It is. I am proud to be in command of an EPCT company.''

Walden sank down deeper into the bed. The drug Burch had given him dulled his senses slightly and made the room blur occasionally. In addition to this sense-twisting disorientation, he realized how exhausted he was.

"What do you want, Major? I'm very tired.''

"Of course, sir." The officer snapped to attention as if he were on a parade ground. "Departure time has been changed. We will not starlift for seventy-two hours while the investigation is conducted.''

"What? I don't want to spend one millisecond longer in this bucket. We're cut off from our work, the quarters are cramped—''

"Please," interrupted Zacharias. "I understand your concerns, Dr. Tarleton. However, this act of sabotage will not go unpunished.''

"Why do you think it's sabotage?" Walden asked. He fought to keep his eyelids from drooping. Zacharias sounded more and more distant, and a warm, fuzzy feeling wrapped him. The drug Burch had given him now took full hold of his senses and made even talking difficult.

"There are indications of tampering with the safety circuits. Nakamura claims it is shoddy maintenance and attributes it to Western quality control. I think the malfunction was caused. The cargo hold sensors should have prevented the outer lock doors from opening. They did not."

"He's still recovering, Major. Could we continue later?"

"Very well." The man somehow stiffened his already rigid spine, did a smart about-face, and marched to the door. Anita had it open for him. Zacharias never broke step as he left.

"Are you really tired or was it just a ploy to get rid of our military friend?"

"Not much of a trick," admitted Walden. "But I need to see the others. Can you arrange for a staff meeting in a couple hours?"

"Your speech is slurred. Leo never mentioned that happening."

"Just tired. Just so dog-tired." Walden's voice trailed off.

"I watch him," promised Egad. Anita patted the dog's head and left, worrying about Walden and a dozen other matters.

"This is ridiculous!" flared Walden. "There's no need to hold up departure because of this."

"I think otherwise," Zacharias said smugly. "A forensic team is investigating. When they are finished and the malefactor is placed under arrest, *then* we will lift for Delta Cygnus 4."

Walden looked around the meeting room. His research team waited with ill-concealed anger at the officer. They were anxious to return to their routines. Walden didn't blame them. Research was a waiting game at times, but the occasional bursts of insight and even genius were not to be denied. The inability to follow up immediately on such a promising line of thought might be costly. Some ideas never—quite—returned.

He tried to formulate the best line of argument to use against

Zacharias. As he thought, he studied the scientists. He amended his earlier notion that they were all nervous and eager to leave. As always, Doris Yerrow sat placidly, hands folded in her lap. Her dull-brown hair boiled up in an improbable nest of tangles and knots. Walden wondered if she ever combed it. With some of the cosmetic products available Doris could have been a decent-looking woman.

Walden couldn't fault her talent, though. Of the entire team, she worked the hardest. Patient research paid off frequently for her. The others might depend on inspiration; Yerrow worked with unrelenting logic.

Chin, Burnowski, and the diminutive Marni Donelli whispered among themselves, occasionally giving Zacharias a cold look. The trio worked together often. Walden wondered how long it would be before Donelli was appointed the spokesman to protest for this group within a group.

To his surprise, Chin presented the case for immediate departure.

"Major," the man said in a clear, precise, clipped tone. "There is much more at stake then petty damage."

Walden bristled. He didn't consider almost dying to be petty, but he knew what Chin meant and held his silence.

"We must leave on schedule. We all have experiments in progress. Delay reaching Schwann will jeopardize the results."

"You were instructed to begin once we reached Delta Cygnus 4," Zacharias said. "You were specifically forbidden to experiment while we are in transit."

"The delay," cut in Miko Nakamura, "is unavoidable. Two escort ships have been assigned to accompany us to prevent other . . . untoward incidents." Her dark eyes worked around the room, evaluating each person. Most of the scientists ignored her. Walden knew they were wrong doing that. Nakamura, not Major Zacharias, wielded the real power aboard the *Hippocrates*.

"What class of escort?" Walden asked.

"Two destroyers," Zacharias snapped.

Walden didn't have a comeback. Two destroyers were capable of laying to waste an entire world. More than protection, such an armada posed the threat of an invasion force.

"Yes," said Nakamura, smiling crookedly, "and Major Zacharias' command has swelled, also. He now commands a company of EPCT soldiers, with full combat equipment."

"What *is* going on? We were supposed to be ferried to Schwann and relieve the researchers there. Nothing was said about making an invasion of the planet. Have the Sov-Lats done something on Schwann to warrant this?"

Walden had visions of being in the center of a full-scale battle. The Sov-Lats would never permit such armed might from orbiting Schwann without reply—and he feared it might be in kind.

He went cold inside. The destroyers and full company of EPCTs might be in response to a move already taken by the Sov-Lat Pact. A benign world circling a distant sun might quickly become the seed that blossomed into all-out war.

CHAPTER

"You can't see them," said Anita Tarleton.

"I can feel them. There," said Walden, pointing at a spot on the blank vidscreen. "The destroyers are *there*."

Anita shrugged. "This is only making you crazy."

"Everything is doing that." He turned away from the feature-less vidscreen showing nothing but the unchanging gray liftspace bubble around the *Hippocrates*. "Everything but you." He put his arms around her waist and drew the red-haired woman close to give her a quick kiss.

"I'd hate to think I was contributing to your troubles." Anita pulled free. "But I am. I made a quick circuit through the contagion ward and found Paul Preston in the middle of some experiment. He had smuggled several test tubes aboard in his pockets."

Walden groaned. Preston worked on angiogenesis factors. A strain of infected test bacteria loosed aboard could kill everyone within hours. The angiogenesis factor not only prevented blood clotting, it encouraged bleeding. Any specimen exposed to it died of internal hemorrhaging—and Preston had carried the deadly vials in his pocket. Any mishap, even someone bumping into him, would have turned a medical ship into a mortuary.

"You're going to have to talk to him about safety procedures.

Once we get to Schwann, to hell with him. We can put him in a lab in the middle of a desert and not care what he does. Until then . . .'' Anita let the sentence trail off.

"Between him and Willie, I've got my hands full. I'll talk to his assistant. She might have more control over him than I would.''

"You just want to be alone with Claudette. She's pretty, isn't she?''

"She is, but you're beautiful. Now quit fishing for compliments. What else do I have to do?'' Walden turned back to stare at the blank vidscreen. In normal space stars shone unblinking and cold. The vidscreen pickups mounted on the hull of the *Hippocrates* became confused once the ship's engines engaged and the starlift field energized. Although he wasn't a physicist and thought them quite insane, Walden wished he understood the process of faster-than-light travel. When he was lecturing at Cal Tech, a graduate student had attempted to convince him of the Christoffel tensors and twisted space and other highly improbable geometrical configurations. It had left Walden feeling thankful he only meddled with life.

Physics twisted the brain.

"Captain Belford wants to see you, too.''

"Really? We've been in this morass for three entire days. Why did he choose this instant?''

"He talked with Leo and found that your headache from the drug had gone. He's probably been busy getting the *Hippocrates* moving in the right direction. There're no guides out here.''

"Only Pierce pinholes and Dru locks and all the other realities that exist only in a mathematician's nightmare.''

"Are you all right, Jerome? You aren't getting into the routine very well. I'm worried about you.''

"I'm fine,'' he said. Physically he had recovered from the ordeal in the cargo hold, and Leo Burch had told the captain the truth. The drug-induced headaches were a day in the past. What bothered him most was that he had yet to find the proper tactic for dealing with the military presence aboard the ship.

And the destroyers. They were in their own starlift bubbles, millimeters away—or was it light-years? He forgot the explanation he had heard. But that wasn't what mattered. Such awesome power accompanied them to Delta Cygnus 4 for a reason, and it wasn't because some bio-engineer had almost died of asphyxiation in a hold. Authorization to send two destroyers had come before he had set foot on the cargo deck.

"I'll see Captain Belford, then check on Preston. Anything else?"

"One thing," she said. "Get yourself a secretary. I've got work of my own to do."

"The new project that you won't tell me about."

"Can't, not won't. Orders from on high."

"All right. I'll see what I can find in the way of help. It's a pity my assistant wouldn't come along."

"You can't blame Kuniko too much. His wife was expecting their first child, and this mission is set for a minimum of three years."

"I don't blame him; I *do* miss him, though. And I don't like to use the ship's computer as a secretary."

Anita nodded. They had electronically bug-swept their quarters twice a day since lifting from Earth orbit. The first two days had been wasted effort. This morning they found two small pinhead-sized cameras. Without sophisticated equipment, they hadn't been able to trace back to whomever had planted them.

"You'll do just fine. You always do." Anita gave him a quick kiss and left. Walden tapped his fingers against the cool ceramic vidscreen as if he could reach through it and touch the fragile gray energy bubble surrounding the ship.

He jumped when a rough, cold, wet tongue thrust into his ear.

"Egad! Don't sneak up on me like that!" He wrestled with the big hound and got him between his legs to hold him firmly. "What are you up to, old dog?"

Egad licked at his face. From the transducer came almost indiscernible words, "Safe to talk?"

"As safe as it'll get. I destroyed two spy devices this morning and just swept the place an hour ago."

"Much work in soldiers' kennel. Dangerous hunters. No prey. They are getting restless. Kill for no reason."

"That's not my worry. What about my staff?"

Egad started a rambling discussion of the smells and personal habits of Walden's research team. He finished, saying, "The Doris bitch. She smells like medicine. Bad smells. Plastic."

"What kind of medicine?"

"Don't know. Nothing I remember."

This startled Walden. Egad's canine nose was a million times more sensitive than a human's. The dog could scent one molecule per billion and remember it precisely years later. That he had encountered an aroma he couldn't recognize made Walden curious. Doris Yerrow wasn't the type to be wearing a new perfume.

"What about the ship's crew? Anything unusual among them?"

"None eat meat. No odor of meat."

Walden had heard that most space crews were vegetarians. Bringing along enough frozen meat for long trips through liftspace was possible; storage was not severely restricted on modern ships. However, nutritional efficiency was a phrase he heard often among spacemen. Being self-sufficient and growing most of their food in aqua-culture and hydroponics tanks gave them a sense of reliability and safety while they were cut off from planetary bonds.

He didn't like thinking about it, but the starlift engines failed one in a thousand ignitions, sending the benighted ship off in a random direction. Sometimes it took years for the crew to find its way home—if it ever did.

"What about Major Zacharias?"

"Can I rip out his throat? He kicked me."

"I'll talk to him about it. Not everyone appreciates such a smart, handsome dog like you." Walden patted the animal's massive head and stood. "I've got to see the captain. You keep prowling around the ship and see what you can find out."

"Spy?"

"Yes." Walden hated himself for putting Egad in the position of spy-hunting, but the paranoia from Earth and endless tedious security drills carried over into space. This was just one penalty he paid for working on restricted access projects.

Walden let Egad take off down the narrow corridor. He watched the misshapen canine vanish around a bend before going to the wardroom. Captain Belford sat at the head of a table.

Seldom had Walden seen a man who looked the part of a liftship captain. Wavy gray hair gave Captain Belford a distinguished air. The creases on his forehead left no doubt that this man carried a heavy burden, but the strong, broad shoulders and the thick-fingered, powerful hands told that Captain Belford was more than capable of bearing it.

"Dr. Walden, you're looking better than the last time I saw you. Sit down." The captain pointed to a vacant seat next to his first officer. Walden nodded to the second-in-command, who pointedly ignored him.

"I don't remember us meeting before, sir."

"You were almost comatose. Dr. Burch said it was a result of the medication he gave you."

"Thanks for your concern. You didn't have to stop by to see me."

"Major Zacharias insisted." The captain's tone changed subtly. Walden got the impression that the officious major was no more in favor with the liftship's crew than he was among the scientists.

"How can I help you?" asked Walden. "I'm just now getting in touch with my team."

"I understand," Captain Belford said briskly, indicating that Walden should be quiet and let him have his say. "My med officer says that your Dr. Preston is engaged in dangerous activity in the ward. Although we have no patients, my medico claims there is extreme danger." The captain pushed across a computer block memory.

"I'll read his report with interest."

"See that Preston is stopped or put in a quarantine ward. I do not want my crew cutting themselves and finding that their immune systems refuse to heal the wound."

Walden raised an eyebrow in surprise. The captain understood Preston's research goals more thoroughly than he had thought.

"The *Hippocrates* is my responsibility, Doctor. I have to know everything happening aboard. I *will* know it. Also, you aren't the first researchers to ship out with us. My training is in other fields, but I pick up enough to know what is potentially serious and what is space gas."

"I'll see to it immediately," promised Walden. "Is there anything more?"

"Well, yes." The hesitation on Captain Belford's part struck Walden as odd. Everything prior had been firm, crisp, precise. "I find myself caught between Major Zacharias and his claim of a saboteur and spy aboard and Nakamura saying there is nothing to worry about."

"You're worrying who is right?"

"Something like that. The *Hippocrates* is a good ship and I keep a firm rein on crew and mechanism. This saboteur business is annoying. Please inform me immediately if you come across anything of importance."

"Of course, sir."

"Dismissed." Captain Belford turned back to a computer vidscreen, his first officer hunched over next to him. Walden knew complete termination of a meeting when he saw it. He left, puzzling over the captain's request.

With complete access to the ship's computer and a trained crew, the captain should know everything before it happened. That was his job. What had occurred to make him ask a mere passenger to keep him abreast of illicit activities?

Walden wandered the halls, finally coming to the section marked off by painted red stripes on the floor and walls and an armed guard.

"Sir, you are not permitted access in this area," the guard said.

"That's all right." Walden glanced around. Through an open door a few meters down the corridor he saw Zacharias and two officers duplicating the scene he had just left with Captain Belford. They hunched over the computer vidscreen working on some esoteric problem.

He turned his attention back to the EPCT guard. Young, hard, well-trained, every movement radiated competence and barely restrained death. Walden found it a little frightening to think that a pompous peacock like Zacharias commanded men like this guard.

"Have you been on many combat missions?" he asked. "I can't read your ribbons."

The guard never glanced down at his own chest; he was *very* well trained. Distracting him would be difficult, should Walden ever want to do so.

"Yes, sir. Four missions. Three on Alphacent in the desert campaign against the Latinos' Fourth Legion and one airless mission on Phobos." A small smile lifted the corner of his mouth. "That moon's well named. Fear. I've never been more scared in my life."

Walden remembered reading sketchy accounts. The Sov-Lats' dominance on Mars was a fact. Some armchair general in the NAA had decided to launch a preemptive attack on their base on Phobos. Four companies of EPCT had gone in. Fewer than fifty soldiers had escaped. The Sov-Lats had nuked their own troops on the moon rather than let it be taken and used as a base orbiting above their heads.

"I know something about the mission. You're one hell of a soldier to have escaped."

"I'm one damned lucky soldier, sir. Skill had nothing to do with it. The germ-bombs they dropped on the Sov base bought us enough time to retreat."

"How did they work?"

"Sir, that is classified information."

"No, no, not *how* did the bombs affect the base? I know that. I helped design the microbe that ate the composite material used in their ships. I want to know how well they worked. How fast."

"You designed the germ-bombs? I guess I owe you my life then, sir. Thanks." The guard smiled even more broadly. "But what you ask is *still* classified."

Walden turned when he heard a clicking behind him. Egad trotted up and nuzzled him until he petted the dog. When he had received enough attention from his master, Egad turned to the guard. For the first time, the guard broke discipline. He bent and scratched behind Egad's floppy ears.

"Is this your dog, sir? He shouldn't be running around loose. Some of the guys get twitchy after a few days in space. They might use him for target practice."

"Egad will be all right. He knows who likes him and who doesn't."

"You may be right, sir. A couple of the non-coms have taken quite a fancy to him."

"I hope they're not feeding him table scraps. It ruins his coat." This brought Egad's head around. The dog glared at Walden and started to growl. Walden smiled, silently telling the dog he was only joking. Egad pulled away from the guard and trotted off into the secured area. Walden saw that none of the officers noticed the canine as he began sniffing around.

Satisfied that he had a spy among the military, he nodded to the guard and went off, whistling off-key and feeling more in control than he had since the ordeal in the airless cargo hold.

All he had to do was convince Klugel and Preston—and probably the rest of his team—not to start any experiment that would jeopardize the *Hippocrates*. He had dealt with the prima donnas before. He could do it again.

Jerome Walden even allowed himself to hope that the stint on Schwann would go smoothly and produce wonderful results. This optimism let him momentarily forget the two destroyers and the full battle-equipped company of Extra-Planetary Combat Team soldiers that accompanied them.

CHAPTER

"You worry too much," said Anita Tarleton. She put her arm around Walden's shoulder and hugged him. "The trip hasn't been *that* bad, has it?"

"Klugel's T-odd phages were released in the hold because of the decompression that almost did me in," he said. "Preston used the cooking utensils for brewing up his agar for an experiment."

"It wasn't the angiogenesis factor, though."

"Thank our lucky stars for that and the decompression containing the released phages. Chin and Burnowski have been at each other's throats constantly. The only one I haven't had trouble with is Doris."

"She's been very withdrawn. I tried to talk to her a few times and she always snubbed me."

"Doris prides herself on being a hermit and hiding in her work. She made Chin mad when she ignored his request to borrow some glassware. I wish there was some way to make her more outgoing. Or at least more polite."

"She's not intentionally rude, Jerome. She just doesn't cope with people well. Research is everything to her."

"She didn't do much of that, either. I checked the computer records for access time charged against her. The others hogged the computer, as I figured they would. She used less than an hour's time over the past month.''

''You haven't done much computer work yourself.'' Anita motioned toward the corner of their room. A new spy-eye had appeared this morning. A micro-drill had bored through the wall during the night and the unknown shipboard snoop had inserted the camera carefully. Without their extensive electronic bug-sweeping they would never have detected it. Walden began to wonder who the snoop was and if he had an inexhaustible supply of equipment.

Walden hadn't wanted his computer work read by others—and computer security in this group was a farce. The most incompetent among them could crack standard protection techniques in a few hours. Just to keep in practice, Walden had entered the restricted liftship navigational computer and idly searched through the database.

He wondered if it would be any more difficult gaining access to the computer systems of the accompanying destroyers. He doubted it. The security structure needed to keep meddlers out slowed the execution of commands. A war vessel required instantaneous response to danger. They used RISC—Reduced Instruction Set Computers—to minimize computation speed, and this made onboard security a joke. All anyone needed do was tap into a single instruction and the rest fell into place like a jigsaw puzzle.

''We should be relaxing and planning. That's probably what Doris is doing.''

''A good point, Anita. Preston and the others haven't accomplished much, except giving me headaches.'' He rubbed the back of his neck. Tension rippled the muscles and knotted his shoulders. He stared at the blank vidscreen showing liftspace. For an entire month the pattern had not changed noticeably. An occasional sparkle showed in the blank gray field. He had asked a ship's engineer what caused the flare and had been told random noise in the vidscreen circuit.

Walden wanted it to be more. Anything. The notion that they drifted in a bubble of nothingness bothered him.

''You're just anxious to get back into a routine,'' the woman told him. ''You can't stop working any more than Willie or Paul.

The only dilemma you have is balancing your own research with administrative duties.''

He jerked when his wristwatch hummed. He touched a stud on the side and read the message flashing across the face.

"Captain Belford wants section heads present. We must be nearing the transition point."

"Good," said Anita. "I want to see stars again. This is getting on my nerves." She cast a hurried glance at the vidscreen, then turned away. Walden's bushy eyebrows rose in surprise. She hadn't mentioned any uneasiness to him. She had believed he was the only one bothered by the notion of encapsulation in an ashen bubble that didn't really exist and thrown faster-than-light across fifteen parsecs.

"Want to come along?" he asked.

"No, I've got to be sure my equipment is stored. The lift didn't bother it too much, but I've been repacking the past couple weeks and want to be sure nothing gets broken. It's a long way to restock."

Walden kissed her quickly, then went to the wardroom, looking down branching corridors for Egad. The dog had been prowling for several hours, and Walden wanted to be certain that he was prepared for the transition back to normal space. When he didn't find the dog, he went into the meeting.

"Dr. Walden, please be seated. You are the last one to arrive." Captain Belford's tone was neutral, but the set of his burly body told that he was in no mood to be delayed, especially by a mere passenger.

"The *Hippocrates* is due to enter the Delta Cygnus 4 system in less than four hours. Each department head is responsible for crew preparation and safety. Dr. Walden, please conduct an immediate examination of the cargo hold with Mr. Luria. He has mentioned that many of your people have spent the trip rooting about in the storage crates. I want no more trouble in this area." Captain Belford glared at the cargo officer, who stoically took the criticism.

"As you know, we cannot communicate with our escort ships during starlift, even though the mathematics tells us we are only millimeters apart. The quality of the starlift bubble prevents even visual contact. The reasons are too complex to detail."

The captain looked directly at Walden. The crew knew everything being said. This was for the benefit of the *Hippocrates'* passengers.

"Continuing." Captain Belford touched a control on his desk computer. The vidscreen blinked, casting an eerie glow on his face from below, turning him into a flickering, demonic creature. Walden forced the image away. Captain Belford had been stern but fair throughout the trip. He was no demon conjured from the depths of liftspace.

"We have one item of concern, however. We do not ordinarily travel in convoy. We locked computers with our escorts before lifting to ensure precise course calculations. We do not foresee difficulty in transition into the destination star system, but all departments will be on red alert status."

"Sir," spoke up the chief engineer. "We need to maintain a ten-light-second interval to prevent overlapping and misalignment of our drive fields. Can the military yahoos comply?"

"Of course they can," snapped Zacharias. "Those crews are the best in space."

Walden leaned back and watched the animosity flow around the table. The ship's officers had little good to say about Zacharias or his EPCT company. Their mere presence aboard what had been designed as a hospital ship must have created a deep, festering dislike whose intensity Walden had misjudged.

"I am sure they are, Major," the captain said dryly. "We need to observe every precaution before transition, however." His tone carried a hint of worry. And this made Walden even edgier than he had been. The destroyers and a full company of EPCTs had not come all this distance for training.

The captain continued giving his orders, then abruptly dismissed everyone. "Thank you, ladies and gentlemen. We will enter the Delta Cygnus 4 system in three hours, twenty-one minutes." He stood and left, trailing his senior officers like gas clouds behind a comet's head.

Zacharias sat for a moment, his face florid with anger. Without a word, he shot to his feet and stormed from the wardroom.

"He is in danger of developing high blood pressure," came Miko Nakamura's low, cold voice.

"Why is he so angry?" asked Walden.

"He had a presentation. Graphics, numbers, a full month's workup to be delivered at this meeting. Captain Belford denied him the privilege of giving his rehearsed message."

"What did Zacharias have to say?"

"Not much." Nakamura chuckled. "I should not make light of this. He is my colleague and I advise him."

"What about the saboteur he was so sure had sneaked aboard the *Hippocrates*?"

"A figment of his active imagination. Phantoms often rise and flutter about when there is nothing better to occupy one's mind."

Nakamura bowed slightly and left. Walden went to find Egad and make sure that his team members had lashed down whatever they were working on. He knew it was too much to hope that they would give up entirely on their research until they landed on Schwann.

It took longer to find Egad than he'd intended. Less than ten minutes before transition, he, the dog, and Anita secured the safety webbing to protect them from sudden radial acceleration.

"It was a strange meeting. Captain Belford seemed preoccupied with business he wouldn't share."

"You're making too much of it, Jerome. He's a busy man, and this is his busiest time. From all you and Egad have told me, the captain is going out of his way to avoid Zacharias. The major is enough to irritate anyone."

"Two minutes until we get back to a good view." Walden had swung the vidscreen around so that he could watch the starfields reappear. He reached out and took Anita's hand. "You ready?"

"The starlift into the bubble wasn't too difficult. I don't think getting out will be, either."

Even as she spoke, Walden felt his insides surge in all directions. Then what felt like intense acceleration seized him. As quickly as it had come, it passed.

"There!" he cried. "Stars! We made it!"

"From the data on the screen, the navigator hit the target volume, too. Less than a thousandth of one percent off. I'd call that great shooting over forty-seven light-years."

Walden loosened the safety webbing and adjusted the vidscreen to accept voice commands. "Vid: full circle scan of the exterior," he ordered.

"That spot. That's one destroyer. Where is the other?" Anita slipped free of her couch and sat beside him.

"Vid: Find the other destroyer."

The screen image spun crazily. Walden instinctively grabbed the sides of the couch to keep his balance. Closing his eyes and opening them again in a few seconds kept him from a bad vertigo attack.

"Why did it do that? The destroyer captain must have—"

Anita's words cut off just as strident alarms sounded and Walden shouted, "That's not one of ours. It's not even a destroyer!"

His vidscreen winked off, a flashing warning message replacing the starfield.

PREPARE FOR MISSILE ATTACK . . .

The explosion against the hull sent shock waves throughout the *Hippocrates*. Anita Tarleton was flung across the small cabin and crashed hard into the far bulkhead. Egad whimpered and struggled to free himself from his safety harness. The straps left behind bloody ribbons where he had been thrown about.

Walden moaned as he released the straps around his own waist and shoulders. The violent motion had given him bruises that would turn all the colors of a rainbow soon.

Panic gripped Walden. He was worrying about trivial matters. They were under attack! What they had seen on the vidscreen had been an incoming missile, not the second destroyer.

"Anita, are you hurt?"

"Just shaken up." She moved so that her back was against the bulkhead. "There's one good thing about this. We don't have to worry about spy devices." She reached over to pluck out the newest spy-eye from its hiding place. The composite material bulkhead had buckled and snapped. In places holes gaped as if giant fists had been driven through the wall.

"Egad?"

"Hurt," the dog whimpered. He circled around three times and curled up in the corner of the room, head stuck under his tail. Walden quickly examined him and found nothing serious. The dog's abrasions would heal without complications.

"We'd better find out what's going on. Who fired on us?"

"I think we collided with the second destroyer," said Anita.

"You didn't see the computer warning. We were fired on by another ship—and I don't think it was either of our escort ships."

"Then who?" A horrified expression crossed Anita's face as she came to the conclusion that Walden had already reached. "The Sov-Lats wouldn't dare!"

"They might do it," Walden said grimly. "They might justify blowing up the *Hippocrates* as a preventive measure. Why were we coming to Schwann?"

"Research," she said in a weak voice.

"Bioweapons research," he corrected. "Their efforts are years behind ours. They might be afraid we'll come up with something that can turn the tide."

"The team on-planet. They might have been killed."

Shock washed across Walden in cold waves. He needed to know more of the situation. The two destroyers accompanying them had been unusual. The full company of EPCTs should have been a giveaway that conditions in the Delta Cygnus 4 system were not peaceful.

He had known that, yet had spent the past month denying it. Vague nagging at the edge of his mind also told him Zacharias might have been right about the cargo hold incident being sabotage and attempted murder.

He shook himself. Paranoia solved nothing. "Let's find out what we can." He helped Anita to her feet. She wobbled for a few steps, then regained her strength.

"What about Egad?"

"He'll be as safe here as he would be anywhere else in the ship."

Lights flashed and sirens howled within the ship. The emergency lights gave first warning of disaster. In the *Hippocrates*, as in any spaceship, the threat of loss of atmosphere dictated visual rather than auditory warnings. Walden considered breaking open an emergency locker and getting into a pressure suit. Since the air seemed normal and he clearly heard the distant sirens, he refused to take the time to don a clumsy emergency suit.

He dragged Anita along behind until they got to the passage-way leading to the control room. Three senior officers lay in the corridor, pools of blood surrounding them. Walden quickly checked for pulses in two; both were dead. Anita, white-faced and shaking, whispered, "He's dead, too."

They rushed into the control room and were immediately taken by surprise. Walden had expected confusion, even panic. For all the rush and tension, the entire crew might be anticipating their lunch break.

Captain Belford sat in the command chair, his strong fingers working over the array of contacts. Indicators blinked in a colorful symphony of light and the captain spoke into a throat mike as he worked. The first officer had pushed aside an injured computer officer and worked through endless problems.

Miko Nakamura stood to one side and silently observed.

"What happened?" Walden asked her.

Nakamura's attention remained on the control boards. "An array of weapons was brought to bear against us. Some modes of attack proved ineffectual. Others have severely damaged our ability to maneuver."

"I saw the missile warning."

Nakamura dismissed it with a chop of her hand. "That was nothing. Our sensors detected it. It was destroyed quickly, as were the other four missiles. They were poorly built and did not evade our counter-weapons."

"What did all the damage?"

"Radiation weapons. An energy field or plasma. We have nothing like it and could not defend against it."

"How did the Sov-Lats manage to build such a secret weapon? Surely our spies are as good as theirs. They know everything we do."

"Yes, that is so," Nakamura said in a strange tone. "Now, please leave the bridge. We have much work to do. We are still under engagement."

The words had barely left her lips when the *Hippocrates* rocked again under a new barrage. Walden watched wide-eyed as bank after bank of instrumentation went dark. Another attack of this magnitude would destroy them completely.

CHAPTER

"Full evasive tactics," barked Captain Belford. He swung around in his chair and touched several of the contacts on a panel to his side. The controls that had gone dark flickered, brightened, and then returned to their normal state. He worked the controls like a virtuoso playing a synthesizer. Tiny hums grew and collided with a deeper bass vibrating through the liftship's decking.

"Damage control, report."

The captain cocked his head to one side and acted on the information fed into his left earphone. Gradually the red indicators winked to amber and finally turned to a more serene green.

"You should leave immediately," Nakamura said. "He works well to regain control of the ship. He should not be distracted by your petty concerns."

Walden took Anita's arm and guided her off the bridge. The flame-haired woman's temper had risen at Nakamura's suggestion that what they sought had to be of little importance. They stopped just beyond the hatchway and looked back in.

"You wouldn't know it to look at him but the captain's hair is artificially gray."

"What?"

54

"He uses a dye to give him that distinguished appearance. I saw him in the commissary rummaging through the chemicals. I made a list of what he took. Actually, my computer run shows the dye to be a rather sophisticated formulation."

"I don't care if he shaves his head," said Walden. "He's getting us back into survivable condition." Only a few red lights blinked on the control panels now, showing the systems were damaged but minimally functional.

"Look, Jerome. In here." Anita pointed to the communications room set off from the bridge. The officer in charge had died when a bulkhead snapped. A sharp sliver of the composite material had severed his throat. Walden held down his rising gorge. He preferred dealing with neat, clean dissections, when necessary. This much blood—and all of it human—bothered him. His parents had wanted him to become a surgeon; they had barely accepted it when he had received his Ph.D. and gone into gen-gineering.

"He never knew what hit him," he said.

"Forget him," Anita said impatiently. "The vidscreen. Look at it! This is the master control for all communications in and out of the *Hippocrates*."

"There are the destroyers." In spite of the bloody pool, Walden took a step forward to get a better view of the vidscreen. The escorts worked in a pattern he had read about when he had worked on the germ-bombs that had worked so well on Phobos. They intertwined their flight vectors to concentrate their fire on a target while never getting close enough to present an easy single prey for the enemy.

"They're going away from us. The Doppler shift shows it." He pointed to a readout panel showing relative motion.

"There's something else out there. The destroyers are working on it. See?"

"You're right. That's got to be the Sov-Lats' ship."

"It isn't, though." Anita reached over the communications officer's corpse and worried at the controls for a few seconds. "The computer recognition program drew a blank. That's an unknown vessel."

"Who knows what has been happening on Schwann? The Sov-Lats might have built a prototype for a new warship." He shivered at the notion. If liftdrive engines weren't required, the Sov-Lats ship might be able to outrun and outgun them.

"They're doing a good job ganging up on the enemy," said Anita. "There! They fired a double barrage of kinetics. Those babies will blow the hell out of 'em!"

Thousands of fragmenting steel balls loaded with high explosives erupted from the warheads of two huge missiles. No hull could withstand such a fusillade.

The vidscreen turned all the colors of the rainbow, then faded. Elements of the CCD camera on the hull had burned out. Anita switched in auxiliary circuits and restored most of the picture. The two destroyers continued their attack, but the enemy vessel cruised along unharmed by the kinetics.

"What happened? Did they miss?"

"The enemy ship did something. A plasma field. I don't know." Anita turned to Walden. "Jerome, I'm frightened. I've never seen anything like that before. They destroyed all the explosive bearings with a single zap from some type of energy weapon. We don't have anything like that!"

"They do. Damn!"

The two destroyers jockeyed for position as they raced past their target. Inertial guidance mechanisms swung turrets and prepared a new volley. A creeping missile inched across toward one destroyer. The missile was easily countered.

"I don't understand. The Sov-Lats know sublight missiles are almost worthless against a destroyer. If they have such a potent energy weapon, why not use it again?"

"It might require recharging. Who knows what type of collectors they use to power it," said Anita. Even as she spoke the rainbow arced across the vidscreen again. This time she was unable to restore more than half of the charge-coupled device elements that acted as an electronic lens.

Even getting half the scene of battle, it was obvious there was one fewer player in the deadly drama.

"A destroyer blew up. The energy weapon hit it."

"No, wait, it's still there. Its engines are dead, though. No power indications." Walden didn't want to think about the consequences of the starlift engines being wrecked. Deadly ionizing radiation would bathe the ship and kill everyone aboard as surely as the strange energy weapon.

Death from enemy fire or death from their own engine leakage hardly mattered. Dead was dead.

"Egad, come here. Good dog. Are you hurt?" Anita knelt and scratched behind the dog's floppy ears. He was covered in blood from head to tail.

"Not hurt. Others. Structure of ship crunched. Walls gone. Some places howl."

"Howl? Is there air leakage?" demanded Walden.

The dog turned his blue and brown eyes on the scientist, not really understanding. He dropped to the deck and put his head on his crossed paws and simply stared.

"You've done well, Egad. Thank you," said Walden. "Can you go into the control room and listen to what Captain Belford is saying? We need to find out all we can."

"There's no need," protested Anita. "We can—" She glanced out and saw Major Zacharias arrive with four armed guards. Two posted themselves outside the hatchway leading to the bridge. The other two followed their superior.

"Egad, find out what's going on. We don't want Zacharias taking over."

"Can I rip out his throat?" The dog's tongue lolled as he panted at the notion.

Walden surprised himself when he answered, "Yes, *if* he's trying to take over from Captain Belford. Otherwise, just watch and report back when you get something definite about whoever's attacking us." The dog sprang to his feet and raced from the communications room.

"Why'd you tell him that? You know he'll do it. He hates Zacharias."

"I'd rather take my chances on my own with a ruined ship and an instruction manual than let Zacharias assume command."

"You might be right," Anita admitted. "I forgot to tell you. I looked up his record. It's everything he said. He was a hero, and he got that chestful of medals honestly."

Walden shook his head. He found it hard to believe.

"Accidents happen all the time. That might have been one."

He shrugged it off. A new battle took form on the damaged vidscreen. Only parts of it came through, but he saw enough to realize that the enemy ship outmaneuvered the surviving destroyer. The enemy vessel must bristle with launch tubes to be able to fire in all directions. The ludicrously slow missiles posed no threat. The energy weapons did.

Egad trotted back into the room and tugged at Walden's hand. "They agree."

"What are you talking about?" Walden knelt and looked the dog squarely in the eyes. "Take it slow and tell me what they agree on."

"Bad ship is not yours."

Walden held back a surge of irrational anger. "We know that," he said as patiently as possible.

"It is not of your kind," amended Egad.

"It's an *alien* warship?" The dog bobbed his head in agreement, then licked Walden's hand. The man patted the dog as his mind raced. Humanity had explored other systems for almost a hundred years and had found only three worlds with even rudimentary life. Delta Cygnus 4 was an important find because lower lifeforms had evolved and gave enough oxygen for humans to breathe, if they used respirators. On every new planet found, the exploratory team sought out life, hoping to find intelligence.

There had never been a trace. And now that more than a trace was discovered, the aliens proved themselves to be treacherous and warlike.

"It hardly seems fair. We find them, and they hate our guts."

"They must have found Schwann," said Anita. "Who knows what they were looking for—or what they found below."

"You're saying that this attack might have been provoked by something we did?"

"The Sov-Lats might have fired on them." Anita's lips thinned to a grim line. "*We* might have, for that matter. Our base might have thought they were some Sov-Lat trick."

"There's more to it than that. The NAA high command didn't send two destroyers and Zacharias' killers along for fun. They must have expected trouble."

"That doesn't make sense. If they did, the destroyers would have preceded us. We all made the transition together."

"Other ship wants us as a decoy," cut in Egad.

"Great. An unarmed hospital ship is going to draw out a warship with who knows what kind of weaponry. Haven't they noticed that the *Hippocrates* is damaged? We can't take any more fire without ending up like that." Walden tapped the vidscreen where the powerless destroyer's image seemed trapped in glue. The battle raged in other parts of space, letting the victim continue helplessly along its last vector.

"Are they sure of the identification?" asked Walden. "It *is* an alien ship and not some new Sov-Lat class?"

"The bitch without smell is sure," said Egad.

As far as Walden was concerned, Nakamura's opinion made it true. He didn't think their "advisor" made mistakes like this.

The *Hippocrates* shifted beneath their feet, throwing them around the small communications room. Walden gingerly lifted himself away from the dead officer still in the control chair. He wiped bloodied hands on his shirt, as if this would erase everything including death.

"Egad, stop that!" he bellowed. The dog looked up from where he had been lapping at the pool of coagulating blood. He didn't understand what upset his master. Walden grabbed the dog's collar and pulled him away. "And don't eat any of the dead, either," he said.

"Won't," promised Egad. "Human meat tastes bad."

Walden didn't want to find out how the dog knew. He stopped in front of the two guards. They moved to block his entry onto the bridge.

"Sir, no one is to enter."

"We will. Tell Nakamura we want to see her. We know we're under attack by another intelligent species."

The guards exchanged puzzled looks. One shrugged and ducked inside. A few seconds later, he returned and motioned them inside.

Zacharias and Captain Belford argued by the main control boards. The captain had discarded his throat mike and had gone back to a variable light command wand. He used the laser to touch photocells on the boards with uncanny skill. Nowhere did a red light shine. Full control had been returned to him.

"You make an odd claim. On what do you base this?" asked Nakamura.

"You let us in when we said we faced an alien warship. That makes it true. You wouldn't have seen us if it had been a Sov-Lat vessel."

This logic brought a tiny smile to Nakamura's lips. "You are a worthy opponent, Dr. Walden." She glanced down at Egad and started to speak. She came to a conclusion that had nothing to do with the dog. "You have any ideas about these creatures?"

"Did we start it? Or did they attack us without warning?"

"You ask a difficult question. We did not know they existed. Zacharias had permission to wipe out the Sov-Lat base on-planet in retaliation for other, uh, shall we call it indiscretions on our Soviet opponent's part. It is not covered in standing orders what to do when attacked by an alien."

"We can't engage the ship. Anita and I watched the alien use its energy weapon against one escort. It's dead in space now."

"We received a feeble transmission from an emergency radio. Several still live aboard the *Tannhauser*. The *Winston* sustained damage but is carrying on the fight."

"We can't match the alien!" cried Anita. Both the captain and Zacharias turned to glare at her. "We can't!"

"We do not need to do so," Nakamura assured her. "We merely draw away the enemy's attention. The *Winston* will do what it must."

"You have seen the damage reports," said Walden. "Just looking at the structural damage, you know we can't take even a near miss. They'll blow us out of space!"

Nakamura's tiny smile turned into a sneer. "We die with honor then. How is it you develop fearsome bioweapons that rot the flesh and destroy the mind and body, yet you turn squeamish at other forms of killing?"

"The sight of blood makes me sick," Walden said. Nakamura mistook his honesty for a joke. She laughed.

"I misjudged you once more, Doctor. Accept my apologies." She bowed slightly more than she had the last time. "It is now time to place our destiny in the capable hands of the *Winston*'s captain and gunnery officer."

Captain Belford pushed Nakamura away and aimed the command wand at a bank of controls behind her. Deep within the *Hippocrates* stirred rocket engines. The ship jerked about, then settled down. The captain changed frequencies on the laser wand and gave new instructions to the computer-driven board.

Nakamura watched impassively. Zacharias shifted nervously, wiping his lips with his left hand and leaving his right on the butt of a holstered pistol. The two guards behind him fingered their own laserifles. Walden moved closer to Anita and put his arm around her.

Walden found his mouth filled with gummy cotton. His heart almost exploded in his chest when he saw the tiny image on the captain's vidscreen whirl and spin and launch four missiles. Against a destroyer, those were puny weapons. Against the *Hippocrates*, they were deadly.

The vidscreen exploded in a flare of eye-searing color. When Walden's vision returned and he had wiped away the tears running down his cheeks, he saw only green lights. Captain Belford sagged back in his command chair, fingers laxly holding the laser command wand.

"What happened?" asked Anita. "Did the *Winston* get the alien ship?"

"Of course," came Nakamura's calm voice. "My tactics seldom fail. From the first encounter, it was obvious that the enemy could not differentiate between the destroyers and us. We posed a threat, or so they thought. This allowed the *Winston* to turn full batteries against them."

"No further damage," Captain Belford said. "The destroyer caught all four of the missiles launched at us." He sat up and ran a hand through his sweat-lank gray hair. Walden found himself wondering if the protein dye would come off on the man's fingers. It didn't.

"I'm glad it's over." Anita sighed.

Something caused Walden to turn toward Miko Nakamura. The woman worked at a computer console diligently, her fingers flying over the keyboard. She did not rely on voice programming, which made him suspicious.

"What are you doing?" he asked.

"There are other aliens in this system. Check this, Captain."

She touched a key on the board to transmit her data to the command console.

"That does it," Captain Belford said angrily. "We're going to starlift back to Earth immediately. I will not risk my ship in another engagement. This is *not* a warship!"

"There're more?" Anita asked numbly.

"At least one, possibly two," said Zacharias, peering over the captain's shoulder to see the display. "We can take them. We know they're here. No more sneak attacks on us!"

"We lift for Earth," Captain Belford said. "As long as I command this ship, my orders will be followed. Is that understood?" He stared at the two young marines behind Zacharias. Their heads moved the slightest amount in nods. Zacharias might be their commander but Captain Belford was in charge while they were aboard his ship. Few dictators carried the power of a ship's captain—and even new recruits understood this.

The men in the EPCT were far from newly enlisted.

"Prepare for the bubble," Captain Belford barked. He worked with his command wand to position the *Hippocrates*.

"Sir, no response from the navigation computer," came the first officer's disturbing report. "We might have sustained damage to the database. I can't find Earth coordinates to home in on."

"Auxiliary," ordered the captain.

"Gone, sir. It's as if the computer has been wiped clean of what we need."

Walden turned to Nakamura. She held a computer memory block circuit in her hand. She spoke before Walden could ask the obvious question.

"I have erased the information you require, Captain. We will not return to Earth."

"Give me that," ordered Captain Belford. To the marines he said, "If she doesn't surrender it immediately, shoot her!"

Miko Nakamura faced the leveled laserifles with a calm that frightened Walden. The woman was prepared to die. And for what? He didn't understand her motives.

CHAPTER

"This is mutiny," Captain Belford told the woman. Miko Nakamura looked at him impassively. "You will obey a direct order or be placed under immediate arrest!"

"There are reasons for what I do, Captain," Nakamura said. "You have worked with me during the past month. You know I am not subject to fantasy."

Walden couldn't keep from glancing at Major Zacharias for his reaction. The officer had drawn his pistol and worked to one side to catch the woman in a cross fire.

"I have no desire to examine psych profiles. Take the memory block from her." He motioned to his first officer. The man stood and took one step in Nakamura's direction. He stopped suddenly. Sweat broke out on his forehead and gleamed in the subdued light from the control panels.

"She's got a bomb. Look at it!"

Walden saw Nakamura place a cylinder on top of the ceramic computer memory unit. A red dot glowed at the tip of the shaft.

"It is keyed to me," Nakamura said. "A colorful term for the device is a deadman's switch. Shoot me and you will destroy the block. Try to forcibly arrest me and I release the trigger. The block is destroyed in this circumstance, also."

"That doesn't matter," Captain Belford said. "I can get replacement programs from the library."

"I have destroyed them. My month has been spent planning for any foreseeable problem."

"She's bluffing," said Zacharias.

"It doesn't matter. The *Winston* is still navigable. We can get the necessary data from her computer."

"Hear me out, Captain. What I have to say is of extreme importance to the Earth's continued safety."

Captain Belford motioned for the marines to stand at ease. Zacharias kept his pistol trained on the woman. From the twitches along his trigger finger, he longed to open fire. Walden had seen the way Nakamura maneuvered him to do her bidding during the trip. Technically, Zacharias commanded the military unit. Practically, Nakamura controlled the EPCT company through manipulation and subtle pressures on both officers and enlisted men.

"Each starlift leaves behind residue in the mathematical sense," she said. "This residue can be detected and from it an accurate flight vector determined. If we leave, the aliens will be able to determine not only the direction of Earth but its distance from Delta Cygnus 4. You will be posting signs showing where our home world is."

"We can fight them off. Look how easily we defeated their missiles." Zacharias' lips curled into a sneer. "I never thought you'd turn chicken."

"She wants to stay and fight, you fool," spoke up Anita. "By running we might save ourselves and endanger Earth."

"Just so," agreed Nakamura.

Walden knew nothing about sophisticated detection methods or if Nakamura was right. He suspected that she was. She had nothing to gain and everything to lose by staying in a planetary system where hostile aliens were establishing a foothold. It also struck Walden as plausible that Nakamura would place the interests of Earth ahead of her own well-being. She was a patriot, certainly loyal to the Japanese Hegemony and possibly to the NAA since the political interests overlapped. An Earth destroyed meant no more Emperor, no more Japan, and total failure on her part.

"We don't have to engage. The *Winston* used us as a cat's-paw and it worked," said Walden. "Can't we just cruise around until we know what the situation really is?"

"We are in danger if we do so," said Captain Belford. His tone indicated that he had begun to doubt a return to Earth was in their best interests.

"We need to do damage estimates," said Walden. "You know what condition the *Hippocrates* is in better than I ever could, but I'd need a few hours to check my staff and be certain that everything is . . . under control." Walden didn't want to come out and warn against starlifting with deadly experiments unsecured. There had been enough friction on this point.

"You feel strongly enough on this matter that you would die?" Captain Belford asked Nakamura. The set of the woman's face gave the answer more eloquently than words.

The captain turned to his first officer. "Get the block and put it back into our computer database. We'll have sufficient protection from the *Winston* until we can verify her claims. This isn't something I had ever considered. Get the numbers from her and check them out, too. Report in one hour on the matter."

Nakamura handed over the memory block and touched a stud on the end of the cylinder, disarming the small bomb. "We must protect our home," she said. "Death comes to everyone eventually. We need to insure that our race survives."

Walden saw that they were staying in the Delta Cygnus 4 system. He signaled Egad to accompany him. Anita edged from the room and joined them in the corridor.

"We're in for a world of trouble," she said. "The tension in there was thick enough to slice with a cutting beam."

"Captain Belford isn't a soldier and doesn't see this as his fight. I don't think he wanted to ferry either Zacharias' company or us."

"Who can blame him? We've given him nothing but headaches since lifting." Anita took his arm and leaned her head against his shoulder as they made their way into the depths of the *Hippocrates*. Walden tried to evaluate the damage as they sought out the members of his research team. Although walls had splintered and some bulkheads had buckled and bent in half, the superstructure appeared intact. They were safe enough, even if the ship was no longer pleasing to look at.

"Doris!" called Walden, seeing the woman digging through a pile of debris at the far end of the main dining room. "Are you hurt?"

"I'm fine," the woman said, running a gnarled hand through her tangled, dirty brown hair. "My cat ran off when everything started falling apart." She hunted in vain for the pudgy feline. Walden had seen it several times and it had always been asleep. The shock of battle must have sent it racing off in panic to find a safe spot to hide.

"I'll have someone look for the cat." He glanced at Egad. The dog bared his fangs showing what he thought of the task.

"No!" Doris' eyes shot wide open. "I mean, that's all right. I'll find Tabby Hayes by myself. He . . . he's a bit skittish."

Walden shook his head. The cat was more comatose than skittish under normal circumstances.

"What happened?" Doris Yerrow perched on the back of a chair and looked around the ruined cabin. For all her dishevelment, she held her composure well, except on the subject of her runaway cat.

Walden quickly outlined all they knew. He was startled by how easily she accepted news that had stunned him.

"Imagine," Yerrow said, "my first off-planet trip and we find intelligent aliens. I wonder what the odds are on that? I need to consider what this means."

"The odds against finding any intelligent life are high. Remember Fermi's Paradox—why haven't we found the aliens long ago, or at least heard them calling? This must be the answer: they were lying in wait for us, ready to ambush us. If you see any of the others, tell them I'm holding a meeting for all personnel in one hour." Walden looked around. "Here is as good a place as any. And tell them to stay out of the way of the crew. I don't want reports of interfering with repairs."

Doris nodded and returned to her search for her bloated cat.

"She smells like plastic," Egad said in an aggrieved tone when they were out of Doris' earshot.

"You just don't like cats," said Anita.

"Her cat smells bad, too. Ugly. Like her, like plastic. Not

even worth ripping apart.'' Egad snapped his teeth firmly to emphasis his point.

"Never mind that. We've got to check the others. I can imagine what Willie has done. We might all be swimming in bacteriophages if his experiment was damaged.''

"I'll track down Preston. You can find the others. I'm not getting paid to be your assistant, after all.''

"But you do it so well." Walden caught Anita by the arm and held her back for an instant. "Thanks.''

She flashed him a bright smile, kissed him and went off, Egad trotting alongside. Walden didn't know what he would do without them—man's best friend and the woman he loved. He began clearing a spot in the debris to hold his meeting. When he had finished he found Willie Klugel and several others in the cargo hold complaining about the damage to their packing crates. They were oblivious to anything else that had happened, totally engrossed in their own research and personal misfortunes.

"How close to a usable weapon are you, Willie?''

"Months, years, who can tell?'' The balding man squinted in Walden's direction. "You're not turning into one of those 'produce or be damned' types are you?''

"We might need it. I've been thinking of delivery systems. Even though the *Hippocrates* isn't equipped as a war vessel, there has to be some way of fighting back.''

"In space?'' scoffed Marni Donelli. She rubbed her callused hands together in an unconscious washing gesture, showing she wanted no part of combat. "Impossible. You need sophisticated missiles. Laser tracking, inertial guidance, all those things plus countermeasures. You don't want the enemy blowing up your germ-bomb on your own doorstep.''

"We have enough aerosol canisters aboard to propel some type of bomb system,'' spoke up Chin. "If Willie's T-odd phages are useful, let's use them.''

"We'd have to penetrate a hull and explode the bombs inside their ships,'' said Burnowski, rubbing his stubbled chin as he spoke. "Not impossible. We can corner a drive engineer and find out more. We might zap and slap—hit with radiation to soften them, then follow with the penetrating warhead. I don't like any of this, though. It's too dangerous to us.''

"Let's adjourn to the main dining room," Walden said, "and discuss it further. I wanted to be sure everyone had their experiments well contained. I don't want any surprises, especially if we're attacked again."

"Again?" asked Donelli. The small woman ran both of her hands through sandy hair to get a lock out of her eyes. "We might be shot at again?"

"Captain Belford has detected another alien ship orbiting Schwann. Our escorts are preceding us, so there shouldn't be any trouble as far as we're concerned."

"We can't count on that, though. Is that what you're telling us?" Marni Donelli appeared distraught over the notion of combat. Walden saw this as another instance of a scientist working on weaponry and never believing it will be used—or wanting to know if it is.

He controlled the shaking in his hands as he moved to stand at the end of a long table. He couldn't fault Donelli for that. He felt the same way.

A quick head count showed that his entire research team had assembled. He rapped smartly on the table for attention. Only when Egad growled deep in his throat did silence fall. Walden looked around the table and tried to come to a decision about their mood.

It ran the gamut from stark fright in Paul Preston's dark-haired assistant, Claudette Wyse, to a curious anticipation in Doris Yerrow, who held her cat and stroked it almost savagely. Her pale eyes blazed with a light that Walden interpreted to be passion. Doris' life had been dull and sheltered, he knew; did this present her an opportunity for adventure? He wished she had found it somewhere else, if she believed fierce space battle with aliens to be a grand and noble undertaking.

Jerome Walden was scared of what might happen.

"We are in a combat zone," he said, his voice strong in spite of the inner quaking he felt. "The *Hippocrates* came through the first battle in good shape, although one escort, the *Tannhauser*, didn't fare as well. I don't think the *Winston* sustained any damage."

"Jerome, why don't we get the bloody hell out of here and go home? Why stay where we might get our asses blown off?"

Burnowski sat with arms folded across his chest and his legs tightly intertwined around the chair's base. He looked like a compressed beryllium spring ready to explode.

"There are reasons we will not," came Zacharias' booming voice. The major strode up, his two marine guards a step behind. Walden thought the officer looked like a Roman emperor arriving to address the Senate. Even worse, Zacharias probably thought of himself in those terms.

"Give me one," said Burnowski. "I've got work to do, and this is disruptive. I can't concentrate, and with the ship bouncing all over space I can't even set a beaker down without having it thrown across the lab."

"The first alien vessel has been destroyed totally. There is a second in orbit around Delta Cygnus 4." He turned and used a laser wand similar to Captain Belford's to activate a large vidscreen at the far end of the room. Walden wondered if the major had tested this earlier. The dramatic effect caused breaths to be sucked in and held.

The screen showed a blue-white water world hung on the sable backdrop of space. Schwann looked enough like Earth at first glance to give them all a pang of homesickness. Only after a few seconds of study did the world give up details not belonging to Earth. The misshapen continents were in the wrong places. There wasn't nearly as much water and the clouds looked . . . different.

How water vapor viewed from space could appear different, Walden couldn't say. First impression aside, this was *not* home.

"There is no question that this ship is another alien war craft." Zacharias pointed out a tiny bright speck moving around the planet, coming from the night side. "We are concerned that the aliens are in league with the Sov-Lats."

"What?" Walden didn't know whether to laugh or get sick at such a notion. Zacharias' paranoia knew no bounds. "That's absurd!"

"Maybe not. They *did* attack the *Hippocrates*."

"Your logic is shaky, Major," said Anita. "If we have two enemies, there's no reason that they have to be allies."

Walden pulled Zacharias aside. "Are you holding back any information?"

"No, why? That is the reason for this conference. We want the entire crew to understand what we're up against."

"Nakamura made a good point about an alien vessel getting a lock on Earth if we starlifted out of the system. If the aliens are allied with the Sov-Lats, that wouldn't matter. The Soviet Pact *knows* where Earth is. It's their home, too. I can't believe they'd enter any alliance with an alien race against us. They know how dangerous that would be for them."

Zacharias sneered at such naivete. "They're devious. The Sov-Lats might be stringing the aliens along, using them to do their dirty work. We've seen it before."

Walden threw up his hands in disgust. The officer had an idea firmly fixed in his mind and neither God nor a full revolution of the galaxy would shake it loose.

"What have you decided?" Walden asked. "We should know how to best prepare. Several of us have come up with preliminary ideas for weapons systems."

"Those won't be needed," Zacharias said brusquely. "The *Winston* can defeat the alien warship now orbiting Delta Cygnus 4."

Walden looked over Zacharias' shoulder. Doris Yerrow had walked the length of the room to stand a few paces from the large vidscreen. She was engrossed in watching the display, her fingers rubbing her cat's neck with almost manic frenzy. The cat hardly stirred in her fierce grip.

Zacharias rattled on about duty to Earth and how Nakamura needlessly complicated the issue with her meddling. Walden wasn't listening. He stopped a meter behind Yerrow.

He saw what had drawn her attention. The speck representing the alien ship glowed with all the colors of the rainbow. Arching down to the planet's surface, a shimmering energy toroid of the purest silver caused the vidscreen to blank out momentarily.

"Give us more magnification, Major," snapped Walden. Startled, the man obeyed without thinking.

"Their MCG is aimed at the surface." Walden experienced an instant of vertigo as Zacharias increased magnification to the limits of the *Hippocrates'* external CCD cameras.

"That's Homeport!"

Walden didn't try to see who had recognized Schwann's most

populous city. The deceptively fragile shimmery silver micro-wave curtain from space moved along the ground, chewing up dirt and turning it into slag. When it reached the perimeter of the city, it did not stop. Dirt and vegetation had turned to molten glass. Now buildings wobbled and flowed as the plasma field touched them.

The pulsed microwaves swept across the city with frightful speed. In front were homes and offices, schools and hospitals, for almost a half million people. Behind, the beam left only smoldering ruin and death.

"Homeport. They're destroying it!"

"No," Walden said in a choked voice. "They've *destroyed* it. There's nothing left. Nothing!"

CHAPTER

"There won't be anyone left alive on the whole damned planet!"

Walden swung, startled at Doris Yerrow's exultation. "The microwave weapons are scouring the planet. There's no reason to be happy about that. Those are our colleagues." He took a deep breath and let it out slowly. "A few are old friends of mine."

"I didn't mean anything by it," Yerrow said contritely. "It . . . it is just such a display of stark power. It frightened me."

She hadn't sounded scared. She had been in awe—and Walden thought there might have been more than a touch of admiration, too. Had the quiet, mousy woman lived too long with her own thoughts as company and abandoned her humanity?

"Major, what can you tell us about that weapon?" Walden had no reason to ask. His expertise lay in other areas, but they *were* scientists. Any data might prove useful. If they learned something of the alien weaponry, they might also learn something of the aliens themselves. What did they breathe? Oxygen? Were they humanoid? What bacteria lived in their guts? Would Willie Klugel's T-odd bacteriophage work against them? What of Preston's angiogenesis factor? Internal bleeding would kill a human in a few minutes. What was the key to an alien enemy's biochemistry?

Even Walden's own work might prove useful, if they learned enough of alien physiology. He could slow signal transmission in nerve dendrites in humans, scrambling thought processes and causing poor decisions to be made. How could he apply this to the aliens?

In his research team, Walden had enough brainpower—even genius—to win a war before it spread from Schwann. He agreed with Miko Nakamura in one regard. They dared not allow the aliens the opportunity to use their deadly plasma cannon against Earth.

He tried to take his eyes off the vidscreen showing the destruction wrought on Schwann's surface. He failed. The ghastly scene burned itself permanently into his memory. Those had been men and women on the planet. Friends in some cases, fellow scientists, humans. Homeport had been an NAA city, the largest on the world.

"They employ two weapons. In space, they use a charged compact torus of plasma. They fire it at almost 3000 kilometers per second—it comes at us at close to ten billion gravities of acceleration. It punches through anything it touches. They don't use it on the ground. They use a simple MCG—microwave compression generator. They burn hell out of anything they hit with it." Zacharias seemed pleased with his small presentation.

"What of the Sov-Lats' base?" Walden asked.

"The *Winston* has reported," came Nakamura's level voice from behind. He glanced over his shoulder, not wanting to take his eyes off the horror displayed on the screen but finding the excuse in the woman's entry. "The Sov-Lat base was hit first. The aliens used missiles tipped with nuclear warheads."

"How crude," muttered Zacharias. "What size?"

"Small. No more than one megaton. We are trying to learn more of the devices, but it is difficult without accurate monitoring of the explosions."

Walden wondered if Nakamura used the "we" in a royal sense. Who else aboard the *Hippocrates* could do such analysis except her and Zacharias?

"We are spiraling inward toward the planet. The *Winston* is in a lower orbit than the alien vessel, will come up from behind faster, then brake and rise to slip in from behind. In this way we hope to take the alien by surprise. The alien ship's own exhaust will shield the *Winston* on its attack run. They shouldn't be able to fire their compact toroid device.''

Walden nodded. He had been briefed on such tactics years before. Although he had little interest in tactics, he needed to know something about the military's needs to better design the bioweapons.

"What about the *Tannhauser*?'' asked Yerrow. "It looks as if it might blow up at any instant.''

"Damage was severe. A compact toroid struck its lift engines. Preliminary report from the ship is not promising. It will never leave this system.''

"What about—'' Yerrow began. Nakamura cut her off with a wave of her hand.

"There is nothing more to report.''

Walden knew that a considerable amount of intelligence had been gathered. Two destroyers laden with sensors and whatever equipment Nakamura and Zacharias had placed aboard the *Hippocrates* poured out continuous streams of data. The woman simply didn't want to be bothered with further questions.

"Need to know,'' she said softly to Walden as she walked past him.

Walden swore under his breath. It never changed. Anita had a project and could not share it with him. He didn't have any reason for knowing. What he had never learned, he could never divulge accidentally. Even now, the same rules applied.

Walden moved to one side of the large dining area and studied his staff members. He and Anita had been plagued by a never-ending stream of spy devices. Had one of his own team been responsible? Egad had tried to sniff out the hiding place for what had to be a large store of the electronic devices. The dog had failed in a full month of effort.

A more likely source for the spying was Miko Nakamura. Walden had watched her enough to know she missed nothing. Her cold eyes took in hints, and her logical mind produced answers.

He wondered what the questions were.

Egad had reported fully on Edouard Zacharias. The man had spent his every waking minute working with his company of

EPCTs. He might have dispatched a well-trained soldier to plant the devices, but he had no reason to spy on either Walden or Anita. The major considered them mere scientists and beneath his contempt.

Doubts crept in as he considered all angles. Walden had assumed he was the victim of the spy probes. Anita might have been the target—her and the damned secret project. She had made minute notes in a special notebook keyed to her fingerprints. Anyone but her opening the book would destroy the contents. The cameras might have been an attempt to read over her shoulder.

Walden wished he had a better idea what went on among his own kind. Trying to deal with them and the warlike aliens gave him a headache that throbbed and burned in his temples.

"Secure yourselves, as if we were getting ready to lift," ordered Zacharias.

"Major, you're not in command," Anita said, indignant at the man's tone. "When I hear that from Captain Belford, *then* I'll obey. Right now, I've got work to do." She shot Walden a hot look accusing him of not standing up to the officer before stalking out of the dining room. The others drifted away, muttering among themselves. Walden had lost control of his meeting, not that he had anything more to say. Nakamura and Zacharias had given him all the information he could use.

He stared at the vidscreen until it rippled and went black. The captain might have shut it off or an electronics failure had burned it out. Walden couldn't tell.

He patted Egad as the last of his staff left the room. Doris Yerrow gave one longing look at the darkened vidscreen, as if wishing to see more of the destruction caused on the planet's surface. Walden didn't understand the woman. He didn't understand anything. All he wanted was some peace and quiet.

He wasn't likely to get either.

Egad turned his head to one side, listening hard. The dog strained to get away from him. Walden released his hold on the dog's collar. Egad raced off in the direction of the control room. Walden followed at a distance, not wanting to tangle with Zacharias' armed marines.

To his surprise, the guards were gone. He noted with relief

that the officers' bodies had been removed, too. Although much of the dried blood remained to stain the composite decking and bulkheads, Walden forced himself to ignore the grim reminder of the first encounter with the aliens.

Standing just outside the hatchway gave him a narrow field of vision. It also hid him from the room's occupants. Nakamura and Zacharias spoke in guarded tones too low for him to overhear. He'd have to rely on Egad to report their conversation.

The first officer, the captain, and the other three men on the bridge made no attempt to keep their voices down. Walden jerked in surprise when he heard Captain Belford say, "You're certain?"

"Yes, sir. An SOS from planetside."

"It might be a trap. The aliens might be luring us into an ambush."

The captain seemed skeptical of this. He asked his detection officer, "What of the other ship?"

"Still incoming, sir. This system's Oort Cloud is almost twelve light-hours away, and they were on the edge of it. They're decelerating fast, but it'll be days before they can reinforce the orbiting ship."

Walden slipped away, then whistled for Egad. The dog obediently trotted from the bridge and came to him.

"Let's go to my quarters," Walden said. "I want you to repeat everything you heard."

The scientist worried over what he had heard and what plans might be brewing for the *Hippocrates*. He didn't want to be in a combat zone. They hadn't done well in the first encounter. The bulkheads had turned to dust in places, and the crew was not trained for full-fledged warfare. Still, Walden had to admit they had few other options. Leaving this system was out of the question if an alien might observe their departure and learn Earth's location.

Had they already found out the coordinates? Reducing the planet's surface to glassy plains indicated that they had everything they wanted. They weren't taking prisoners.

Walden took a deep breath in a vain attempt to steady himself. He was used to working with death—but it could only be seen through a microscope. In some cases, his work had to be viewed by computer-enhanced magnification. The death confronting them now was visible, open, vicious. If he survived Walden wasn't sure he could ever get rid of the image of the gentle silver microwave beam erupting from the alien ship and causing such massive destruction on Schwann.

Too many had died already for him to cut and run. They had to fight to the death here or no one—no human anywhere—might be alive by the time the next New Year's day came around.

Walden pushed past crew members cleaning the passageways. Most of the deaths from their brush in combat had been centered in the control and communications rooms.

Walden hunted through his clothing until he found the electronic bug-sweeper wrapped in a spare pair of pants. He used the compact device to run over the walls and ceiling again. If any spy-eyes had been planted, they waited passively. He began talking and checked once more. The room was as clean as possible.

"All right," he said to Egad. "It looks safe for you to tell me what they were saying on the bridge."

"Captain Belford got faint help request from survivors," the dog said. He tossed his head and got his collar with the computer-driven voice box into a more comfortable position. He settled down, head on outstretched paws. "Bad smelling officer thinks it is a trap."

"Zacharias?" Egad lifted his head and nodded. His tongue lolled to one side and he panted.

"Bite his leg? If you won't let me kill him, can I maim him?"

"Not now," Walden said. "What of Nakamura?"

"The one without smell cautions the captain. Says rescue is necessary to learn what happened. Also says aliens must be killed first. We attack like we should. All three go after one alien."

Egad's pack mentality rose to color his thinking. Walden knew that their best hope was for the *Winston* to maneuver behind, as Nakamura had planned. The other destroyer and the *Hippocrates* couldn't mount any real threat and would get in the way more than they could help.

"Other escort to dock."

Walden snapped out of his reverie. "We're going to help them with repairs?" The dog nodded. "That makes the pair of us an easy target for the alien. The *Winston* had better not foul up its attack.''

''Cat smells like plastic. Can I kill it?''

''What? You mean Doris' cat?'' The abrupt change of topic confused him for a moment. It wasn't like Egad to switch subjects like this. The dog was usually single-minded.

''She smells like plastic. Can I kill her, too?''

''What's your sudden dislike of plastic? Never mind. We've got more important matters to tend to.'' Walden sat on the small bed he shared with Anita and thought hard.

He said, ''Go back to the control room and listen to what they're saying. I'm going down to the cargo bay. That's the only spot where the ships can lock together and exchange crew.''

''Can't bite the major?''

''No!''

Egad trotted over and shoved his head into Walden's hand. The scientist knew that the dog had been joking. He patted Egad and said, ''You be careful. Things are getting dangerous around here—and will get even worse.''

''Always careful. You know me.'' With that Egad raced off, his legs pumping hard to keep his outsized body moving.

Walden wished he could do more to control the situation. When they were aboard the *Hippocrates*, Captain Belford was in command. The man seemed to withstand the combined urgings of Zacharias and Nakamura well, although the Japanese advisor swayed him with outrageous acts. So far, they had been based on logic. Walden hoped that the woman continued to think carefully about what she did. Otherwise, she would be a time bomb in their midst set to explode.

''Mr. Luria,'' he called when he saw the cargo officer. ''I'm here for the inspection the captain ordered.''

The swarthy man looked as if he had bitten into something caustic. His lips rippled and then pulled back in a thin line. ''I don't have time now, Doctor.''

''Docking with the *Tannhauser* is difficult, isn't it?''

Luria glared at him. ''There aren't many secrets on this ship since you people came onboard. The destroyer is within magnetic grappler range.''

Walden heard sharp hissing sounds. He jumped, afraid that the cargo bay doors had opened to vacuum once more.

"Those are the grapple guns. The *Tannhauser* will pluck the cables and affix the magnets to tow plates. We should dock in a few minutes."

Walden waited nervously while Luria silently watched a small vidscreen. The exterior pictures revealed little other than the vastness of space. Only when the destroyer came within a few hundred meters did it take on definition and give Walden a sense of its size.

"They really got blasted," he exclaimed when he saw the extensive melting on the surface. The Ultimate Strength Steel plating around the liftdrive engines had flowed like putty. Forward, the carbon composite hull had sublimated from the intense heat. "How did anyone survive when the aliens did that to the ship?"

"Not many made it," said Luria. He used a laser wand to program the docking computer. Thick, flexible tubes grew from the side of the *Hippocrates* and touched the destroyer near its airlocks. "The locks are fused. They're drilling through just aft to get out."

"They won't be rebuilding the *Tannhauser*," Walden said. "Spare parts for the *Winston* is the only service it's going to give."

"You're probably right," Luria said. "There. There they come. The survivors."

Leo Burch and a dozen large medbots pushed through the crates. "Ah, I've found you at last, Mr. Luria. Are the survivors safely inside yet?"

"Almost here, Doctor."

"How are you doing, Jerome? You didn't show up for your tests this morning. Wondered if something had happened."

"Your nurse told me you were out playing golf and had canceled," Walden said.

"I was out playing with my nurse." Burch worked a few seconds on a portable control board. His medbots rolled to the entry lock and waited for the *Tannhauser*'s crew to get inside. "I'm afraid old age is creeping up on me. My drive has turned into a putt."

"You lack inspiration. I've seen your nurse."

"Ugly bucket of bolts, isn't she? I'm trading her in for next year's model when we get back to Earth. Albert's starting to look better to me." He patted his robot's chrome head, then worked his controls. The medbots loaded the crew onto auto-gurneys and rolled off to the wards.

"Is that it?" asked Walden. "Only eleven from the destroyer?"

"That's all," said Luria, his voice almost breaking. He straightened and got back control. "The engineer and I are going into the *Tannhauser*. Please remain clear of the lock, Doctor." Luria hurried toward the docking tube linking the ships.

"He's taking it well," said Burch.

"What?"

"His sister was on the *T*. She's still in the liftdrive section. Or rather, her body is. Well, I've got to go. If you won't come see me, I'll have to get to work on those eleven and see if I can't split some fees along the way. Good thing I brought the extra medbot." Burch tapped out a command. The remaining robot wheeled up beside him and the doctor climbed on. "Beats walking around. That's one reason I never liked golf. Drop in sometime and see me."

Burch tapped in the final command on the control and the medbot rolled away, the doctor lounging on the padded surface. Albert trailed at a respectful distance.

Walden didn't know where to go. When he heard Egad barking, he knew something important had been resolved in the control room. The dog skidded to a halt and stood panting, waiting for the order to speak.

Walden knelt and put his head next to Egad's. "Softly," he said. "What did you learn?"

"Captain Belford has ordered the major to land combat team and rescue survivors. We go in now!"

Walden looked up and saw a dozen fully armed EPCT marines march into the cargo bay. They would soon be under the alien ship's guns unless the *Winston* had been successful. After seeing the destruction wrought on their other escort, Walden doubted the *Winston*'s chances of complete victory.

One direct hit from the potent microwaves and the *Hippocrates* would be a footnote in history.

CHAPTER
10

Jerome Walden stepped back and watched as the combat team prepared itself. The sergeant in charge moved deliberately from soldier to soldier, checking equipment, studying air filtration systems, making certain that the proper attitude was shown.

"Are they going down now?" he asked Egad. "How are they landing on Schwann?"

"Check ship first. Then we go down. Can't move when the other ship is locked onto us."

Even as the dog uttered the words, the sergeant marched his squad into the *Tannhauser* through the connecting tube. Walden hesitated. Luria and two others had already entered. There couldn't be much danger, except for possible radiation leakage from the starlift engines. Something held him back. What other weapons were aboard the destroyer? There might have been many unlaunched antimissile warheads. Radiation might bathe the entire ship.

Walden dropped to one knee and held Egad's shaggy head between his hands. "Listen carefully. I'm going into the destroyer. It is dangerous, and I don't want you coming along unless you want to."

"Dangerous?"

"Very dangerous. We've talked about this before. Things neither of us can see might be loose. Radiation can kill us. Poisonous gases from their coolant systems are a danger, too. The entire ship is a death trap.''

''I go with you.''

Walden hugged the animal to him. ''You're more than a friend, Egad. I don't know what I'd do without you.''

''You watch for things we can't see or smell or hear. I will do rest of sniffing.''

Walden cautiously peered down the connecting tube. The magnetic grapples held the two ships together firmly, but the tube still swayed and bucked. Walden had a momentary vision of entering and finding a hole in the bottom. A fall through that hole would send him tumbling through to infinity. He shoved the notion away as ridiculous. It could never happen. He knew it.

It still worried him as he gingerly stepped into the flexible tunnel. Ahead he saw a pale yellow circle cut through the *Tannhauser*'s hull from inside. The airlocks had been turned to slag by the potent enemy beams.

Egad almost tripped him when the dog shot forward, sensitive nose twitching.

''Smell anything?''

''Like home.''

''You mean like my lab?'' The dog's head bobbed up and down. Walden went cold inside. Of all the odors he had expected aboard a destroyer, chemical and biomass effluvia were not high on the list. ''Show me where they are strongest.''

Egad hopped through the smoothly cut hole and dashed off toward the stern. Walden followed more clumsily. How the dog managed to coordinate four legs when he had such problems with two always amazed him. Getting his feet under him, Walden ran after the dog.

His heart almost exploded when he saw the locked door where Egad stopped and sniffed.

''This is their master magazine,'' he said.

''Read this? I do not understand. How can you read?''

''It's not a magazine you read. It's a place where dangerous things are stored.'' Walden ran his hands over the metal door. He found the print lock. A series of hollow depressions accepted his fingers. He didn't expect the door to open; only authorized, recognized fingerprints should have worked.

Silently the door swung inward. The dangers in the room beyond hid in absolute darkness.

Walden grabbed Egad's collar and kept the dog from entering. "What do you smell?"

"Not like soldiers' quarters. Like home."

Walden fumbled along the wall seeking a light switch. The slick inner bulkhead had been specially treated with a rubberizing paint to further seal the room against biologic hazards. Egad had said it smelled like home—a biowarfare laboratory.

Walden carefully moved into the darkness, sure that the dog was right. Research wouldn't be conducted aboard a destroyer. That meant the finished products were stored here. The *Tannhauser* carried its full complement of conventional offensive and defensive systems—and the NAA had added one more offensive system.

"Can you see?" he asked the dog.

"Too dark."

"Wait in the corridor. If I tell you, go find the sergeant leading the marines and warn him of a biohazard."

"Speak to someone not you or Anita?"

"Only if I tell you." Walden fumbled in the dark, finding the edge of storage bins with his forearm. He cursed and rubbed the injury. Moving even slower, he traced along the compartment until he found an auxiliary light.

The sudden intense glare blinded him for a few seconds. He squinted and shielded his eyes as he looked for the regular room lighting. A power surge had burned out the overhead sockets, leaving behind only charred, blackened quartz tubes. Walden had to rely completely on the dazzling emergency lights.

He let his eyes adjust before examining the storage compartments. His stomach knotted tightly when he saw what lay behind the glasteel windows.

"Come over here, Egad."

"You want me to talk to others?"

"No. Forget me even saying that. Can you smell anything? Something that might burn at your nose?"

The dog sniffed around the bases of the compartments. "Bad odor but not burning bad."

"That's sealant. Nothing is leaking from the compartments." He didn't know if he should feel relieved. The bioweapons inside were intact, but he had no idea what they did.

"You, freeze!"

Walden glanced up. A marine trained a laserifle on him.

"What are you doing here?"

"Get your commander here immediately. I'm Dr. Walden, in charge of the research team. This . . . this is extremely hazardous bioweaponry. I don't even know what it's supposed to do."

The marine had already touched a communicator on his shirt collar. In seconds, the bandy-legged sergeant appeared in the doorway, laserifle leveled.

"Sergeant, get me information on the *Tannhauser*'s armament. This is a bio-bomb of some kind. My dog detected laboratory odors, although I don't think there's any leakage. Was there a biowarfare officer aboard?"

"She's dead," the sergeant answered. He touched his own communicator and spoke quietly for several seconds. Only then did he lower his rifle and enter. He motioned for the other marine to stand guard while he investigated further.

"That's bad news. Do you have any idea what might be in this container?"

"Standard burrow-and-explode canister," the sergeant said. "They put the damnedest things inside. Explosives are usual, even nukes. When we use them planetside, we can put in poison gas for ferreting out dug-in troops or even—"

"Bioweapons," Walden finished for him.

The sergeant shrugged. "Just another way of killing," he said.

"This might kill *us*," Walden said uneasily. "There is a chance some has leaked into the containment compartment. You don't have any idea what it is or its effects?"

"Who's going to tell a sergeant anything?"

"This is as dangerous as radiation leakage from the lift engines. More," Walden said. "Radiation can be detected easily. This might be designed to be hard to analyze."

"I've notified Major Zacharias. He'll be here in a few minutes. I got work to do. Don't go leaving the ship, sir. Leastwise, not until you have permission.''

"Egad, go tell Anita what we've found." The dog shot past the sergeant and the guard at the door before either could react.

"That your dog? He's a crazy-looking mutt, but smart. Sometimes I think he's listening to everything we're saying—and understanding it.''

"He's mine," said Walden. "And if he ever gives you advice during a poker game, take it. He's a better player than I am.''

The marine laughed, not knowing Walden meant what he said. After teaching Egad to play five-card draw, Walden had never been able to win consistently. He had stopped playing with the dog, claiming he didn't like using cards with dog spit on them.

The scientist examined the room carefully for clues that might reveal the nature of the bioweapons stored in the compartments. The delivery system had been damaged; if the fire control officer on the *Tannhauser* had launched these weapons, they would have blown up in the tubes.

"Jerome?"

"Anita, did you bring containment?''

"Suits, handlers, the works. The EPCTs almost didn't let me in.''

"How—''

"I convinced them that these weapons might be useful," broke in Miko Nakamura. The advisor had already donned protective gear. Walden took the suit from Anita and quickly slipped into it. The itchy sensation he felt along his spine was only nerves. Every time he worked with hazardous biomass he had the same reaction. Still, he tried to settle the suit so that it didn't chafe.

"Why bother opening the containers?" asked Anita. "The *T* is going to be sealed and abandoned.''

"Possibly not," he said. Of Nakamura he asked, "Is there any chance the ship will be needed for spare parts? The *Winston* isn't going to come through the fight untouched.''

"We will need much from this vessel," Nakamura admitted. "We will need these weapons. Can you release them from their berth and transport them to the *Hippocrates*?''

"We don't even know what is inside. I have some guesses, but we have to be sure.''

"I brought along a small analyzer." Behind Anita stood a robotic unit designed for use in contamination zones.

Walden unfastened the controller wand and spent a few minutes giving the robot instructions. He motioned with the laser wand, and the unit dutifully went to the suspect compartment.

Walden moved Anita and Nakamura back, then allowed the robot to work at its own pace.

"It'll be a few minutes before it gets inside the case. It is analyzing the air as it works. I'm getting a thirty-second update on its findings. So far there's nothing out of the ordinary. The missiles—burrow-and-exploders, the sergeant called them—are packed with an argon atmosphere to prevent growth of the biomaterial should they crack open."

"They are aerobic bacteria inside?"

"Probably. A few use an anaerobic bacteria, such as the composite hull-eating missiles designed for use in hard vacuum, but we mostly stick with bacteria that can be sprayed in an aerosol."

"Aerobic bacteria tend to be easier to control," explained Anita. "We have a devil of a time keeping our own troops from becoming contaminated. A bacillus with an accompanying prophage—"

"It's open now. There's leakage." Walden backed up involuntarily, even though the containment suit protected him fully. He checked the readouts from the analyzer. "What the hell were they going to use *that* for?"

"You have identified it?"

"Anthrax. Why in the hell are they loaded with *that*?"

"It is a favorite of the Sov-Lats," said Nakamura. Walden spun and faced her. Through the clear visor he saw her expression turn impassive.

"These were going to be used against the Soviet research facility on Schwann. You wanted it to appear as if they had contaminated themselves."

"You have an active imagination, Doctor. What you describe might be construed as an act of war."

"Not if you got away with it. It might be months before independent investigators arrived to find out what happened," said Anita.

"What 'independent investigators'?" snapped Walden. "The

Sov-Lats might think they'd done it to themselves and never even report losing their lab. Think of the loss of face if they did. That could have put us months or even years ahead of them.''

"We live in a dangerous universe," said Nakamura.

"I'm not sure we don't go out of our way making it more dangerous," he said.

"What are we going to do with the missile?"

"This one gets jettisoned," Walden said. "The others, too, for all I care."

"A moment, Dr. Walden. There are nine remaining undamaged B-and-E smart missiles. They might prove useful in the forthcoming planetary assault.''

"What assault?" Walden tried to ferret out the tiniest bit of information and failed. Nakamura revealed only what she wanted him to know.

"We land a party of marines to rescue those under attack by the aliens. These B-and-Es might be important. We can jury-rig a launcher to use on the *Hippocrates*."

"You're turning a hospital ship into a launch platform for anthrax-laden missiles?''

"We fight for our survival. Any weapon is important. This might be the one that turns the battle to our favor." She edged closer and stood on tiptoe to peer into the compartment cradling the damaged missile. "Without the B-and-Es we might be unable to rescue the surviving researchers.''

Walden's mind raced, considering possibilities and discarding many courses of action. He looked at Anita. "We can get them safely into the *Hippocrates*, but storing them is going to be difficult without the proper compartments.''

"We didn't bring anything this large with us. The containment facilities were supposed to be in the on-planet labs.''

"They must be near the cargo bay," said Nakamura. "We do not wish to risk transportation through the ship. They must remain close to their launch tubes.''

"We ought to see what Willie Klugel has bollixed together. His work with the bacteriophages requires similar containment. Hell, he'd get a kick out of seeing the end product of our work.''

"He might have been the principal scientist on this project," pointed out Anita. "Didn't he come to us from the new Fort Detrick facility, just before it was blown up by terrorists?"

"This looks like their handiwork," Walden said. "Contact him. See what he can throw together. I want a Level 5 containment or these missiles don't budge from here."

"He has been notified and is complying with your request," said Nakamura. She touched the small communicator fastened to her lapel. "Your surmise concerning Dr. Klugel's participation in this project is in error, however."

"Score one for Willie."

"Your Dr. Yerrow worked on it more than ten years ago."

"Doris?" Anita was taken aback. Walden had passed beyond surprise at anything.

"One day I might be able to screen the records of my own staff. How do you know what I can't find out? I assembled the team from at least two recommendations and published papers. No one let me see past classified research."

"A sorry situation, Doctor. I sympathize with you. Often, it makes my job more difficult, too."

"You can at least eavesdrop until you find out what you need to know to do your job." Bitterness welled up inside him. He enjoyed the research he did. That it might end up in a missile, such as Doris Yerrow's had, did not bother him. The continual secrecy and the paranoid fear surrounding the work did, though. He couldn't even find out what project Anita had been sent to Schwann to work on.

"Here are cargo robots," said Nakamura. "Are they sensitive enough to use for handling the missiles?"

Walden examined them, made a few adjustments to their controls, and finally let the robots begin their work.

"The analyzer will follow to be sure there's no leakage. At least the missiles will be used for something worthwhile. We can rescue some of our friends from the aliens."

Nakamura hesitated for a moment when he spoke. Walden swung around and shoved his visor squarely against the woman's.

"We *will* use the missiles to rescue our researchers?"

"They will be used in the rescue," Nakamura said. "But those we rescue are not ours. They are Sov-Lat Scientists."

CHAPTER
11

"We're all dead," Jerome Walden said tiredly. "These clamps will never hold. The missiles will go rolling around the first time the *Hippocrates* tries to maneuver."

Nakamura laughed. "You have little faith in yourself or others. The B-and-E missiles will remain where they are until we use them. They are smart missiles and know when not to detonate."

Walden looked at the racks skeptically. They had been jury-rigged and were too flimsy for use in combat. The other choices available were even less palatable. Leaving such dangerous weapons aboard the *Tannhauser* had occurred to him, but Nakamura said they were needed on-planet for the assault. He didn't know enough about the situation on Schwann's surface to dispute her claim. Worst of all, the *T* might crash onto the planet's surface. He didn't want to be the one to loose anthrax on the world.

"We can destroy the bombs. Launch them toward the sun. The missile engines have enough push to get them out of Schwann-orbit and begin to fall inward."

"We need them," Nakamura said.

Walden grabbed for support when the ship lurched. They had begun their own descent toward the ravaged planet. Within an hour Major Zacharias' marines would land and attempt to rescue the beleaguered Sov-Lat scientists.

"Captain Belford is unused to the maneuvering required for such positioning," Nakamura said. "This vessel lacks the steering capability of a destroyer or drop ship."

"How comforting."

Walden tried to regain some of the dignity he had sacrificed in his wild grab for support. Remaining on his feet had allowed him to hold onto a few shards of composure in front of the unflappable Nakamura. The scientist walked slowly back to his makeshift laboratory where Anita and Egad awaited them.

"The *Winston* begins its attack soon," said Nakamura, nodding in Anita's direction. "That will keep the alien vessel busy and cover our descent."

"How will we do it?" Anita asked. She perched on an acid-resistant black-topped worktable in the laboratory, long legs swinging restlessly. "Nobody up top will talk to me."

"They are busy," said Nakamura.

"They're busy worrying. The computers do all the work after they program them." Walden paced to relieve the tension he felt. It did not work. Knots formed in his stomach and cold fingers squeezed at his heart, threatening to stop it.

"There are small deviations to correct. However, Dr. Walden, you are correct. The strategy has been planned and programmed. We need only adopt the proper tactics to accomplish our goal."

"You're not telling us everything," accused Anita. She glanced at Egad, who cocked his head to one side. A blue eye fixed on the military advisor, as if studying her reaction.

"The Sov-Lat facility has been severely damaged."

"Do you mean the planet might be contaminated? You can't send the EPCTs into that without full hazard suits!"

"There's something else, isn't there?" Anita dropped to the floor and stood beside Walden. "You're planning on using the B-and-E missiles, and it's not against the Sov-Lats. Not any longer."

"We need information about the aliens. Those trapped in the underground laboratory can provide us with essential data unobtainable through other channels."

"The aliens have landed and are attacking the lab. *That's* the problem. They've left orbit and are on Schwann!"

"You have touched on the kernel of this problem, Doctor." Nakamura bowed deeply. "I must speak with the major and be certain his troops are adequately briefed for the mission." She left the room with a movement that made Walden wonder if her feet even touched the deck. Nakamura didn't walk as much as she glided like a silent, sallow ghost.

"We're in one hell of a mess. The *Hippocrates* might be fired on from above if the *Winston* can't fully engage the alien ship, and now we find out they've got the lab under siege."

"How long could a scientific party hold out?" asked Anita. "They aren't equipped for a long battle."

"The Sov-Lat base might be. They're as apprehensive about their security as Zacharias is about ours."

"If they're no better, the aliens have already overrun their position," Anita said in disgust.

"No," said Egad. "Sovs holding on hard and fast. Huge fight. Aliens could not defeat with microwave beam so they try to rip out throat in pack attack."

The dog dropped flat on the deck and panted harshly. Walden saw how agitated the animal was. He knelt and petted the shaggy head.

"We're not going to be hurt," he assured the dog.

"You lie," Egad accused. "I smell the lie!"

"It's hard to have a pet who can argue with you—and win," Walden said, smiling weakly. "You're right, Egad. I don't know if we're going to come through this with our skins intact."

"There's more, isn't there?" asked Anita. "You were trying to hide this from Egad. Now you're trying to hide something from me. What is it?"

"Nakamura wants to use the anthrax bacillus against the aliens. We have no idea if it would work. We know nothing about them, so it might be worse firing those B-and-Es than waiting for more data. Why use weapons that might be useless against the enemy and would hinder our own forces?"

"There's more," pressed Anita. "You're not thinking of going down yourself, are you?"

"It might be the only way we can be sure we can get to those trapped in the base," he said. "We don't know what damage has been caused, or what might have been released. The Sov-Lats aren't as conscientious about containment as we are."

"I remember Baikonur," Anita said. "That launch accident wiped out their major port, Star City, and a hundred thousand hectares."

"They never should have tried to get that much virus into orbit." He tried to force the accident from his mind. The Soviets had decided to risk transporting several metric tons of mycotoxin in one launch rather than increasing the risk over six or more. Their cargo ship had blown up, and the deadly fungus-derived toxin had killed almost two million of their own people.

Even the most elementary containment precautions had been ignored. What was their research facility on Schwann like? Walden expected the worst, if the aliens had peeled back even one layer of the underground laboratory.

"We don't have to write off the entire world. We might be able to contain some of the damage," he said.

"Jerome Walden, World Saver." Anita's bitterness caused Egad to cringe and slide under a table. He hid his head under his paws. He didn't like it when they argued.

"That's a better role than playing Shiva. Destroying worlds—genocide!—isn't to my liking."

"Have they asked you to land with them? Zacharias doesn't strike me as the sort to invite civilians to his parties." Anita snorted and crossed her arms. "For that matter, Nakamura doesn't seem the type to volunteer to go, either."

"So why me? I'm best suited for it. For better or for worse, I'm in charge. This is my responsibility."

Anita said nothing for several seconds. "They won't want you along."

"You hope they won't. I'd better go see."

"Damn all volunteers. Haven't you learned *anything* being around the military all these years?"

"It doesn't look that way, does it?" He touched her cheek. She flinched away and glared at him. "Get a field unit ready for me. I don't think I'll be able to take more than that."

"Full contamination suit, too, I suppose." Anita's bitterness hurt him.

"Of course." He started to leave when Egad came up and nuzzled him. "What is it, old boy?"

"Want to go with you. You don't smell good."

"You mean my nose isn't as sensitive as yours?" The dog nodded and wagged his rat-thin tail. "I don't think so. This is going to be dangerous."

"Want to go."

"We have a suit for him. Remember? You made it before we left."

"I suppose you want to go along, too?" He looked at the flame-haired woman and couldn't read her expression.

"This isn't for the fainthearted. Only heroes need apply. I'll stay behind, thank you."

"All right." Walden looked down at Egad. "Let Anita get you outfitted in the suit and we'll drop with the marines."

The dog bounced up and down. Walden wondered if the animal had any idea what he was getting into. For that matter, Walden wondered if he knew what he was doing. Landing in a combat zone was stark foolishness. Landing with aliens shooting unknown weapons *and* trying to find biological weapons leakage was even stupider.

He went directly to the bridge. Along the way he saw few crew members. The *Hippocrates* had been placed on a high alert status with most posts doubled up for safety. Should one crewman in a post be killed, the second could take over immediately—or so went the theory. Walden knew that if any station sustained such a loss, the entire ship would be lost.

The *Hippocrates* wasn't built like a war vessel. Major damage meant more fatalities than were "acceptable."

"Nakamura, I want a word with you." He stopped the military advisor as she came from the communications room.

"We are preparing for the landing, Doctor. Make it brief."

He outlined his concern for worldwide contamination and finished, saying, "Dr. Burch might be able to treat traumatic injuries, but he isn't going to be equipped to recognize or analyze the biohazards that might have been released."

"Your expertise gives a shortcut in this, eh?"

Walden said nothing. The woman considered his request from

angles he had never weighed. Whatever proved most advantageous for the success of the mission would decide her.

"Zacharias will not like having a civilian accompanying him."

"I want to take along my dog, also."

"Indeed?" A thin eyebrow arched and cold black eyes bored into him. "A strange request."

"Egad's nose is more sensitive than even our best surface acoustic wave detectors. A combat team doesn't usually carry SAW-dets, do they?"

"Hardly. Such equipment is bulky and difficult to power without leakage that might betray tactical positions. There is even discussion about wearing full hazard suits. They are clumsy and mobility will be important."

"Without the suits, they might not have to worry about mobility. Some offensive viruses can kill within seconds."

"I am aware of this. So is the major."

She spun and left him standing in the corridor. He trailed her into the bridge. Nakamura spoke earnestly with Captain Belford, who glanced over his shoulder. The man had aged a dozen years in the past few hours. His lined face had a gray pallor that Walden associated with death. In the hollowed pits of his red-rimmed eyes he blinked, then gestured in a vague way that encompassed everything and nothing.

"Very well, Dr. Walden. You will be allowed ten kilos of equipment, your dog, and any level hazard suit you want. Be in the cargo bay in ten minutes. Clearance has been given."

"Do you want a continuous direct report? It might be helpful."

Nakamura's cold eyes lit like panel indicators. She reached into a hidden pocket and pulled out a slender cylinder. Handing it to him, she said, "Use this. It is a scrambled vari-frequency transmitter. You can send tri-dee pictures as well as full sound. If you cannot leave it on as you work, be sure to use it frequently. All data goes directly into my computer for analysis."

"If I leave it on, it won't run down?"

"There is a superconducting battery inside. Very small, almost undetectable."

"You'll get your tour of the planet."

"Thank you. Perhaps I misjudged you, Doctor."

"I don't think so."

Walden had no desire to spy for the woman, yet she afforded the best chance for defeating the aliens. Whatever data she received would be put to good use. From all he had seen of Zacharias, the major wanted only to make a bigger name for himself and get a few more medals.

Walden arrived two minutes before the marines loaded into their armored landing craft. Walden had nosed around the cargo hold for a month checking on his staff's boxed equipment and looking for dangerous experiments in progress, but he had missed the sleek landing vehicles.

A blunted boron-composite prow showed that the craft could descent through an atmosphere at a steep angle. Small wings gave some maneuverability and body jets enabled a powered landing. From the exterior, Walden saw no way the craft could ever lift from the surface once it had landed.

"There's no need," Zacharias said, as if reading his mind. "We either win or we die. I don't like retreats. This attack might be one I thought up."

"The *Winston* has pickup shuttles, doesn't it?"

"So did the *Tannhauser*," the major acknowledged. "We can't count on either. The *Winston* has just begun its engagement of the alien warship."

"And?"

"It's too early to tell."

"You mean sneaking up on the ship didn't work as well as you'd hoped."

"No, it didn't. There is a real battle in progress. We have to get in and find the Sovs as fast as we can."

Walden shuddered. He had a flash of premonition. The *Winston* blown apart. The silver beam of microwave energy arching downward to lick across their column. Death. Men burned beyond recognition. The Sov-Lat base nothing but a crater five hundred meters deep, the sides slickened black volcanic glass.

"You don't look too cheerful about dying, Doctor. You want to back out? There won't be another chance."

"You're probably going into a biological hell, Major. I'm volunteering to do what I can to hold down casualties."

"We don't know that, though the Sov-Lats are sloppy. My

men don't function well in the hazard suits. The damned things have a radar cross-section you can't believe. Makes them easy targets for automated gun batteries.''

''Where do we sit?''

''We?'' For the first time, Zacharias noticed Egad standing patiently beside them. ''You're not taking that damned dog with us. I won't allow it!''

''I can't take all the equipment I need. He's mobile, quick, and his nose is more sensitive than anything you could carry down with a dozen armed men aboard.''

Nakamura stepped up just as Zacharias started to deny Egad permission to board. The woman's cold eyes fixed on the officer. ''Get aboard,'' Zacharias said with distaste. ''Both of you.'' He glared at Nakamura, then ducked into the hatch.

Walden and Egad followed. It took the human several seconds for his eyes to adjust to the dim lighting inside. More than two dozen couches lined the walls. The ones in the center of the craft had been filled already. He dropped into one beside the door.

''That's bad luck, Doc,'' came a soft voice in his headphones. ''The guy nearest the door has to be the first out. Not one in ten survive the mission. Real bad luck.''

Walden jumped as if the couch had burned him. He moved forward and found an empty couch near the small enclosed pilot's cabin. With two quick tugs, he had Egad secured in a couch across from his. As he fastened his own straps, he listened hard for further warnings. No one commented now. He cinched himself down firmly.

''Listen up, men,'' boomed Zacharias. ''We hit, we shoot anything that moves before it shoots us. If it isn't moving, check it out. We want dead enemy and no heroes. Sergeant Tanner's squad is first out. Mine follows. Dr. Walden is in between. Let's drop and kick alien ass!''

The sudden acceleration took Walden by surprise. He had expected a few minutes warning. The instant Zacharias stopped speaking, the pilot blasted free at top speed.

The assault craft twisted like a corkscrew, or so it felt to Walden. The heat mounted quickly and the walls became too hot to touch, even wearing his insulated hazard suit gloves. Before he could worry too much about this, another sharp kick of acceleration threatened to black him out. Wind screamed in his ears, even past the headphones and through the suit's helmet.

The landing—and Walden hesitated to call it more than a controlled crash—took him by surprise, too. The pilot had given no warning at any stage of the flight. They had left the *Hippocrates* and landed in less than ten minutes.

"By the numbers, odd out, even follow!" The echoes in his head from the landing had barely died out when commands came his direction.

"You're next, Doc. Move it or lose it."

Walden got Egad free. The dog had tolerated the flight better than he had. Brown and blue eyes peered up at him through the transparent visor. The dog's tongue hung out to one side as he panted in the hot suit. With Egad's help, he stumbled to the hatch, retrieved his analyzer, and fell into the bright sunlight of Delta Cygnus 4.

His polarizers flared the instant he looked up. They had landed in the middle of a major battle.

CHAPTER

12

Someone hit Walden from behind and knocked him flat on his face. Along his back danced intense heat. He kicked free of the craft and started rolling.

"Egad!" he cried. "Are you there?"

The dog yelped. Even in the midst of such confusion, Egad did not reveal his speaking ability. Walden had drummed it into the animal's head that to do so might jeopardize his life.

"Walden, stay where you are. Tanner, circle, code red, code three, code zenith."

Walden recognized Zacharias' voice. He rolled a half turn more and came up to his elbows. The polarizer hummed and faded, giving him a better view of the land. Huge gouts of molten rock had splashed over the landing craft. Even if it had been capable of flight, this bath would have destroyed it. One wing had been burned through and the engine compartment hissed and vented noxious vapors. Walden was glad he'd insisted on everyone wearing the hazard suits. They protected against chemical as well as biological dangers.

"Where are they firing from?" an aggrieved voice demanded. "I can't zero in on them. My damned sensors are going crazy."

"No chitchat," came Sgt. Tanner's voice. "Major, where are you? We got cut off."

Walden wiggled around and got away from the steaming rock that partially covered the landing craft. His knees were rubbed raw by the time he managed to find shelter behind a substantial boulder. The dirt around it had been blasted away but it looked secure.

"Egad!" he called. "Can you get over to me?"

A loud bark told him the dog was on his way. Walden pressed close to the rock, taking comfort in its solidity. Examining a pain in his side revealed the cylindrical camera Nakamura had given him. He remembered his promise to use it to give the military advisor a clear picture of conditions on Schwann. He inserted the slender camera in a holder on the side of his helmet before swinging the analyzer around and getting to work on its tiny keypad. The numbers from the machine refused to turn into meaningful information. He ran a self-test and found the analyzer in good working condition. Using a computerized test probe, he sampled the air for the slightest hint of living material or free-floating virus.

Nothing.

He changed the sensitivity setting and shook the unit, but the readings did not change.

A heavy weight rested on his shoulder. Walden jerked around guiltily, then smiled sheepishly when he recognized his assailant. Egad had found him. The dog banged his paw against the side of Walden's helmet until the man got the idea.

"What frequency?" he asked. Egad turned and showed one they could use for private communication. Some frequencies were assigned for everyone's use. Others had been reserved for command, between officers, between officers and non-coms, and between non-coms and the troops. The one Egad indicated hadn't been taken for use during this mission.

"We can talk now," he said to the dog. "But be careful. Who knows who might be listening."

"Cannot sniff. Suit blocks my nose," the dog complained. "Itches." Egad shook all over, as if trying to shed an unwanted skin.

"We need it."

"Soldiers are fighting hard," the dog said. "Fifty paces ahead. Alien fighting machine."

Walden chanced a look past the edge of his boulder and saw a marine wiggling forward on his belly, pushing a large tube ahead of him. The EPCT got to his knees, set a tripod, then dived to the side. Walden closed his eyes even though the polarizer in his helmet protected his vision better. The tube roared and shook the ground.

Then came an earsplitting eruption followed by deathly silence.

It took Walden several seconds to realize his hearing had been impaired in spite of cut-out circuits in the helmet's exterior pickup. An almost unbearable ringing faded and he heard voices through the background buzz.

"All units advance. Heyward took out their damned mech. Tanner, get around to the side."

"Sir, we're encountering stiff resistance. It'd be better—"

"Do as you're ordered, Sergeant!"

"Sir!"

A click marked the change to an officer-non-com circuit. Walden heard the marines muttering on their open channel. They sided with their sergeant.

"He doesn't want to risk his own ass, that's why," came one caustic voice. Walden didn't have to know what the question had been. The marines thought Zacharias chose the easy path while he sent his sergeant along the harder one.

Walden stood and cautiously surveyed the terrain for the first time since tumbling onto Schwann's surface. It looked like the surface of the Moon. Huge craters had been dug as if by meteor impact. Tiny, sharp-edged hills rose to block his view. All vegetation had been seared and a few clumps of grass burned fitfully.

"Scout to the left," he ordered Egad. The dog obediently trotted ahead. Walden followed, worrying over the analyzer's malfunctioning. With so much charred vegetation, he should have a dozen different readings. He got nothing.

"Alien mech," warned Egad. "Stay down."

Walden dived just as a humming sounded in his headphones. The noise turned into a series of explosions.

"Got 'em with the pipes," came an exultant voice. "That's going to stop 'em dead in their tracks."

"You blew up a pile of bolts, vacuum brain. That's nothing more than a robot fighter."

"No, it isn't!" protested the first voice. "My sensors show living beings inside. High readings."

Walden frowned. He worked at his analyzer and got nothing.

"They're blanketing the field with varying EM pulses. Screws up the sensors. Turns them into space debris."

"My pipes locked on fine. I blew up *something*."

"You blew up our own landing craft."

The argument raged. Walden shifted to another frequency and spoke quickly with Egad. "The aliens have covered the place with fighter robots. Can you get us through to the Sov-Lats' lab?"

"Can't sniff out the aliens," protested the dog. "Can't sniff anything!"

Walden worried even more. He didn't know how his analyzer had been affected by the blanketing electromagnetic radiation the one marine claimed. His electronics might be fused inside, no matter that the self-test showed optimal operating levels. Risking Egad to sniff around when the air might be laden with any of a thousand different forms of instant bio-death was out of the question.

He didn't know what the Sov-Lats had worked on in their lab. They might have developed a virus that his field analyzer couldn't detect. If so, they fought in the midst of death from more directions than he cared to consider.

"Smell humans," came the dog's voice.

"How? Egad, no, don't take off the helmet!" Walden's plea came too late. The dog pawed hard and untoggled the helmet, sticking his shaggy head up to sample the air. He turned like a weather vane in the direction Sgt. Tanner had taken.

"There. Men there. Strange odors. Vegetable eaters."

"Any different smell? Anything alien?"

"No."

Walden cursed under his breath. He had hoped to recover an alien corpse and work on it. He needed to know if the anthrax in the B-and-E missiles would work. If not, Nakamura would only create unnecessary havoc using them.

His headphones buzzed with conversation. "More EM jumbles coming our way. They send 'em in waves. Here it comes!"

The volume dropped suddenly to keep him from being deafened by the static. As quickly as it had come, the interference vanished.

"Odd numbers forward, even numbers cover us," came Sgt. Tanner's voice. He had given in to his superior and acted as a lightning rod for the aliens' attack.

Walden got into position to watch. The alien mechs squatted like pudgy insects. Small rods sprouted from their metallic domes, each sporting a nimbus of a different color. When the colors came together, a silver stream of microwave death blasted forth.

Tanner's squad worked around the perimeter, drawing fire from the emplacements. Walden watched as the even-numbered marines placed their "pipes," a dozen meter-long tubes welded together, and fired them. Each tube spat forth an independently targeted missile. The genius bombs got into the air, found targets, and computed the best trajectory for destruction. Some rocketed out at a hundred times the speed of sound. Others drifted slowly so that Walden was able to watch their inexorable progress. Each flight of bombs coordinated their effort among themselves to produce maximum destruction.

One by one, the robot pillboxes were blown apart and left in ruins. Ugly, oily black smoke rose from them, marking their demise. Again Walden used his analyzer to get a clue to their composition. The analyzer failed him.

"Be careful," he cautioned Egad. "The mechs are giving off poisonous fumes."

"No poison, just bad smells," the dog corrected. "Not like ours."

Walden didn't dispute the dog's opinion. Egad often proved more sensitive than the SAW-det he had in the laboratory. Some biologic systems were still more effective than electronic ones.

They moved from one vantage to another, dodging occasional flying pieces from the exploding alien fighting machines. The marines had learned the secret of setting their pipes and made increasingly short work of the mechs.

"The entrance is over there," said Zacharias, pointing in the general direction of a slagged field. "I'm picking up IR readings showing a doorway."

"Are the aliens still zapping us with EM pulses?" asked Walden. He sat cross-legged on the ground next to the major and worked the analyzer. For the first time since landing, he got credible readings. Ionized vegetable matter predominated. A quick glance across the burned-off field verified this. No indications of rampant deadly viruses or mutated bacilli made the computerized machine beep or flash a warning.

"What do we face?" asked Zacharias.

"Nothing more than you're already handling," said Walden. "The Sov-Lats' facility hasn't been breached."

"The hell it hasn't." Zacharias turned his head, as if listening. Walden decided the major had talked to distant patrols working their way around the slagged plain. "The aliens blew the merry hell out of the entrance. The Sovs had it covered, though. Reports show heavy defensive capability."

"But they didn't use bioweapons. I'm getting nothing to show that."

"They didn't have to." The words had hardly left Zacharias' lips when a ground-shaking explosion knocked the man flat. Walden rolled onto his side, hanging onto the analyzer as if it might support him. In the center of the grassy field rose a small mushroom-shaped cloud.

"A nuke?" Walden was too shaken to check his readouts.

"HE—just conventional high explosive. There are big nukes inside, though. All the dangerous Sov-Lat research centers have them, just in case."

Walden had heard rumors of that for years. Although he didn't discount them, he doubted even the Soviets would be that fearful. He had heard they wanted to avoid the NAA forces from breaking in and stealing their work—he had also heard it was to cleanse in case of a major bio-release. The former might be true. Walden doubted the latter.

Both the Sov-Lats and the NAA had done extensive work on radiation-resistant diseases. Bacteria lived—thrived!—inside the radioactive boiling water pipes in reactors. Using them as host, an elegant bit of gengineering had produced a strain of radiation-impervious adenovirus that produced flulike symptoms. It had never been a practical weapon because the flu was too mild and the lipoprotein envelope broke apart and permitted frequent natural mutation.

To cleanse with nuclear radiation would be more dangerous than trying to contain with more pedestrian procedures.

"The top level is booby-trapped!"

"Can you contact the scientists?"

Zacharias made a sound as if he spat. "What good would that do? They'd think we'd joined forces with the aliens and were trying to steal their work."

Walden shook his head at such rampant paranoia. The Sov-Lats were bad. In various conferences he had seen how their researchers were instilled with fear of anyone outside their bloc. Zacharias displayed the same symptoms. The two sides would have to learn to cooperate if the alien threat became any worse.

Walden glanced up into the bright blue cloudless sky. The MCG energy weapons used by the orbiting alien had momentarily burned away the water vapor. Two shiny dots neared the zenith. Walden thought he saw another hostile exchange between the ships. The alien ship and the *Winston* continued their orbiting dogfight.

"How much time do we have?" he asked the major.

"You mean what's going on up there?" Zacharias jerked his thumb upward indicating the fighting vessels. "Stalemate. The *Winston* got in the first shot and damaged them, then it got dicey. Too bad the *Tannhauser* can't join in. The pair of them'd make quick work of the bastard."

The EPCT officer turned, his gaze farther afield. Walden saw his lips moving as he barked commands on another frequency but heard nothing on his band. Walden worked at his portable analyzer, looking for the smallest hint of released bioweaponry. His instrument gave true readings now—he hoped.

"Egad, what do you smell?"

"Bomb shells. Burning. Human shells."

"Nothing alien?"

The dog shook his head emphatically. Walden looked back at the major to see if he had overheard Egad's report. The officer was too engrossed in moving his squad toward the entrance to the underground laboratory to pay attention to the scientist or his dog.

"Come on. You're going to be the first down the hole. Tanner is reporting booby traps just inside the entrance."

"I don't know anything about traps," protested Walden. Zacharias grabbed him by the shoulders and lifted him to his feet. A hard shove got the scientist moving in the direction of the hidden lab.

"Tanner'll teach you what you need when you need to know it. I've got to patrol the perimeter to keep more alien fighting mechs off your back."

Walden didn't think the aliens had any forces left. From all indications, they had landed a small force and then been attacked by the *Winston*. Unable to reinforce the ground units, the aliens had been removed as a threat on Schwann.

Egad raced alongside Walden as they slipped and ran across the glassy surface. Walden was never happier than when he skidded to a halt beside the marine sergeant. Tanner knelt by a blasted-open door, goggles down and studying the darkened interior.

"I see at least two bomb triggers. We blew the door but didn't touch their booby traps. Don't know how they protected them, but I'd like to know. It's a useful trick."

"What kind of traps?" asked Walden.

The sergeant shrugged. "Never seen anything like 'em." The sergeant gestured that Walden should change com frequency. "You private on this line?" he asked. "Good. Where's the major?"

Walden explained how he was patrolling the edge of the plain.

"Son of a bitch," grumbled the sergeant. "He lets me do all the fun shit."

Walden again got the feeling that Tanner had little respect for his superior. Being given the most dangerous jobs in combat heightened that sentiment.

"I'll try to trigger the traps. You keep a watch out to be sure we're not spraying ourselves with killer gunk."

Walden had to smile. He had heard the soldiers refer to both chemical and biological weapons as "killer gunk" before. To hear it spoken with such fervor now showed how little they really knew of biologic systems work.

"A low-level grenade," said Tanner, tossing a marble-sized sphere into the door.

A tiny *pop!* sounded. Walden started to poke his head around to look in. Egad grabbed him and dragged him back an instant before a geyser of molten metal erupted.

"Sodium!" screamed Tanner. "Get the hell out of here. Run for it!"

Walden didn't have to be told twice. He made sure Egad was well ahead of him before he got his feet moving. He was almost a kilometer away when he ran out of breath and collapsed to his knees. Tanner came back and knelt beside him.

"Diabolical bastards. We ruptured a liquid metal cooling channel to their reactor."

"They'll kill themselves. Their reactor will start running hot."

"It might be shut down. They could have left the turbines on and dropped the control rods. Damned primitive bastards. Why do they always rely on twentieth century technology—and never *good* tech at that?"

"How are we going to get into the lab? We can't swim through the sodium. The fumes are deadly and the metal is corrosive, even if the suits protect us from the heat."

"We burrow." Tanner's lips kept moving, but Walden heard nothing. The sergeant had switched to another frequency. Walden was getting used to this but it still disconcerted him.

"Get down."

Walden dived, not even asking why. Seconds later the ground shook and dirt geysered up.

"Right on the target. That Nakamura knows her stuff."

"She launched a B-and-E missile from the *Hippocrates*?" The notion stunned Walden. He didn't want to cope with the mutated anthrax contained in the warheads.

"She stripped out the killer gunk and put in HE. She carved us a custom-made door. Let's make the most of it. You on auto?"

Walden indicated that he was. The analyzer worked to give a ten-second update on conditions. As Walden thought about Nakamura's accuracy in placing the B-and-E, he reached up and touched the small camera she had given him. He had locked it onto his helmet to give a continuous view. She had used this to target the missile.

He didn't care how she had worked her magic. They had a hole gaping in front of them. He stood and stared down into it. Stygian blackness even his IR goggles couldn't penetrate greeted him.

"Let's win medals. You ready to die, Doc?"

"No, but this has to be done. We've got to find out about the aliens, and the Sov-Lats might know what we need."

Sgt. Tanner helped him down the side of the sloping crater. The marine's grip slipped. Walden grabbed frantically for purchase and found only rubble under his gloves. He heard Egad barking furiously, but this did nothing to help. Night swallowed him, and he fell endlessly in the loose debris.

CHAPTER

Walden cried out as he fell. The screams echoed inside his helmet and deafened him. When he slammed hard against something unyielding and unseen, it almost came as a relief. The sensation of falling endlessly wasn't one he cherished.

"You in one piece, Doc?"

"I think so." He cautiously worked around in the rubble to be sure he had a good footing, then stood. Checking himself, he found no obvious injuries, though he knew he'd have bruises all over his body in a few hours.

Just as he recovered fully from his slide, he was bowled over by a heavy form. The immediate barking told him Egad had joined him.

"Smell chemicals," the dog told him without preamble. "Bad smells. No humans."

"Sergeant, can you get a light down to me?"

"Even better, Doc." In a few seconds Tanner and five other EPCTs joined him. Walden marveled at the amount of equipment the men carried. Enough firepower rested in their arms to fight a small war—and after what they had been through, it had proven barely adequate.

"My IR goggles aren't good enough for me to see the analyzer readout."

"It's not plugged in directly to your helmet display?"

"I don't have that kind of output." Walden almost added, "I don't think." He had used the field until too infrequently to know its full capability. He had always relied on the more automated and better equipped laboratory analyzer.

"Give me a second." Tanner worked with patch cords and a small reset probe. "Try it."

"I . . . it's working. I'm getting a heads-up display of the readouts."

"You should have better IR vision, too. That hazard suit of yours isn't up to EPCT specs."

Walden didn't point out it wasn't intended for combat. He turned slowly, studying the eerie, ghostlike images generated by the infrared lenses. He wondered if the small camera mounted on the side of his helmet gave Miko Nakamura any better view. He thought that it must. The way she had handled the device and had so reluctantly given it to him showed that it was state-of-the-art spy equipment.

"Can we contact the *Hippocrates*?" he asked.

"We're putting in relay boxes as we go." Tanner held up a signal pistol. In its magazine were slender cylinders smaller than roofing nails. He shot one into the wall so that it was in line-of-sight with the surface.

Enough of the relays would insure uninterrupted communication—Walden hoped. He remembered how the alien electromagnetic pulses had blanked his analyzer functions.

"Can the Sov-Lats pick up the relays?" he asked.

"Doubt it," the sergeant answered. "The gadgets switch and split frequencies constantly. Harder'n any iceteroid to detect. I don't want to go to the bother of unwinding foptic cable. This is going to have to do us."

Walden understood the sergeant's reluctance to unwind the fiber optic communications cable. Light, tiny, virtually untappable and jammable, it still presented a foot-tangling obstacle if a retreat proved necessary. He decided to let the military operate as they saw fit and studied the tunnels. The hole Nakamura had blown might have blocked off other options, but the tunnel extending to the right or to the left offered enough choice for him.

"Egad, which way to the elevators?"

The dog hurried off without answering. Walden followed, keeping a close watch on the readouts hovering in front of him like netherworld spirits. He didn't want the dog blundering into biologically active areas without his helmet on. One sniff and the proper virus in the lungs could kill within seconds.

"Halt!" The sharp command froze Walden in his tracks.

"Stop your damned dog, unless you want to lose him," Tanner said, pushing past Walden.

"Egad, heel." The dog had obeyed the sergeant's first order and sat on his haunches in the middle of the dark corridor.

"Don't move, dog," Tanner said. "Hecht, Giovanni, disarm the bomb. Standard Sov-Lat issue."

The two marines crowded by Walden and went to stand on either side of Egad. The dog's head turned up, as if he watched with rapt fascination. Walden wasn't sure Egad could even see in the dark. The ghostly outlines of the two EPCTs drifted to and fro across his IR display. Once Walden thought he saw a tiny core of intense heat. As quickly as the flare appeared, it vanished.

"They lasered it," explained Tanner. "Not too hard a trap to avoid, but in the dark they can get messy."

"What else do we have to fight our way through to get to the elevators?"

"Those are likely to be booby-trapped, too," the sergeant said. "It might be better to find emergency stairs and descend that way, if they even have them."

"They must. They'd be trapped below if they didn't and the power failed."

Tanner snorted but said nothing. Walden began to worry that the marine knew the Sov-Lats better than he did. They might seal their contaminated area and condemn their scientists to death if a major accident occurred. He tried to shake off this gloomy thought and found that he couldn't. The misgivings Zacharias and the others demonstrated on a daily basis had begun to work on his usual optimism.

"Stairs," came Egad's voice. "What? Down?"

"Who spoke?" demanded Tanner. "I ordered com silence."

"Sorry," Walden said. "I didn't hear the order."

"It wasn't intended for you—and you weren't the one speaking."

"Just a catch in my voice." Walden reached down and patted Egad to assure the animal everything was all right. The sergeant subsided and moved to examine the stairwell door.

"It's dangerous to do it this way."

"Hell's bells, Sarge, you want to try their damned elevator? I don't want to have the floor blown out from under me. It might be a couple hundred meters to the bottom of the shaft. That's one hell of a ways to fall."

"Shut up, Hecht." Tanner paced around, then shone a light through the doorway. Simple metal stairs spiraled downward. Walden flipped his IR goggles to full power and saw no heat sources. A quick check of the analyzer made his gut turn to ice.

"There's bio-leakage below," he said, his voice choked enough to unintentionally sound like Egad's. "Bioweapons grade. Some sort of mutated endospore of *Clostridium botulinum*."

"What's that do?"

"The bacterium causes botulism. I can't tell you exactly what would happen or how fast, but you want to be sure your hazard suits are working properly—no tears, nothing wrong with the gas exchange or filtration system."

Walden jerked Egad around and fixed the animal's helmet. Egad complained by growling deep in his throat.

"This might not affect you like it would a human, but it's bad stuff, old boy. Trust me." He patted the dog through the suit and got a tail wag in response. Egad might not like being imprisoned, but he accepted it. He had spent too much time watching Walden's experiments to doubt the danger.

"Take the point, Hecht. I'll go next. The doc can follow me with his mutt. The rest of you keep alert and keep putting in the relays. I don't want to lose contact with the major, unless it's necessary."

Walden almost laughed at this. Tanner had already thought of a way to do what was necessary without having any interference from the above-ground Major Zacharias. They started down the spiraling staircase, stopping at the first landing and doing a full instrument check.

The levels of airborne spores increased. Walden shivered. Botulism was a terrible way to die. The bacteria grew inside the body, producing a deadly nerve toxin. Paralysis might be the least of a victim's problems. Autonomic response was thwarted and suffocation would occur without immediate medical intervention.

"Sarge, want me to check the levels as we go?" asked the one Walden identified as Hecht.

"What do you think, Doc? We have to go through an airlock and decontamination each time. That takes maybe ten minutes total. Is it worth it?"

Walden peered through a heavy glasteel portal into the first subterranean level. Emergency lights gave a dull appearance to the corridor, as if it had been turned out of some strange silver cloth rather than cast in plastic. A quick check with the IR goggles in place failed to turn up any sign of life.

"We don't know how many levels there are," he said. "I don't want to plunge all the way to the bottom and find ourselves cut off because we passed someone by."

"You mean you don't want any of the aliens getting between us and the surface," said Hecht. "Don't worry, Doc. We can take care of them." He swung a heavy laserifle around. "This baby'll blow'em fourteen ways to hell and gone."

"Hecht, toggle off," Tanner said tiredly. "The doc's got the right idea. We don't want to fight upstairs. Better check each level as we go. It'll take an eternity, but I want to tell my grandkids about this."

"You don't even have kids, Sarge," came a protest from one of the others in the squad.

"At least I've got balls, which is more than you'll have if you don't keep com silence like you were ordered."

Walden ignored the byplay between the marines. He knelt and pressed his helmet against Egad's. By speaking loudly the dog could hear. They didn't need to use the radio.

"When we get inside, go find any humans," ordered Walden. "Be careful, though. They're all Sov-Lats."

"Find and come back? Find and fetch?"

"Find and return," Walden told the dog. He knew Egad's fighting ability was limited in the hazard suit. The suit had been designed for mobility, and Walden wanted to make the most of it. A human might shoot at another. It was less likely they would open fire on a dog, especially if they were not expecting to see one. That gave Egad a slight edge.

Walden realized it was a very slight one, but he could not shake off the feeling that time mattered to them. The release of the botulism spores told of major breakdowns in the facility. He didn't want to find out what else had failed—but he knew he would.

"Doc, you mind risking your neck a bit?" asked Tanner.

"You want me to go through and look around?"

"I'll send a couple men with you, but I don't want to commit the entire squad."

Walden nodded. His worry about enemy forces springing from an unexplored level still applied. To be trapped within a level might be as bad. Better to lose a few than the entire squad.

"Decontamination won't take long. The Sov-Lats' equipment isn't as thorough as ours. Five minutes max."

"Hecht. You're volunteered to go with the doc. Watch his back and do as he says. You're going to be cut off on the boss-man circuit, so he's in command."

"The dog," asked Hecht. "Can he give me orders, too?"

"Sure, why not?" Tanner laughed and Hecht joined in. Egad started to speak but stopped when Walden restrained him. He signaled to the animal to enter the small decon chamber. Hecht crowded in beside them and cycled the door shut.

The room filled with foam that made Walden feel giddy and buoyant. As quickly as the floating sensation came, it passed and the foam vanished beneath heavy antiseptic sprays of red and green liquid.

"What is this shit, Doc?"

"Something specific for what they were doing on this level. I can't say. Might be radioactive debris around. Watch your counters."

"I always watch my ass. That takes *everything* into account."

The marine sounded confident, but Walden saw the way he gripped his laserifle a bit tighter. The muscles along his shoulders probably knotted from the strain. By the time the antiseptics had drained and a bright UV light clicked on, Hecht was wound-up tighter than wire around a transformer coil.

Walden stepped into the corridor beyond the decon chamber. The lights came up as he moved slowly past the first office door. Hecht pushed past him and kicked in the door. The room was empty.

"An office. Section head. Natasha Romanov," reported Hecht.

Walden's eyebrows rose in surprise. Hecht read the Cyrillic nameplate on the desk with ease. Zacharias has trained his EPCTs better than expected. Walden motioned for Egad to explore while he went through the files in the office. A section head had access to more information than anyone else in the research section.

Walden settled in front of the computer terminal and worked slowly at the keyboard. His Russian was rusty but proved good enough to bring up the main menu displays.

"They didn't do anything worth mentioning," Walden said after a few minutes studying what he had retrieved. "The next three levels are mostly administrative, also. Level five is the first research laboratory."

"Why have the decontamination equipment installed?" asked Hecht. "They weren't doing anything to worry about it."

"Not here. Lower. That the section head's office is next to the unit tells me she worried about bioactive spills from below."

"She wanted out fast if there's trouble? Is that it, Doc?"

"Exactly." Walden half listened as Hecht went on talking. He studies the files, trying to decide what had happened in the research facility. Unconsciously touching the side of his helmet, as if to scratch his head, his hand came to rest on the slender camera Nakamura had given him. It had run constantly, giving the advisor a comprehensive look at everything he had seen.

He kept forgetting it. Walden fought down the coldness inside. Had Nakamura heard him giving the orders to Egad? He wanted to keep the dog's abilities secret, not only for the edge it gave him but because of the implied guilt. The research responsible for Egad's abilities had not been sanctioned—and even worse, when he had succeeded, the data had not been reported.

Egad trotted up and sat beside him. Through the dog's helmet he saw the animal's tongue lolling. Egad had been working hard and was trying to cool off.

"What is it, old fellow?" he asked, pulling the dog close. He turned off Nakamura's tiny spy camera and pressed his helmet close to Egad's.

"No one alive. More than five dead. All shot."

Walden had not been able to get Egad to count higher than five. The concept of numbers still eluded the dog, but details weren't needed. That the level's occupants had perished was all that mattered now.

"I can't make head nor tail out of this," Walden said, turning back on the camera. "Have Tanner begin searches on lower levels, but it'll be at five where the labs start that we'll get our answer."

Walden made a quick check with his analyzer and found the air clean of botulism spores. Egad had said those who had died had been shot. He wondered if they had died at the hands of the alien invasion force? From the battle raging on the surface he had supposed the aliens had been turned away before gaining entry.

"Make a quick check," Walden told the marine. "Find a corpse and call me."

"Should we split up?"

"Do it. We're by ourselves and there aren't any biohazards running around loose."

The marine left, his step less than confident. Walden nosed around a bit more before going into the corridor. Hecht gestured for him. Walden glanced into the room. Four bodies were slumped over a table.

"Looks like suicide," the marine said distastefully.

"All like this," spoke up Egad.

"How do you know, Doc?"

"Intuition," Walden said, trying to sound as much like the dog's computer-generated voice as he could. "Let's forget the other levels and get to the labs. The administrative personnel didn't make it. Maybe the scientific staff did."

Worry dogged his steps as they retreated through the decontamination unit. What had caused the Sov-Lats to kill themselves? Egad had said all died in the same fashion. Fear of capture by the aliens? That hardly seemed plausible. He knew the Soviets' mental toughness too well and respected it.

Something had been released below that made it easier for them to take their own lives rather than face. . . . What had the Sov-Lats brewed up in their bioweapons research?

Back in the stairwell, Walden told Tanner, "Have spare hazard suits ready. I don't want to get halfway down to find that they released something that eats through these."

"I thought these shucked off everything, acid, bio, cuts, everything."

"They're supposed to," said Walden. "I don't know what we're up against." His analyzer showed increased levels of the airborne botulism spores. He worried less about this and more about what other bioweapons they faced.

"I had Giovanni check out level two. One body, apparent suicide. Want to go on to the third floor?"

"Let's try level five. Time is working against us," Walden said. Tanner checked the integrity of his suit and then ordered his men to do likewise. "I'm not trying to scare you, Sergeant," Walden explained. "This isn't going to be a safe training maneuver with a dozen observers waiting to bail us out."

"We don't train like that. We're EPCT. More of us die in training than in combat—we're ready for anything out here."

Walden started down the stairs, not sure that meant much now. The very air carried weapons no human could fight—not with a laser or projectile weapon or genius bomb. Avoidance was the safest way of fighting.

And they were walking down into the center of the infection.

"Interference on the com-link, Sarge," came a quick report. "Faint radio transmissions from below."

Walden stared though the glasteel window onto level five. Two deeper levels completed the extent of the Sov-Lats research base.

"We keep going. Down to level seven. That's where I'd hole up if there were trouble."

"Not me," said Hecht. "I'd hightail it for the surface."

"You'd get your tail blow off doing it, too," snapped Tanner. He correctly interpreted the man's words as the beginning of hysteria. "We stay together. We're a unit, dammit!"

"More static, a few words. Can't make them out."

"Can you patch them through to my headphones?" asked Walden.

The hissing and popping and sizzling noise like bacon in a microwave beam startled him. He turned down the volume with a swipe of his chin and listened hard. Through the interference he heard a voice pleading in Russian for help.

"Should we answer?" asked Tanner.

"Find our where they are. Don't tell them we're NAA."

Tanner rapped out a guttural reply and waited. Walden strained for the answer.

"They're here. Level seven." Tanner faced the decontamination unit and paused. "It's more complex than the ones on the upper levels," he said.

"I found the source of the botulism," said Walden. He stared in disbelief at small valves along the walls. The Sov-Lats had intentionally released the toxin-producing spores. "It must be a defensive measure they took."

"Just like a skunk," commented Hecht.

Walden yelped in pain when his headphones blared a siren warning.

"Now hear this, now hear this. Major Zacharias speaking. The alien force has brought up reinforcements from a hidden base. They've blasted through the ground in four locations and are entering the Sov-Lat facility. All units, retreat. I say again, all units retreat. Code green, code x-ray, code niner."

Walden hesitated. The scientists trapped inside still lived and begged for rescue. They could answer questions about the research—and about the aliens. What had caused the aliens to begin using their microwave weapons on the planet's surface? The firsthand information would go far in combating the threat posed by the aliens.

"We go in," Walden said. "Blast open the door. Use that diode laserifle you're so proud of, Hecht."

Tanner pushed the scientist out of the way. The entire squad turned their weapons against the heavy decontamination chamber door. It blew apart under the combined assault. Walden waited for them to blast the inner door, too. The deliberate construction required such violent measures. A timer prevented the doors from opening and closing without a full decon cycle elapsing.

"Where are they?" demanded Tanner.

Egad raced between their legs and rocketed forward. Walden pointed and took off behind the dog. He hoped the dog's sensitive hearing had picked up a clue that they had missed. All he got on his headphones on the Sov-Lats' frequency was static.

Walden kept his head swiveling around as he ran, making sure that Nakamura's camera pointed at everything. He wished he could have paused to look at their labs. He could have learned a great deal about their projects—and their progress.

"A sealed chamber," panted Tanner, sliding to a hault behind Egad. Walden skidded on the smooth floor and peered inside. Three women and a man huddled inside.

"How do we communicate with them?" demanded Walden.

"Radio com is out," came the disturbing message. "Not getting any transmission at all. Their power supply must have died."

One woman turned frightened, haunted eyes toward Walden. She looked at him—and through him. Her lips moved in a pattern over and over. Then she reached over and picked up a box.

The others in the room simply looked on with the resigned contemplation of those sentenced to die. She opened the lid and worked inside for a moment. Then she sagged against the thick metal wall, her head bowed.

"What did she do?" Tanner motioned his men back and began lasering at the chamber door. The armor plating proved too obdurate for hand-held weapons.

Walden took a deep, steadying breath. He tried not to panic. Egad nuzzled against him.

"What?" he asked the dog.

"She said two words again and again."

"What were they?"

"Infinity plague!"

CHAPTER

Walden paled as he watched the dismal, bent women and man inside the sealed chamber. He couldn't take his eyes off the small box the woman had opened. "She pressed the cleanse button," he said in a voice almost too low to hear.

"What? What did you say, Doc?" Tanner turned from his futile attempts to open the sealed safety chamber.

"She pushed the button to blow up the entire complex. There must be a nuclear device buried below us."

"Why'n the bloody hell didn't you say so?" Sgt. Tanner's lips moved soundlessly as he cut off Walden and barked orders on frequencies closed to the scientist.

Walden reached out and shook the marine's arm. "We've got time—maybe fifteen minutes."

"It'll take more than that to get them out of the chamber. They don't seem to be cooperating." Tanner touched a control on his helmet and spoke rapidly, his orders again going to his squad and not to Walden. The marines raced off in the direction of the elevators. Tanner had come to a wise decision: obey Zacharias' command to retreat. They couldn't get the Sov-Lats out before the entire lab complex vanished in a nuclear firestorm.

"You coming, Doc? We're getting out of here."

"I'm coming." He glanced through the window again. The

woman's entire body shuddered with her hysterical sobbing. Walden quietly asked, knowing she couldn't hear, "What have you done? What is your Infinity Plague?"

Egad nudged him into motion. A quick check of his chronometer showed that precious seconds ticked away. All his readings about the Sov-Lats stated they used a fifteen-minute delay on their nuclear cleansers. He had no way of knowing if they followed accepted procedure on Schwann. Walden ran as hard as he could to catch up with the retreating marines. They stood impatiently waiting for the elevator cage to arrive.

"Everyone into the first car to arrive," ordered Tanner. "No stragglers, no splitting forces."

The elevator doors slid open. For the span of a heartbeat no one moved. A solitary gasp came from Tanner at the sight of the alien inside the cage.

Egad recovered faster than either human or alien. The dog leaped, his whipcord-thin body striking the alien just below the knees. The alien lost balance and reached out to catch himself. This gave Tanner and two others time to recover their wits. The marine sergeant grabbed an outflung wrist and twisted viciously. At the same instant, he stepped forward.

Walden winced when he heard alien bones breaking. The others crowded into the elevator. By the time Walden turned around, the doors had closed and the elevator had started for the surface.

"We might be going into a nest of them," said Tanner. "I'm not getting anything on the command circuit. Laserifles at ready. Shoot'em if you got'em in your sights."

Walden let the marines do what they could to prepare for a possible alien ambush. He worked around the wall and stared down at the alien. Egad stood guard, his bandy legs straddling their enemy.

The scientist almost laughed aloud. This hardly looked like the caliber enemy to prove your worth against. The bone structure was small, delicate, even fragile. The high cheekbones supported heavier bony ridges for a snout like an earthly pig's. The lipless mouth hung slack and a pale purple tongue lolled out to one side, as if the alien did a bad impersonation of Egad trying to cool off. The eyes flickered open and shut. Walden had only a glimpse of cat-slitted green and gold. Without a doubt, the

eyes were the alien's loveliest feature. From the eyelids, the forehead bulged slightly, then sailed back in the manner of the ancient Maya Indians. Rough skin rather than hair covered the
dome. Beyond this Walden couldn't see because of the alien's
helmet.

"They must breathe a mixture similar to ours," he said.
"Their coloration is close, except for the purple tongue."

"No air?" suggested Egad. The dog had seen hypoxia in laboratory animals and the cyanotic blue tongues produced.

Walden frowned and motioned Egad to silence. The sergeant
and the rest of the squad were too preoccupied to notice. They
nervously pushed back and forth, as if this would make the elevator move faster.

Walden tried to help the alien sit up. Hecht roughly pushed
the being flat. "Don't, Doc. He can't do much flat on his ass."

"He's not even armed." Walden had looked in vain for a
weapon and had discovered nothing that looked dangerous.

"Can't say. We'll be sure when we get him to interrogation."

The alien's slitted eyes blinked at this. Walden had the feeling
that he understood everything being said. That told the scientist
many things. The aliens communicated using the same radio
frequencies, which implied their technology was on a par with
Earth's. Their auditory organs had to be similar, too. Even more
to the point, the alien *understood* NAA English.

"You're not going to be hurt if you cooperate," Walden told
the alien. The eyes turned on him and stared. He had no sense
of what thoughts raced through that potentially hostile mind. The
creature belonged to a species that had systematically destroyed
all life on Schwann.

This shook Walden. He had based his feelings of harmlessness
on the alien's appearance. Another entity of the same race had
ordered the deaths of untold researchers and their families. Delta
Cygnus 4 had become a barren wasteland because of their energy weapon—and their ruthless willingness to use it against
unarmed humans.

"Sergeant, did our research facility have any weapons?"

"What? Sure, Doc, they had plenty." He hefted his laserifle.
"A small detachment of EPCTs with these can hold off anything
the Sov-Lats had."

"I meant heavy armor. Antisatellite cannon. Missiles."

"They might, but it costs too much to transport forty-seven lights. Dammit, when's this elevator going to get to the top?"

Walden didn't feel any better about knowing the research center had likely been unarmed and unable to fight the alien warship. There might have been *some* armament, but not as much as that carried aboard the *Hippocrates* and under Zacharias' command.

The innocuous, funny-looking alien had to be a cold-blooded murderer.

"At last!" Tanner burst out of the elevator, laserifle leveled. The wall of heat surging into the elevator took Walden by surprise. Egad whimpered and the others in the squad let out curses as they forced their way out to get their laserifles into the fight.

"Don't even think of escaping," Walden warned the alien. The piglike being looked from Walden to Egad. The dog stood a few centimeters away, fangs bared. This had the effect of convincing the alien not to resist, even though Egad could have done little with those teeth through his hazard suit helmet.

Walden peered around the door of the elevator and saw Tanner dispersing his squad to catch the enemy in a crossfire. This was the only tactic that might get them out of the research center—and Walden saw that it wasn't working. Two of the squad had been cut down and the boiling heat from the enemy weapons caused him to sweat, even inside the insulated hazard suit.

"Sergeant, what's happening?" he shouted. Walden tried to get better control of his nerves. There wasn't any reason to shout. Tanner wasn't deaf and he wasn't far off. The radio would provide ample amplification, even at distances up to fifty kilometers.

"We're fighting for our bleeping lives, that's what's happening, dammit," the man flared. "How much longer until the freaking device goes off?"

Walden glanced at his timer display. They had less than ten minutes—if his information about the duration before detonation was accurate. The Sov-Lats might have planted a device with a shorter det delay.

"The only consolation is that the pigs will get it, too," grunted Tanner. He rolled into the corridor, came to a halt flat on his belly, and turned his weapon to full beam. The plastic walls began to blister and pop, filling the air with noxious vapor. Walden did not hear the sergeant's command to the others in the squad to duplicate his attack.

Such an effort was dangerous. The laserifles would discharge quickly and leave them at the aliens' mercy if it didn't work.

It did. The walls melted down into a small bottleneck, opening ceiling and floor as they contracted.

"Up. Get upstairs. Now!"

Walden put his arm around the alien's thin shoulders and heaved him erect. The being stumbled and tried to resist. Egad herded him like a sheepdog with a flock. The alien obeyed the silent command to climb up and through the damaged ceiling. Walden followed as fast as he could. Egad bounded past and stood guard over their captive.

"Tanner, there are small tanks waiting for us!" cried Walden.

Tanner didn't answer. Hecht blundered up behind, pushing him out of the way. Two others, hazard suits smoldering and coated in a hot veneer of plastic from the walls, followed quickly. Of Sergeant Tanner there wasn't any trace.

"Get over to the lead vehicle, Doc," Hecht ordered.

"What's wrong with Tanner?"

"He bought it. Get your ass moving or we're all dog food." Hecht took a swipe at the alien with the butt of his blackened and twisted laserifle. "Make that hog slop."

Walden and Egad escorted their prisoner toward the lightly armored vehicle in the front of the column. A hatch popped open when they were within a few meters. Two EPCTs piled out, their weapons swinging in restless arcs, ready for action.

"In," came a voice Walden remembered well. He dived headfirst through the hatch. Miko Nakamura grabbed his arms and skidded him deeper into the vehicle. Behind him came the alien. At the creature's heels Egad bumped and nudged with his head.

"What about Sgt. Tanner?" demanded Walden.

"He died well. His sacrifice allowed you and the survivors in his squad to escape. The alien presence on the upper levels of the research complex developed rapidly and unexpectedly."

"They invaded the labs?"

Nakamura looked at him as if he had suffered brain damage. "I said this."

"The Sov-Lats triggered a cleanser."

"We are aware of this. I ordered these vehicles in for pickup. Our instruments show less than fourteen minutes until explosion."

Walden tipped his head to one side and checked his elapsed timer. He showed only three minutes. "Are you sure?"

"They use a long count for off-world complexes. There will be ample warning. We will detect a preliminary neutron burst before the final sequence begins."

Walden had to trust her. And he had to admire Nakamura for coming personally to fetch them.

"Where's Zacharias?"

The woman's neutral tone, for the briefest instant, changed to a bitterness he had never heard. "The major is conducting peripheral cleanup. There will soon be no aliens in the field—only in the laboratory complex."

Nakamura turned to the prisoner and examined him with her cold, dark eyes. She said nothing, turned and went back to the hatch. Hecht and three others scrambled in, followed by the two guards. The armored vehicle lurched and roared as it started across the barren plain. Walden was thrown flat.

In that instant, the alien jerked around and tried to open a rear hatchway. Egad had maintained his balance. The dog dived between the alien's legs, sending him to his knees. Moving with deceptive slowness, Nakamura went to the prisoner's side and reached out.

The alien screamed like any Earth child experiencing pain. Nakamura's grip on the alien's good arm did not seem as if it could inflict such agony. When Nakamura turned to one side, the alien tumbled head over heels and landed flat on his back at the woman's feet.

"Do not do that again." She bent her knees slightly and increased the pressure on the trapped arm. The alien's eyes screwed tightly shut, then the entire face went slack.

"They have a low threshold of pain," Nakamura observed clinically. "That might prove useful in questioning. Then again, they might perish swiftly, too. We will conduct a full physical examination before asking what we need to know of our . . . guest.'' She glanced at Egad, the corners of her mouth turning up in a wry smile. Nakamura bowed in the dog's direction and returned to the front of the vehicle.

In a few seconds, both EPCTs who had protected their entry into the vehicle came back and sat on either side of the unconscious prisoner.

"He's not going anywhere," said Walden.

Neither man spoke. One fondled a wicked-looking, sixty-centimeter-long, diamond-sputtered blade and the other cradled a long-barreled laser in the crook of his elbow. Walden saw that the prisoner was never going to attempt another escape. He left Egad to watch over the alien. They could learn too much about the aliens and their attack—he had no desire to see the captive killed senselessly.

"How far are we from the complex?" he asked Nakamura. The woman ignored him. He scooted farther into the front of the armored vehicle and pushed his back against an outer wall for support. The dim lighting turned the occupants into strange and ominous shadow figures swaying with the vehicle's motion.

The driver's face was illuminated from below by the panel lights. Of them all, he looked the most demonic. Walden didn't bother the man for information. If Nakamura wouldn't tell him what he needed to know, the driver wouldn't either. Besides, the less the driver was distracted the more likely he was to get them away from ground zero before nuclear cleansing.

"It's going just fine, Doc," spoke up Hecht.

"How can you say that? We lost Tanner and half the squad."

"I'm gonna miss him. He was one hell of a fine sergeant. But you know how it is. They treat us like mules, loading us until our backs break. Then they eat us. Giovanni was an okay sort, too." Hecht stretched. "It's not all bad, though. I'm due for stripes and my own squad now, being senior. I'll take good care of you, Doc. Tanner would've wanted it that way."

"Thanks," Walden said dryly.

"And your mutt, too. We all like him. What'd you say his name was?"

"Egad."

Hecht laughed. "Fits. The first time I looked at that mismatched collection of legs and body and head and those crazy eyes, that's what I said. Egad."

Walden tried to get some sense of how far they had come. The vehicle lacked windows. The driver worked through exterior sensors and information provided by aerial and space surveillance. Only a small PLZT window high above the driver gave any hint of the outside world.

As Walden stood to peer out, the window flashed black. The vehicle rocked lightly, and Walden lost his balance. He sat down heavily, holding onto the loop of webbing that provided both seat and safety belt.

"Close one," muttered the pilot. "The damned pigs are dropping stuff on us from orbit. The *Winston* couldn't hold them long enough for us to hightail it."

The driver and Nakamura switched to a different frequency and shut off Walden. The scientist turned to Hecht.

"What'd he mean?"

"The pigs are better than we thought. The *Winston* only damaged their ship. Leastwise, that's what I heard."

"The driver called them pigs. How'd he know what they look like? We didn't know until we caught that one." Walden pointed to the rear of the armored vehicle.

"Word gets around fast. You got to call 'em something. They look like pigs, so we'll call 'em that."

Walden sat in silence. Few things traveled faster in military circles than a rumor—or a description of the enemy. He wondered if there were any EPCTs in the company who wouldn't recognize the alien from the brief description given by the driver?

He doubted it.

"How far are we from the complex?"

"Not far enough." Hecht's light bantering tone darkened. "I don't like being around the big nukes. Nakamura says it's a big one, too. Damned big. Maybe eight hundred megatons."

"Eight *hundred*?" Walden sat in shocked silence. There had never been a nuclear device this large detonated. He wasn't even sure if computer modeling had mapped out the effects of such a large bomb. Testing had stopped at two hundred fifty megatons. This device would not only vaporize the research facility, it might crack open the planet.

What was the Infinity Plague and why did it require such hellish measures to eradicate it?

"We can't get far enough away before the bang," the driver said on an open frequency. "We're having a pickup meet us. Everyone get ready to bail out."

The vehicle rocked again. Walden sat up in surprise when the wall began glowing a cherry red.

"Damn, the pigs got us with the edge of a microwave beam."

"They're firing on us?"

"Leastwise," said Hecht, "they'll go up with the Sov-Lats. That's only fair."

Walden watched apprehensively as the hot spot spread along the side of the armor and began to show the passing terrain as pinholes developed. The vehicle wasn't going to be good for anything in a few more seconds—and they'd be exposed to the full might of the alien maser beams.

The driver jerked the heavy vehicle around and sent Walden tumbling into Hecht. The marine righted him and roughly tossed him back into his seat.

"Don't buckle in, but hold on tight," Hecht advised. "We're almost there." He motioned to the marines in the rear of the vehicle. They crouched, getting ready for a hasty exit.

Walden swung from side to side as the vehicle slued to a halt. The hatch popped open and Hecht vanished outside. The marines followed him quickly. Nakamura, Egad, and their alien prisoner trailed them more carefully.

"Come along, Dr. Walden," the advisor said. "We do not stay much longer where we are not wanted."

Walden shot a quick look at the driver. The man had stripped off his command helmet and donned a standard-issue hazard unit. Everyone was abandoning ship.

He piled out and stared up into the off-color blue sky. A bright speck blossomed and grew. In seconds, the pickup ship landed. Walden didn't need any urging to scramble into the tiny, needle-prowed ship. He made certain Egad was strapped in. He had barely finished when he was slammed back into the pads. The pilot had not been on the ground longer than two minutes.

Walden let out a deep sigh. They had made it.

Then the blast wave from the exploding atomic bomb caught the light ship and tossed it about like a leaf on a hurricane.

CHAPTER

15

Jerome Walden cried out in panic as he felt the pickup ship sliding sideways. Egad let out a pitiful whine and several of the marines shouted and cursed at the pilot, who was forward and oblivious to their demands for a smoother flight.

"Are we all right?" demanded Walden of Hecht.

The marine nodded, his face pale. "We had a close one. The Sov-Lat facility went up, and it was bigger than Nakamura thought it'd be. If we'd stuck around on-planet even another few minutes . . ." He spread his hands and made a vague gesture showing that they'd be memories and plasma.

Walden shuddered. "Tanner and the others? Their bodies were left down below?"

"We didn't have time to get them out. Damned shame. A marine ought to be buried on his home planet. Or at least in space." Hecht rubbed his face and screwed his eyes tightly shut. "Not too bad going up like that, though. The corps won't forget them."

Walden held onto the padded arms of the acceleration couch, fearing new waves would assault the pickup ship. The pilot had recovered quickly and well, switching systems damaged by EMP and ignoring the worst of the damage by using manual controls. For all the damage, the rest of the lift went smoothly.

Nakamura made her way back from the cockpit after the scream of atmosphere died and they were in the hard vacuum of space. She settled into an empty couch beside Walden.

"There is considerable damage to the ship," she said without preamble. "The blast and EM pulse reduced many of our outer sensors to fused glass."

"What can I do?" Walden wasn't sure he could do anything to help. Repairing equipment aboard a combat vessel was more in the field of the EPCTs.

"We might required immediate interrogation of the prisoner." Nakamura's cold dark eyes flashed back to the alien.

"Why?" The reason struck Walden like a blow to the stomach. "The alien's ship?"

Nakamura nodded. "It has driven off the *Winston*. Although it sustained damage, it poses a threat. Some mechanism of which we are unfamiliar allows it to home in on our prisoner."

"The ship is tracking us?"

"It is. It attempted to destroy us when the pickup ship touched down. I believe the EMP from the Sov-Lat explosion threw off their sensors and granted us a few extra seconds."

"What good will it do to question him? If they blow us out of space, we can't give the information to anyone who can use it. The time would be better spent—" The woman cut him off.

"Major Zacharias is already aboard the *Hippocrates*. We have established an untappable com-link."

Walden heaved a deep sigh. He was a gengineer, not a torturer. Given time and his lab analyzer, he could create drugs that might loosen the alien's pale purple tongue. Aboard a ship that might be blown out of the sky at any instant, he didn't stand much chance of success. He told Nakamura his misgivings.

"The battle is always decided before it begins," she said. "The loser knows in his heart that he has lost before the first blow is delivered."

This made Walden mad. "I'm not giving up. I just pointed out how difficult it will be to get anything useful from him."

"He understands English. He must also understand Russian. This means he is skilled in, for him, alien endeavor. Let us appeal to him for information and a truce."

"A truce?"

Nakamura's expression became unreadable again. Walden saw what she did. Playing for time would get them back to the *Hippocrates* and allow the *Winston* an opportunity to repair and get into a defensive position. They had been outgunned. Now they had to negotiate with an enemy already shown to be willing to destroy all humans.

"He wasn't armed when we caught him," mused Walden. "Maybe he was trying to contact us. We can't go wrong by asking."

"Minimize his injuries. We meant no harm," said Nakamura.

Walden swung out of his couch and floated back toward their prisoner. Two marines flanked the alien.

"Take off his helmet," ordered Walden. "He either breathes our atmosphere or he dies. It might not matter which if his friends get into position to open up on us."

Nakamura settled behind Walden, one leg anchoring her to a couch stanchion. Walden worked to unfasten the alien's suit and found the catches difficult.

"Go on," he said to the alien. "Undo the rest."

The alien glared at him, cat-slit green eyes blazing pure hatred.

"We've got a big problem," Walden said in an offhand manner, as if speaking to himself. "Your ship wants to vaporize us. If it does, you'll go, too."

"We do not forget. We will fight to the death!"

"You weren't armed. What was your mission in the Sov-Lat base?"

The alien glowered, his pig snout nose wrinkling and his nostrils flaring. He wasn't going to cooperate.

"What do I do now?" Walden asked of Nakamura.

"They exist in our atmosphere. How would he like to breathe . . . nothing?"

"She wants to shove you out the airlock," said Walden, understanding Nakamura's ploy. "I don't want her to, but she outranks me.'

"Rank? You?" The alien looked confused. "You are of different orders. How can she hold rank over you?"

"We're different," Walden said. "We don't go by a caste system. Take my word for it, she can do it—unless you show some cooperation.'' He bent closer to the alien and said in a low, conspiratorial voice, ''You don't have to give away anything important. Just enough so I can keep her from throwing you out.''

''I will die for the Frinn.''

''Is that your superior?''

''It is their race,'' corrected Nakamura. ''Listen more carefully to *how* the words are uttered.''

''She wants your head,'' Walden said. ''She won't take resistance from you without wanting to harm you. What is the name of your ship?''

The Frinn made a snuffling sound. Walden wasn't sure how to interpret it. The alien might have given them a name or he might have made an abusive noise.

''What can we really gain from this?'' Walden asked in exasperation. ''I don't know what to ask or if he's even giving me decent answers.''

''Throw him out,'' Nakamura ordered.

The Frinn's eyes widened in fear. Walden noted this reaction was shared by the two races.

''My vessel is the *Prolum*.'' The captive shrank back in the couch, eyes still wide as he waited for Nakamura's response.

''Contact the *Prolum* and tell them we are a peaceful ship and unarmed,'' she said in her low, menacing voice.

''I will die for the Frinn!''

''Of course you will,'' she agreed. ''We must decide the time. Will it be now—or will it be later?''

The ship shuddered and began to spin slowly around its axis. Walden clutched at a couch for support as weight returned.

''Rolling to maneuver,'' came the pilot's garbled voice over their helmet phones. ''Evasive tactics. All hands secure for runaway, all hands secure!''

Walden swung up and into a couch, fastening the straps an instant before the pilot decelerated. Walden thought they had hit a wall in space. The broad straps cut deeply into his flesh. Just as quickly as it had slowed, the ship accelerated, driving him deep into the pneumatic padding.

The explosion in the aft section sent shock waves rumbling the length of the small craft. Walden clapped his hand over his ears to shut out the roar.

"Put your helmet back on," called Nakamura. "We're losing pressure. The hull has been breached."

Walden swung his helmet back into locking position. It had been a relief letting it dangle freely so he could breathe without its claustrophobic presence. Even as he fastened the toggles, he turned to the alien. The Frinn's hands had been secured at his sides.

"Get his helmet back on!" cried Walden, gesturing wildly. The marines had already fixed their own helmets and listened to orders coming from the pilot.

With the ship tossing and twisting, Walden got free of the straps on his couch and almost cracked his helmet against the prisoner's couch. Walden righted himself and began working as fast as he could to fasten the alien's helmet.

"Turn the other direction," the Frinn said, eyes on Walden.

"I really don't want you to be hurt any more. I'm sorry for the way you've been treated so far." Walden looked at the alien's injured right arm and his tied left wrist. "Are you in much pain?"

"I am Frinn." Walden found another emotion shared by their races: contempt.

The helmet snapped into place. The expression of relief on the Frinn's face showed that the air supply worked satisfactorily. Walden had no more time to check out the alien's suit systems. The ship began cartwheeling.

The forces pushed him forward, then he slid around the smooth walls to the stern until he pressed against the engine compartment bulkhead. Walden knew in that instant how an insect pressed onto a microscope stage felt. Struggle as he might, he couldn't move. Relaxing, letting the centrifugal force hold him, he rode out the worst of the tumbling. By keeping his eyes fixed and ignoring what his inner ear told him, he was able to keep from vomiting inside his helmet.

A toss of his chin gave access to his heads-up display. The atmospheric pressure dropped rapidly. When it passed ten torr, his sensors failed to measure the near vacuum inside the ship. A major leak had occurred.

Another twitch of his chin opened the frequencies most likely to be used by the pilot and Nakamura. As the com unit scanned,

Walden worried. It finally locked onto the one used between the *Hippocrates* and the pickup ship.

". . . can't make it," the pilot was saying.

"You're too far out for grapples. Stabilize your pitch and yaw."

"Steering jets are out. Main engines won't shut off. The tumbling is uncontrollable. Suggestions?"

Walden lost the answer in a burst of interference. Then he lost consciousness as the ship bucked once, split apart, and revealed the vastness of space through sundered bulkheads.

"I've died and gone to Heaven," Walden said, his eyelids flickering open. He reached out and touched Anita Tarleton's cheek. She clutched at his hand and held it tightly.

"You gave me a scare. What happened on the ship? Nakamura won't tell. Classified, she says."

"You should ask Hecht or one of the other EPCTs." Walden closed his eyes for a moment, then sat bolt upright. "What about the Frinn? The alien prisoner? Is he all right?"

"Nakamura and Zacharias have him under wraps. They aren't saying if he's dead or alive. They hustled him off the ship before any of the human casualties."

"Who?" he asked, not wanting to hear.

"The ship's pilot caught a burst of radiation from their MCG weapon. The Frinn?"

"That's what they call themselves. The pilot's dead? Who else?"

"The two marines guarding the alien. The others, the ones who were on-planet with you, are all alive. I don't think any of them are seriously injured."

"What happened?" Walden asked Anita.

"The ship's main engine blew when the Frinn microwaves hit it. The pilot caught a reflected beam and died a few minutes after we got him onboard. Other than this, the radiation shielding held. You're one damned lucky son of a bitch, Jerome." She bent and put her face into his shoulder. Hot tears burned against his skin.

"I'm going to be fine." He looked over her shoulder at the hospital bed readouts. It took a bit of turning to get to see his display, but none of the lights flashed red or blue. Greens meant health and recovery. Blues hinted at future problems and reds warned of immediate and critical conditions.

"I know. I just wanted to fuss over you for a few minutes."

"I've got to see the Frinn. He must be scared witless by now."

"Why the compassion for it?" she demanded. "They blew the hell out of the *Winston*—there are fewer than half the crew uninjured and almost ten percent are dead. And what happened on Schwann? Don't tell me that was a Sunday picnic!"

"The Frinn are the first intelligent alien race we've discovered."

"They found us," Anita said sourly.

"They found us, all right," said Walden, forcing himself upright. His legs wobbled as he took a few tentative steps, but strength returned at a swifter pace as he moved around the hospital ward and dressed. "We've got to sue for peace or none of us will leave the Delta Cygnus 4 system."

"They have us outgunned, that's for sure," she said. "But then they sent a warship."

"And we didn't? What do you call the *Winston* and *Tannhauser*?"

"They bombarded a defenseless planet. They killed men, women, and children who couldn't fire back! What's wrong with you, Jerome? Did that monster damage your brain?"

Walden couldn't argue about what had occurred on Schwann. He had seen the destruction, but the dying Sov-Lat scientist's words haunted him.

The Infinity Plague. What did that *mean*?

"Do you think Zacharias will let you see the alien?" she asked.

"I hope so. I was getting through to him on the pickup ship, establishing a rapport. Another few minutes and I might have gotten something worthwhile out of him. All he told me was the name of his ship. The *Prolum*."

"Wonderful. We know the name of the pig ship that'll turn us into superheated metallic vapor."

"Anita!"

"Sorry," she said. "I was worried about you down there. And rumor has it they look like pigs."

He hugged her. "Where did Egad go? I don't see him around."

"He's with Zacharias. The major tried to throw him out, but Nakamura insisted that the dog stay. I think she knows he's more than a simple canine."

Walden had gotten the same impression. The military advisor watched and evaluated constantly. The smallest slip on Egad's part would have alerted her—and Jerome wasn't sure *he* wasn't the one who had given away the dog's true abilities.

He started out the door when he ran into Edouard Zacharias. The expression on the major's face defied analysis.

"What's wrong?" Walden asked, fearing the worst.

"Come to Ward Nine. That's where we have the Frinn."

Walden and Anita rushed to the ward, pushing past four marine guards standing at attention. Inside, Nakamura stood silently, studying the alien.

"He went into convulsions ten minutes ago," said Zacharias. "We tried to use our automated diagnosis equipment."

"You injected drugs because of a computer program designed for humans?" Anita was aghast at such stupidity.

"Their physiology is not dissimilar," said Nakamura. "I approved. I do not think the drugs caused this . . . reaction."

The Frinn surged and struggled against restraining straps. A hard rubber bar had been placed in his mouth to keep him from biting through his strangely colored tongue. A thin trickle of pale red blood seeped from the corner of his mouth. What worried Walden the most was the cracking noises. The alien's convulsions were so extreme that he was breaking his own bones.

"Relax," he said, his hand on the alien's feverish forehead. "What has Dr. Burch said?"

"We did not consult with Burch," said Zacharias. "We have reason to believe he is not trustworthy."

"Your prisoner is dying, Major," Walden said angrily. "What difference does it make now if Burch is a Communist or a Baptist? You need his expertise."

"Those are not the questionable loyalties," said Nakamura. "Burch sent out a carrier signal the *Prolum* used to attack the *Hippocrates*. Only sacrifice by the *Winston* allowed our temporary escape."

"This is—"

"Jerome!" Anita clutched at Walden's arm.

The Frinn had stopped his violent thrashing. His green and gold eyes opened and he tried to speak. The rubber restraining bar prevented it. Walden worked to free it.

Walden backed off, dropping the rubber mouthpiece to the floor. "He's dead," he said.

From behind he heard Major Zacharias swear. The man finally said, "He died without telling us a damned thing!"

Walden wanted to strike out at the officer. Only Anita's strong grip on his arm prevented it. A life, an alien life, had been snuffed out and all Zacharias thought about was his own reputation.

CHAPTER
16

"He's dead, dammit. Doesn't that mean anything to you?" Walden's anger flared like a supernova. "We could have *learned* from him."

"He was alien and our enemy, but Jerome's right." Anita Tarleton moved closer and pressed against Walden. From across the room Egad whined.

"This was unavoidable. We have no reason to believe we precipitated his demise." Miko Nakamura stared at the body. "An autopsy will prove useful. We need insight into their physiology."

"Too bad he's not alive," said Walden. "We could vivisect him."

"Your anger is misplaced, Dr. Walden." Nakamura bowed slightly and left.

"An autopsy. That'll give us what we need to fight them," said Zacharias. "We don't know enough about them to do a good job of defending ourselves, much less killing them."

"We might not even be able to discover *how* his body functions, much less determine the cause of death," Anita pointed out. She looked with distaste at the alien corpse. Walden read her thoughts as if he had developed telepathy. She found it hard to believe the piglike creature with the fragile skeleton, cat eyes, and the oddly proportioned body could slaughter innocents. They had seen the deadly effect of the alien microwave barrage; now they had to come to grips with the reality of the weapon's creators.

"I'm not interested in the finer points," said Zacharias. "Tear him apart and let me know the simple things. Where to shoot them for maximum effect. If sonic weapons would work. Give me some indication of histamine reaction for designing a nerve gas. I'm not asking for complicated bioweapons. Those can come later."

"I'll need equipment from the cargo bay," Walden said, all strength gone from his body. He had never experienced such complete tiredness as this before.

"The marines will get it for you."

"I want Leo Burch to help us."

"Out of the question." Zacharias' denial came out sharp and complete.

"What's Leo done?" asked Anita. "He's always seemed a decent enough guy to me."

Egad came over and laid across Walden's feet. The man bent and scratched the dog's huge ears. He saw Egad's interest in the major's answer and wondered at it.

"I need not answer," the officer said. He looked around, as if he expected to find spies everywhere. He came to a decision. "Very well. There has been sabotage aboard the ship. Burch has been implicated in those cases. Further, he broke radio silence. The aliens used the carrier wave to home in on us."

"You're saying he's a Frinn spy? That's ridiculous."

"He inadvertently aided them and almost doomed the *Hippocrates*. He attempted to secretly contact the Sov-Lat facility. The aliens intercepted the message and turned it against us."

"I don't know Leo too well," said Walden, "but I find it hard to believe he's a Sov-Lat spy."

"Everyone is suspect. He might have accomplices."

"Paranoid," muttered Anita.

Egad let out a tiny whimper that neither could interpret.

"Get us the equipment—and Leo Burch."

"You cannot threaten me," Zacharias said.

"No threats, Major. This is a promise. We need expert help

in the autopsy. Neither Anita nor I are medical doctors in the strictest sense. We're researchers who happen to know a great deal about human biosystems, but we don't fix broken bones or . . . look for the best places to drive in a knife.''

"He will be watched constantly."

"Sleep with him for all I care." Walden's anger flared again. He turned to perform a cursory examination of the Frinn. The skin had turned tough and dry, its pebbly texture hardening in death. Walden forced open the eyes. The slits had closed, giving the impression of no pupil at all.

"There's an excess of mucosa in the snout—the nose," said Anita.

"Perhaps. What's normal?" Walden started to examine further when the ward door slid back. Leo Burch stormed in, his automed assistant Albert trailing behind.

"What's going on? That jackass Zacharias thinks I'm a spy one minute, then treats me as if I'm a savior the next." Burch stopped and stared at the Frinn. "Is this something out of your lab? Or is it one of *them*?"

"Them," confirmed Anita. "He died in convulsions. We're supposed to find out why."

"The way Zacharias has been treating me, I wish he were on the table." Burch studied the alien for several seconds. "Autopsy? I'm not much of a pathologist. You two can do a better job. You've even got the equipment. All I have is this rust bucket of a diagnostics automedic." He thumped the robot's curved silver dome. A clear, bell-like note sounded. "Albert's just like the major—he's got an empty head, too."

"Do you think you can find anything?"

"Let's look," said Burch. "Even if I am a Commie spy, I'm still damned good at finding broken bones." His strong fingers worked the length of the Frinn's arm, finding where Tanner and Nakamura had manhandled the alien.

With the arrival of more complex analytical equipment from the cargo hold, the three began work in earnest on the Frinn.

Walden was startled when an alarm bell rang; they had been hard at work for almost three hours.

"What's that warning?" he asked, reluctant to leave the analyzer as it developed a more complex computer model of the

Frinn enzyme system. "I don't want Zacharias interrupting us until we have something definite."

"Too late," groaned Burch. The doctor backed away from the stainless steel table, bloodied hands held aloft. "Don't shoot. I confess. I did it."

Zacharias glared at him, then pointedly ignored the doctor. "Walden, you're needed."

"I know. You told me." Walden pointed to the partially dismantled carcass on the table. A half dozen different automated tests were in progress. Albert stood to one side quietly digesting information obtained from the analyzers.

"On-planet."

"What?" The three humans chorused the question. Egad's ears pricked up. The dog rose and shook himself, as if he had just been given an unwanted bath.

Zacharias wiped his mouth with the back of his hand. "I don't like it but we have to go back. We've received a distress message from another research facility."

"But ours was miked into atoms by the aliens," said Walden, "and the Sov-Lats' got blown up."

"They had—have—another. One we had no inkling about." The officer looked even more uncomfortable. "Even Nakamura had no idea they maintained two labs. The second is on the other side of the planet from the known one."

"You're not going to land for another rescue attempt?" The scorn in Anita's voice made Egad growl and bark at the major. The man stepped back and glared at the dog.

"We have to. Nakamura told me about the Infinity Plague."

"What about it?" demanded Walden.

"You were there. You heard. You had to. She only saw and heard what you did since you carried her camera."

"You just know the name? Nothing else?" Walden experienced a strange combination of relief and dread. He had hoped for some idea what the Sov-Lats had feared so much that they would detonate a crust-buster atomic weapon. Whatever it was, he wanted it kept away from the likes of Edouard Zacharias. Now the chance existed for Zacharias to learn about it.

And if he obtained it, would he use it? Walden went even colder inside. Zacharias might hesitate; Walden didn't think the major had a true killer's instinct. Miko Nakamura would use it in an instant, if it suited her arcane purposes. He had never understood exactly what her position was with the expedition or why their Earth-bound superiors had placed her as military advisor.

"The Frinn will be able to use their weapon again," pointed out Walden. His interest in landing once more on the planet's surface had faded.

"We have reason to believe they did not detect the SOS," said Zacharias.

"Why not?"

"The Sov-Lats contacted us on a scrambled band using variable-frequency encoding. The codes change every few seconds and the frequencies alter thousand of times a second."

"Pretty sophisticated. Is this a standard com procedure?" Walden saw the expression on the officer's face change to one of anger.

"No."

Walden didn't have to ask how the Sov-Lats had obtained the information and technique. The spy Zacharias had sought aboard the *Hippocrates* had divulged it. He began to wonder about Leo Burch. He knew little about the man, but if Zacharias suspected him and the Sov-Lats *had* obtained top secret information, there might be something to the charges. Burch's position had been aboard the *Hippocrates* as medical doctor, and Walden had never had much contact with him before the autopsy. The man, even though not a pathologist, had worked quickly and expertly. But was he a spy?

"When was the information leaked?"

"Who knows? It came after you got back. The secondary complex knew details of all that happened while you were inside. You might as well have been broadcasting directly to them."

Walden didn't bother denying that he was the spy. Zacharias wouldn't believe it—and he had homed in on Burch already, for whatever reason.

"How dangerous is this going to be? The last time we had to fight our way through a Frinn field unit and almost got wiped out by their soldiers inside the lab."

"HALO and then a quick I/O."

"What?" Walden stared at the major, not understanding.

Zacharias snorted in disgust that anyone this side of human didn't know what he had said. "High Altitude drop, Low Opening. We go in with power chutes. Then we sneak in and out."

"I/O like in computer I/O," said Walden, realization dawning on him. "So we don't fight off the Frinn?"

"We won't have the armor or equipment to do so," said Zacharias.

"What about the Sov-Lats?"

"We feel that they will come along peacefully. Their interest in leaving Delta Cygnus 4 outweighs the identity of the rescuer."

Walden shook his head in disbelief. Zacharias still thought in terms of "them" and "us"—Sov-Lats them and NAA us. The game had changed. Them had turned to Frinn.

"I wanted to let them rot," Zacharias said unexpectedly.

Walden took a few seconds to follow what the officer meant. Walden had worried over the new enemy being the Frinn. Not so for Zacharias. He still fought the last battle.

"Nakamura convinced me that we rescue humans now, even if they come from the wrong ideology. We drop in one hour. Be ready."

"Wait. I'm going to need some help this time, if we're to get any idea what the other lab released."

"The Infinity Plague? Very well. You may take along one assistant." Zacharias glared at Egad. "The hound stays here. It proved a disrupting influence before. I saw Sgt. Hecht's report."

Walden didn't argue. He needed to select a human staff member to accompany him on this "drop." He wasn't sure what it entailed, but it couldn't be too difficult. Most EPCT maneuvers were planned with microsecond efficiency and were run by computer-activated equipment.

"I'll volunteer."

"What?" Walden pulled out of his thoughts. Anita Tarleton stood just inside the door, arms crossed. "You want to go down into that hell?" He stared at her in disbelief.

"Why not? Beats staying here and feeding Egad." She knelt and scratched the dog's ears. "Not that I won't miss doing that, old fellow." She hugged the dog close, then pushed him away. The animal cast a quick over-the-shoulder glance at Walden, then followed Major Zacharias. Walden would have a full report on the officer's dealings before the drop.

"The power drop chutes are robotic. There won't be anything to do until we land," said Anita. "Then I'm as good down there as you are. Maybe better."

Walden thought about it for several seconds before coming to a decision. "I hate it when you're right. You want to go and let me stay to feed Egad?"

Anita laughed. "We *both* go. I didn't volunteer to let you off the hook."

"Let's get our equipment packed," he said, going to her. His arm circled her shoulders and he pulled her close. "The field unit didn't work out. I need more complete analysis, and I need it in real-time."

"I've got just the thing in my lab," she said. Side by side they went to prepare their equipment.

"We don't do *anything*?" Anita asked, a tremor of fear entering her voice.

"Dr. Tarleton, you're nothing but a passenger. The chute does it all for you." Hecht cleared his throat and added in a lower voice, "It'd better do everything for you. If it doesn't . . ." He shrugged.

Anita cast a worried look at Walden, who experienced similar misgivings. He hung in a sac surrounded by an amniotic fluid. Movement was possible but difficult. A heads-up display showed the condition outside the egg: air pressure, temperature, shell integrity, flight vector. Walden had no controls to alter any of it.

"We do all the dodging," said Hecht. "We can't let a greenie try. Too many smash up by waiting too long to open or opening too soon and getting the shit blown out of them high up."

"Comforting," muttered Walden. He tried to relax. The fluid washed back and forth on the other side of the membrane and soothed him. Its temperature kept him cool, and the linear porosity membrane allowed sweat to diffuse away from his body. He began to wonder if he got really frightened on the way down how much fluid would permeate the membrane, or if he would be really embarrassed when the egg opened.

Walden decided surviving outweighed any considerations of ego and reputation.

"All sealed?" asked Hecht. Walden checked his heads-up display. Greens showed in an arc across his field of vision.

"Ready," he and Anita said simultaneously.

"Put'em into the popgun. You folks go first. Take the pigs by surprise. See you on the ground."

Walden cried out in surprise as the handler moved his egg to a launch tube. In seconds his exterior view vanished. Walden almost panicked until he realized there was nothing to see inside the ceramic-barreled launcher.

"Stay calm, Jerome," came Anita's voice. "They com-linked us up for the drop."

"I'm all right," he lied. He forced himself to control the tremor in his words. He screamed as the launcher fired him toward Schwann's surface. One instant he saw only darkness. The next he saw the off-color blue and white clouds surrounding the planet. Walden closed his eyes to stop the vertigo caused by the whirling images.

This proved worse. He *knew* he fell toward the world. It was better to watch the cause of his anxiety. His stomach stopped gyrating when he found a spot on the planet's surface and stared at it with all the concentration he could muster.

"We're tumbling," Anita said. "Are we supposed to?"

"I don't know. It doesn't seem right. My shell temperature is mounting fast. We're hitting the upper atmosphere."

Walden watched with a mixture of fear and fascination as the heads-up display began to show increasingly deeper shades of red. The egg's shell heated from friction.

"Pieces of the shell are ablating," said Anita. Walden heard the same curious mixture of emotions in her voice. "I've got a drop-timer showing one minute until touchdown. Do you check?"

Walden hadn't seen the chronometer. He scanned the display, forcing his eyes off the increasingly red temperature indicator. "Got it. Check. I'm also picking up another reading. Pale orange, lower right corner."

CHAPTER

Jerome Walden watched in mute horror as the exhaust from the incoming missile filled his display. He tried to shut his eyes and couldn't. He was hypnotized by the inexorable progress of the missile that would snuff out his life.

"It's going to hit!" howled Anita Tarleton.

Walden's display filled with pure white light as the missile detonated. He jerked away as if this would save him. For a fleeting instant, he thought the involuntary movement had done something to preserve his life. Then he realized that the Frinn missile had exploded short of its target—him.

"Anita, are you all right? Did it miss you?" Fear surged again when he realized what this reprieve might mean. If the missile had locked onto the woman's egg and blown her from the sky, it would be a Pyrrhic victory for him.

For several heart-stopping seconds she did not reply. Then came a faint, "I made a terrible mess inside the egg," she said. "How embarrassing."

"Never mind that. Are you all right?"

"Only my dignity is shattered," she said. "A defensive missile took it out before it got within range. My radiation levels soared, but the egg protected me."

Walden checked his own counters. The nuclear warhead on

the Frinn missile had sent out a wavefront of deadly gamma radiation, but the egg's shielding had protected him, too.

"I've got fifteen seconds until chute deployment," he said. "Do you read?"

"Mine's already opened," came her reply. "I'm hitting the ground in another few seconds."

She cut off abruptly when Walden's egg parted. The amniotic fluid blasted in all directions and instantly hardened to confuse any radar tracking him. The sudden jerk of a parachute harness around him almost took his breath away. Then he floated softly like a feather to the ground. He hit the ground running. In seconds the chute collapsed behind him. In less than ten the material began turning to chalky powder. A soft wind blew away the final traces of his landing, leaving him standing alone on a grassy slope and clutching his analyzer.

"Jerome, over the hill. I've found the entrance to the lab."

He hurried to join Anita. She had already unpacked her equipment and studied a tiny direction finder. Pointing in the direction of a rocky red bluff, she silently outlined the entry to the Sov-Lats' facility.

"Your hazard suit intact?" he asked. He bobbed his head around to check the new displays. When the egg had separated and gone on its way, it released the heads-up electronics inside and activated his hazard suit's.

"All intact," she said, not even checking. He started to make her do a complete readout, then stopped. She was as anxious to find the other scientists as he was.

He jerked around and peered into the bright blue sky in time to see steering jets firing. "That must be Sgt. Hecht and the others. He said they were following us down."

"Yeah," Anita said sourly. "They used us as decoys. That missile came too close for comfort. I exceeded my annual radiation limit by fifty millirad."

"Get Doris or one of the others to do your tracer work for you for a few months."

"I ought to make Zacharias do it. He's the one who said there wouldn't be any problems. 'Easy in, easy out,' he said. The damned lying son of a bitch."

"Cool down. We've got our destination in sight. Let's start for it. Hecht and the rest of the squad can track us."

"You can bet Zacharias is sitting pretty up in the *Hippocrates*. How did he ever win all those fancy medals?"

Walden stopped and watched the flares in the sky. When he got to ten, he began to worry. Hecht's new squad only had seven in it. The flares began to magnify, to burn brighter and longer in the air.

"Doc, you there?" He barely heard the sergeant through the static in the headphones.

"What's going on? It looks as if you're landing an entire invasion force."

"Not us, the pigs. The *Winston* caught the missile going to zap you. Something alerted them, though. They gave up trying for us and started sending down their own forces. Nakamura says we're facing almost a company."

Walden had passed fear or caring. What did it matter if they faced a company or the entire Frinn home planet? Either way spelled death for them.

"What about pickup?"

"On schedule. We've got one hour to dig out the Sov-Lats."

"I meant *now*. Forget them."

"We got orders. You come, you stay. It doesn't matter. I have to try to rescue them."

Walden swore. He wanted to get the hell out and let the others fend for themselves. No matter what lay behind the cryptic words "Infinity Plague," it wasn't worth his and Anita's lives finding out.

The first of the Frinn invasion force landed. He dropped a range finder over his IR display and located them at fifteen kilometers. Making out the composition of the force from the heat profile lay beyond his expertise.

"We got big troubles, Doc," came Hecht's worried voice. "They aren't landing organics. They're landing an *automated* force. Nakamura warned us something was wrong. We're fighting damned robots!"

"Is that more difficult?" asked Anita. "Most of your equipment is computer-driven."

"Might be easier, but I don't know. I hate going against machines. Soulless bastards."

All the time they talked, Walden and Anita trudged along toward the cliff. From the left flank came two of Hecht's squad. The tips of their oxygen-iodine laserifles showed corona discharges from use. One marine stopped and adjusted the baffles at the muzzle. The electric blue sparking vanished.

"You got the place sighted, Doc?" asked Sgt. Hecht.

"We're only a kilometer away.. What about the Frinn?"

"All robots, every last one of them. The *Winston* is engaging their ship."

"The *Prolum*."

"That's the name. This time the *Winston*'s doing a better job. It's destroyed half of the armor the pigs launched."

"Half?" cried Anita. "You mean this is only *half* what they sent against us?" She swept her arm across the horizon where the heat profiles of forty tanks crept in their direction.

"They're still thirty klicks off. We got time." The marine didn't sound confident. He worked at his bulky laserifle, then began barking orders on another circuit. Walden saw the EPCT's lips moving.

Two squad members set up the devastating pipes that launched the genius bombs. Hecht sent two more marines with rifles to the top of a rise. The two remaining marines were nowhere to be seen. Walden hoped that they worked their deadly trade and hadn't been killed on the way down.

"We're covered, Doc. Let's the three of us go in and fetch the Commies."

"The six can hold off the Frinn?" asked Anita. Skepticism tinged her voice. Walden shared her suspicion that they would emerge from the underground laboratory and find themselves ringed in by alien armor.

"As good as the entire *Hippocrates*," said Hecht. Walden wasn't sure this gave him new confidence. The Frinn had almost completely destroyed the *Tannhauser*, the *Winston* was damaged severely, and the *Hippocrates* was a hospital ship incongruously laden with an Extra-Planetary Combat Team.

"The door's opening. They must want us inside," said Anita.

She laughed without humor. " 'Step into my parlor, said the spider to the fly.' "

"Let's fly, then." Walden pushed forward, working his head in a constant circle to take in all his ever-changing displays. His analyzer fed information to him about the quality of the air inside the laboratory. He found no spores laden with botulism or other evidence of bioweaponry gone amok.

"They've cut off their defensive circuits for us," said Hecht. His head swiveled around as he checked the sensors and booby traps lining the corridor. "All they have to do to trap us is flip a switch. Want to go on, Doc, or do you want me to go it alone?"

"We're in this together," said Anita. The nervousness she displayed didn't stop her from pressing on.

"She's right. We didn't have to come in the first place. No reason now to quit when the going is getting easy."

Hecht laughed. "You're scared shitless, both of you, aren't you?" He didn't wait for an answer. "The difference between you and Lard Ass is that you don't let it bother you."

Walden didn't have to ask who Lard Ass was. Hecht didn't like Major Zacharias any more than Tanner had.

"My readings are in the green," reported Anita. "Do we have to wear these damned helmets? They make me claustrophobic."

Walden touched the side of his. Nakamura's camera still rode in its bracket. He wondered what new information the advisor got from a quick passage through a super-secret Sov-Lat complex that she hadn't already gleaned from the first excursion.

"We're not even close to being at the lowest level of this facility," Anita said. "I get readings showing at least ten subterranean levels."

"And no time to explore." Walden stopped and stared. Coming toward them down the dimly lit corridor marched six men and women, unprotected by hazard suits or combat armor. A quick pass of his sensors confirmed what he thought; they carried no weapons.

"We hail you, comrades," said the man in the lead, his powerful hand upraised. Walden's throat contracted as he thought of those fingers clamping on his windpipe. He pushed away such a paranoid fear and tried to concentrate on the man himself, not the image.

He couldn't separate fact from fantasy. The Soviet colonel's broad shoulders held up the insignia well, making him look like a recruiting poster in a Latino country. The pale blue eyes bored into Walden's gray ones. The scientist tried not to flinch. He almost succeeded.

"I am Col. Vladimir Sorbatchin, commander of Soviet-Latino Pact Base Twenty-three. These are the surviving comrades." He made a grand, all-encompassing gesture that stopped before a brown-eyed, light brown-haired man of medium height and suspicious nature. His eyes darted about constantly, making Walden think of a trapped rat. "This is our esteemed director of research, Dr. Pedro O'Higgins, from the People's Republic of Chile."

"I've followed your work, Doctor," said Anita. "Your methods are a bit . . . extreme."

"Living specimens must be sacrificed for scientific progress if the greater good is to be served." O'Higgins sounded defensive.

"Hate to interrupt, but the Frinn are circling in for the kill. We've got less than ten minutes to get our butts out of here or get'em shot off."

"Such colorful language," Sorbatchin commented. One pale blond eyebrow rose as he studied Hecht. "He is not an officer? You command this unit, Dr. Walden?"

Walden tensed. How had Sorbatchin known his name? Zacharias might have been right about a spy among the *Hippocrates'* crew or passengers. In the academic and research communities he had maintained a low profile for many years. His published papers had been seen by few outside NAA government circles. Even Anita's reputation was limited to those in defense research.

"We've sustained heavy casualties, Colonel," Walden said. "We all are doing jobs we're not trained for. What happened in your complex? Surely there were more than . . . six?"

"The Frinn, as you call them, have proven adroit at picking off our escape parties. Only we remain. This facility remained secret until your arrival. You have brought them with you, it seems."

"Not our fault, Colonel," said Hecht. "They homed in on us. The major figures we got a spy in our ranks alerting them—and you."

"Sergeant," interrupted Walden. "Let's argue the point after we've returned to the *Hippocrates*."

"Right, Doc."

Hecht spun and led the way outside. Sorbatchin and O'Higgins stood close together, exchanging heated whispers. Walden touched the exterior amplifier on his hazard suit helmet and listened. Their argument came through clearly in a bastard hybrid of Russian and Spanish. He missed the details, but the main thrust was trusting the NAA to get them out unharmed.

Sorbatchin looked squarely at his researcher and said, "We have a friend among them. There is no need to fear. They want to save us."

O'Higgins' skepticism was overridden by the quake that shook the facility so hard that parts of the ceiling tumbled down and filled the corridor with dust. Huge support beams thrust through the cast plastic walls and ceiling, letting in debris and dirt from above.

The sudden rupturing of their secure bubble caused the four scientists in the tight group to run after Hecht. Walden waited for a moment, then took Anita's arm and turned her around. There was no time to spare. The entire Sov-Lat complex was disintegrating from the Frinn attack.

"I need to look around!" Anita protested. "We need information!"

"You're getting to be as bad as Nakamura. We're leaving alive and to hell with what the Soviets were doing here."

"Their labs—they're set up differently. I can find out so much about their progress!"

"Later." Walden guided her to the entrance. The heavy doors that masked the entry had vanished. A quick check of his displays showed elevated radiation levels.

The Frinn had melted the doors off with their microwave cannon.

Walden stepped into the sunlight cast by Delta Cygnus and wondered how such a peaceful afternoon could have turned so deadly. In the distance he saw the brilliant streaks of the genius bombs launched from the war pipes. Flight after flight blasted into the sky to arch down and seek out targets. He saw one Frinn fighting vehicle explode with actinic fury. He started to cheer the destruction until he saw how few of the other bombs reached their targets. The alien tanks deftly countered even the variable flight speed genius bombs.

"We've got big problems, Doc," said Hecht. "Take a gander at the reports I'm getting from the others."

Walden didn't have to ask for an interpretation of what he saw flashing across his displays. The Frinn had circled them and now concentrated all their fire on a small area.

And they were standing squarely in the middle of that target.

CHAPTER
18

"Incoming!" shouted Hecht. The group separated and dived for cover wherever they could find it. Walden found himself with his arms around Anita. They hit hard and rolled twice, coming to a bone-bruising stop behind a jagged upjut of rock.

"Your suit's torn," she said, recovering before he did. She fumbled to get a patch from the tiny repair kit slung at her side.

"Don't worry about it," he said. "The analyzer still shows nothing unusual in the atmosphere. No bioweapons or poison gas."

"I'll patch you," she said firmly. Walden regained his wits as the woman worked. He noted that some of his instrumentation had failed. The familiar green lights in the heads-up display had turned to amber. When he checked his circuits, he found more than a few internal components had been destroyed.

"What did they hit us with?" he asked, not expecting an answer.

Hecht's voice boomed in his ear. "Just got word down from the major. They're throwing all their armor against us. You can't believe the way it's working."

The two sets of pipes Hecht had set up whined and whirred and sent their AI bombs after the Frinn tanks. Walden's polarizer darkened briefly to compensate for the brilliance of a tank ex-

ploding. He saw a stubby cannon sailing through the air in one
direction and the body of the tank melting down as the acid from
one genius bomb went to work on its metal shell. But for every
tank disabled, the Frinn threw two more into the battle.

"We can't fight them," said Hecht. "Nakamura believes
they're all running on expert programs. All robots, no pigs inside."

"Why?" asked Anita. "What difference does it make?"

"Plenty. The *Winston* is making progress against the *Prolum*
because it has gone to a total computer-driven defense system.
Robots don't tire, but they can't go beyond the bounds of their
programming, even the genius circuits."

"We're facing an army that doesn't make mistakes but which
we might be able to outsmart. Is that it?" asked Anita.

"Wonderful," muttered Walden. The tanks rolled relentlessly
toward their position. They might figure out a clever tactic given
time—but that was the only commodity they had too little of.

"Sorbatchin," called Walden, using his external speaker.
"What armaments do you have inside that'll do us any good?
We've got to hold the armor back for— How long, Hecht?"

"Another fifteen minutes. Be that long before the pickup ship
can launch. The *Hippocrates* is in orbit close to the *Prolum* and
can come under fire at any instant."

"Could they launch sooner if the *Winston* destroys the Frinn
ship?" asked Anita.

Hecht only shrugged. He was a field sergeant of marines, not
a combat pilot.

"We have no weapons," Sorbatchin said pompously. "We are
dedicated to peaceful endeavors only. The Soviet-Latino Pact—"

"Flare off, Colonel," snapped Walden. "We all know why
Schwann is so popular. My team didn't come here to develop
improved herbs and spices for cooking. Neither did yours."

"You mistake our intentions," Sorbatchin said, mock hurt in
his voice.

"We have weapons," cut in O'Higgins. "Use them, Colonel,
or I will."

The Soviet officer glared at his director of research, then
shrugged as if saying that nothing could be done about such

security breaches. He unbuttoned the front of his dark blue uniform and fumbled inside. He pulled out a plastic sheet the size of his hand and no thicker than a fingernail. Sorbatchin stroked over the pliable membrane. For several seconds, nothing happened.

Then the top of the butte erupted in flame.

Walden shielded Anita against falling rock. Through the ringing in his ears, he heard Hecht bellowing at his squad.

"That wiped out ten degrees of their entire southern line," Hecht shouted. "Get after the edges of the break. Don't let them roll forward and ring us again. Keep the hole open!" The marine jumped from foot to foot in his eagerness to counterattack. This was the first opportunity to take the fight to the Frinn.

The top of the butte roared anew as missiles blasted from hidden launchers. Walden wasn't expert in such evaluation, but he guessed that this much firepower would have seriously damaged an orbiting destroyer.

The Sov-Lats had protected their secret base well—too well for it to be the peaceful research center Col. Sorbatchin claimed.

"They're trying to close," Hecht said. "Incredible power turning against that section. We can't hold for long." He turned to Sorbatchin. "Any vehicles, Colonel? We can use them to get the hell and gone out of here."

"We have a few miserable surface vehicles," the Soviet officer said, his hands spread in a deprecating gesture.

"Get the turbine-powered trucks." O'Higgins glared at his commander again. "They will do us no good if we die in this hellhole."

"We have a few poorly maintained vehicles garaged over there." Sorbatchin pointed. Hecht was already on the way.

In seconds came a bull-throated roar of a powerful Tesla turbine-powered truck. Hecht wheeled it out of a hidden garage and braked savagely in front of them. "Get in. We've got to move. The hole is closing too fast. The damned robots aren't giving a millimeter."

"The defenses. Use them again," O'Higgins said. Col. Sorbatchin stroked over the membrane controller. New blasts from above came, all directed at the terrain to the south. Walden cringed at the power of the explosion even though it was ten klicks away. Another tank had died in a fiery flash.

Walden didn't need Hecht to tell him to get in. He and Anita scrambled over the rear gate and rolled into the truck bed. Following them came two of Hecht's squad, who helped in the Sov-Lats. Sorbatchin was the last to enter. He sat stolidly at the rear, polar blue eyes fixed on the blown-apart doors to his secret laboratory. Walden went and sat beside him, saying nothing for several seconds.

He finally said, "It's hard to lose a command, isn't it?"

"Ah, yes, that is true. But the loss of life. So many lost to the Frinn. They can never be replaced."

Something in Sorbatchin's tone alerted Walden. "Did you lose someone special?"

"My wife. She was a major in security."

"KGB?"

Sorbatchin turned and smiled crookedly. "No. The GRU. As I am."

Walden realized then that this had been more than a secret base. It had been so well hidden only military security knew of it. The political and mostly civilian Komitet Gosudarstvennoi Bezopasnosti probably had no inkling of its existence. What *had* they researched there?

"I'm sorry," Walden said, startled that he meant it. Sorbatchin and the Soviet-Latino Pact countries were his sworn enemies. They did all they could to destroy the NAA and its allies; they violated treaties and imported an awesome array of offensive weapons to protect this secret base—and his heart went out to a fellow human.

"Yes, I believe you are," Sorbatchin said, startled. "Thank you." He turned back and watched as the complex vanished. Hecht drove with frantic speed—and with good reason.

Dirt and bits of rock flew into the rear of the truck as the Frinn opened fire on them. Walden moved away from the colonel. Let him try to kill himself by being exposed and that close to the rear of the truck. Walden made his way forward, hanging onto the exposed roof braces. The thin sheets of plastic covering the bed flapped and soon blew off; too many nearby explosions tore holes through the flimsy material.

Walden settled beside Anita. "How's it look?" he asked. She gestured that she couldn't hear. He had to reseat his hazard suit helmet. It had shifted enough to make it difficult for him to change to her com frequency using the chin switch.

"Not good." She stared through a long, thin tear in the plastic. Walden went cold inside when he saw the ugly snouts of the Frinn tanks. They looked large enough to drive the truck into.

"They're so close," he said uneasily. Anita only nodded. He held her close, as much for his own comfort as hers.

Hecht skidded to a sudden halt. Two more of his squad jumped in. The sergeant didn't immediately start up again. The two marines worked frantically to get their war pipes inside the truck. They used fastening clamps to secure the weapon. Only when it was ready for use did Hecht roar off again.

Sorbatchin watched critically. He barked out a sharp order. One marine scooted to the back of the pipes and adjusted the tripod. Sorbatchin nodded his approval.

"He's got four of his squad. Two more to go," Anita said.

The marine squatting behind the pipes turned and looked at her. "Sorry, Doctor. The other two bought it. A tank ran over their position. They didn't have a quantum jump of a chance." He turned back and triggered the weapon.

The pipes fired, the air whining and humming with the departure of their genius bombs.

"They're not even trying to pick up the bodies," Walden said numbly. That showed how serious a position they were in. Leaving Tanner and the others behind had bothered the EPCTs. It had been a matter of survival then; it was again.

"Nakamura's giving us the course to follow," came Hecht's voice in the headphones. "The tanks are definitely on full computer control. No organics behind them. I think we can make it if we keep switching direction at random."

The truck swerved from side to side, then put on a burst of speed that threw Walden to the bed. He struggled to get his feet under him and failed. He saw the marines in the rear of the truck begin firing their weapon steadily. One loaded and the other worked furiously at the target finder The truck shuddered from the constant launching—or was it from the Frinn barrage? Walden couldn't tell.

A part of the truck blew off, taking three of the Sov-Lat scientists with it. When Hecht braked suddenly, another tumbled and crashed to the ground outside.

"Wait!" cried Walden. "Man overboard!" He couldn't think of anything else to say.

"Make it quick, Doc. We got big trouble. Even the help we're getting from the *Winston* isn't doing us much good. Those damned robots are *quality*."

Walden wasted no time. He jumped through the hole blown in the truck's side and hit the ground running. He stumbled and went to one knee, then got to the side of the Sov-Lat scientist. The man lay facedown on the ground. Walden rolled him over and checked his pulse in the carotid artery. The thready throbbing showed life still clung tenaciously.

Walden grunted and heaved the man across his shoulders, then staggered back toward the truck. Sorbatchin grabbed a double handful of fabric and lifted the man easily from Walden's shoulders.

"You are a strange one, Doctor," the Soviet colonel said. He offered Walden his meaty hand. With a quick jerk, he lifted him off the ground and sent him reeling the length of the truck just as Hecht gunned it.

Shaken but happy for his minor bout with heroism, Walden got back onto the bench beside Anita. The woman clung to a roof brace with both hands. She screwed her eyes tightly closed and refused to watch. Walden wanted to join her, but the fascination of watching the Frinn fighting machines drew him like a moth to a flame.

Few of the tanks reflected light. The only silvery flashes he saw came from impacts against their armor. The war pipes continued to prove effective in striking the armored giants, but few of the genius bombs carried enough explosive to penetrate. The best they hoped for was a brief scrambling of the enemy computer's sensory input.

The sky rained a steady stream of silvers and golds—the *Winston* turned its full armament against the alien tanks. And still they fought to keep open a tiny segment of the armored ring threatening to strangle them.

Walden pushed aside the admiration he felt for the beings capable of automating such fighting machines.

"Will we make it?" he asked Hecht over the one circuit he had to the squad leader.

"Don't know, Doc. Don't rightly know where we're going. Just want to get on the other side of the machines so all of them can't target us simultaneously."

The turbine whined louder and the truck shot forward. Walden looked out and saw the Frinn tanks pivoting about. They had reached the hole in the advancing wavefront—only the tanks on either side could directly and easily target them now.

Those proved more than enough.

Walden looked from one side to the other. The crackling rainbow discharges from both tanks' main weapons built and slid toward them in a deceptively peaceful arch of shimmering silver. He grabbed for Anita just as the world filled with pain and blackness.

CHAPTER

The polarizer in Walden's helmet worked hard to keep him from being blinded. The fusing circuits inside the hazard suit filled it with thick smoke that forced him to open emergency vents. He rolled and groped, trying to clear his eyes of the dancing yellow and blue dots and the tears from the burned circuit residue. It took several seconds to get a semblance of vision back.

"Anita?" Walden knew instantly his suit radio had joined most of the other instrumentation. He stripped off the helmet and cast it aside. With it he lost what few of his heads-up displays remained, but he gained full vision and hearing.

He stood, stunned. The world around him had changed. Schwann had never been heavily endowed with vegetation. Nowhere he looked showed the sparest twig, the slightest hint of lush green or living matter. The dirt had been burned away and only bare, melted rock remained.

"Anita!"

His words crossed the barren landscape and vanished. No echoes came to haunt him—he had to rely on his own imagination to conjure the image of what must have happened.

He spun around, trying to find the others. He didn't even care if he saw a Frinn fighting machine. Simple movement would have reassured him that he hadn't died and gone to a desolate, lonely personal hell.

A whining sound alerted him. A luminous compact toroid of blazing white plasma crossed the sky and crashed into the horizon. Walden struggled to see where it hit. He trudged up a slight incline and peered into the dusty distance. He saw a towering column from a nuclear detonation. Without hesitation he twisted and threw himself down the hillside.

Seconds later the explosion's wavefront passed over him. He stayed down longer than necessary, doubting his own sanity. Even when ghostlike hands clutched at his shoulder and shook him, he resisted. He dared not turn to look.

"Go away," he sobbed. "Go away!"

"He's shaken but doesn't seem hurt. The blast didn't harm anything. Eyes are focusing."

Walden blinked as a bright light shone into his gray eyes. As quickly as it appeared, it vanished. The hands lifted him to his feet.

"Sergeant?"

"Here, Doc. We did just fine getting through the ring. The machines thought we were goners. They were programmed to go for other robots. When the truck got blown up, the pigs' tanks left us alone."

"Why shouldn't they? We couldn't harm them." Anita Tarleton hugged Walden close. "You gave us a fright. You wandered off."

"I remember seeing the Frinn tanks launch their MCG weapon. Everything's a blur after that."

"Ah, Dr. Walden, the trauma of being tossed about has disoriented you."

"Colonel?" Walden slowly regained his bearings. The tight group around him were all familiar. The Sov-Lat colonel and the director of their research, the man he had saved, one other— all were Soviets. Hecht and Anita were the only others nearby.

"The EPCTs are having a hard time of it on Schwann, Doc," spoke up Hecht. "The only reason I didn't get my balls blown off was the truck cab. It discharged part of the microwave energy. I got thrown clear, just like you and the others."

"The two men on the war pipes died," said Anita. "Their bombs blew and took them out."

"What are we going to do? We can't stay here. The planet is . . ." Words capable of describing the devastation refused to come to his lips. He didn't have the vocabulary to adequately tell of the ruin.

"The Frinn tanks are out of control. They're roving the planet seeking targets. Some fire at random—they've been damaged. When they do, the others return fire. They might keep up their own private civil war for hundreds of years." Anita heaved a deep sigh. "Schwann is lost to us until we return with destroyers and take out the tanks from space. The *Winston* isn't capable of doing it."

"What of the *Prolum*?"

"Who cares?" cut in Hecht. "We got ourselves a ride back to the *Hippocrates*! Look!"

The pickup ship came down fast, rockets blazing. A few stray missiles arched toward it, but the *Winston* countered from orbit. The ship landed a kilometer away and signaled with a primitive light flash.

"That's my baby. Let's get to'er!" Hecht shucked off most of his gear, keeping only his laserifle and the bulky twenty-kilogram pack supplying the activated oxygen-iodine mixture to its lasing chamber. He set a fast pace for the others to keep up with. Walden and Anita were almost exhausted by the time they reached the pickup ship. Sorbatchin and O'Higgins were sweating but otherwise none the worse for the run. The other Sov-Lat arrived by the time Walden had lashed himself down on an acceleration couch.

Walden remembered nothing of the trip back to the *Hippocrates*. He might have passed out from exhaustion. Whatever the cause, he was in the *Hippocrates'* surgery once more before he returned to his senses. Leo Burch stood over him, peering down with a jaundiced eye.

"You ought to be put in isolation," the doctor said.

"What? What's wrong?"

"It's the only way you're ever going to get any rest. Here." Walden winced as Burch gave him an injection.

"What was that?"

"Enough stimulant to keep a rogue bull active for a month—and loving every second of it."

"I'm no rogue bull."

"And you won't enjoy an instant of it, even after the stimulant wears off. Major Zacharias has ordered your presence aboard the alien ship. It's ours now. All ours."

"I don't take orders from him. Neither do you."

"Nakamura has requested your august presence, too."

Walden moaned and heaved his feet over the side of the bed. "Isolation would give me a rest, is that it?"

"You need sleep, not what you're likely to get hanging around those two. And the Sov-Lat colonel is a real pisser, too."

"Sorbatchin has worked his way into our chain of command?"

"He's got Zacharias cowed. I wonder how the man ever won all those shiny medal he's so proud of. Think I can buy them by the kilo through a mail order military supply house?" Burch punched in a new program for the automedic hovering beside the bed. Lights faded and the machine whined to a halt. "Get out of here. I don't think the automed's going to let you go, otherwise. It's the only one of us with any sense."

"Thanks, Leo." Walden stretched and instantly regretted it.

"Just wait till the stimulant *really* hits."

"Don't sound so happy about my misery." Every muscle in Walden's body screamed in agony. He found movement helped. This decided him to go directly to the bridge to find Nakamura. She seemed to be the one with the most information to give.

"Ah, Dr. Walden. We go to the same destination. Please, be my guide so I do not become lost aboard this fine hospital ship." Vladimir Sorbatchin's ironic tone told Walden that the colonel knew intimately the layout of the *Hippocrates*.

"What's happened?"

"Nakamura is to give us this information."

Walden snorted. The Sov-Lat officer lied indirectly. He knew and only wanted the briefing to come from Nakamura. His cockiness in the midst of those who had been enemies only a short time before reinforced Walden's belief that Zacharias was right. There was a Sov-Lat spy aboard.

"Enter," came Nakamura's cool, controlled voice. "Be

seated. We begin immediately. Much has occurred since you dropped onto the planet.''

Walden slipped into an empty seat, Sorbatchin beside him. The briefing room just off the bridge slowly darkened and a hologram of the *Prolum* appeared. The scene unwrapped slowly until Nakamura sped it up. The space battle between the Frinn ship and the *Winston* took on comic overtones, but Walden knew it was recorded in deadly earnest.

The *Winston* slowly beat down the other ship until it no longer fought.

"We were suspicious. We know little of their combat techniques, though there can be only one optimum strategy."

"You are referring to *Book of Five Rings*?" asked Sorbatchin. Nakamura did not answer.

"We sent out a probe," she went on. "We drilled through the *Prolum*'s hull and thus afforded access to more than a hundred independently directed AI camera drones."

Pictures flashed across the end of the briefing room with eye-confusing rapidity. Walden blinked to keep from paralyzing his mind with sensory overload, but he got a fast tour through the alien vessel.

The interior was lit in a fashion similar to human ships, but the amount of purple in the light gave an eerie cast to control surfaces. The Frinn relied more on sound than visual cues. Walden wondered what they did if their ship lost pressure—or if they had a system to prevent it from ever happening. Such a device alone would prove invaluable to humanity. The composite hulls were light and strong but tended to fracture and star like stressed safety glass. One small crack quickly spread and caused explosive decompression. Even plastic liners had proven ineffective.

"They are a private race," said Nakamura. "There are no barracks-style mess halls or sleeping quarters. Each aboard the *Prolum* has individual sleeping, eating, and sanitary facilities."

"This makes for wasted space and overloading," spoke up one of the *Hippocrates'* officers.

"Yes," Nakamura said, not bothering to comment further. "The Frinn enjoy much recreation or possibly education. Their data banks are extensive and programmed toward tests in more fields of learning than we were able to verify before . . .'' Nakamura's words trailed off.

"Are their records intact?" asked Pedro O'Higgins. Walden leaned and peered past Sorbatchin to see the brown-skinned Sov-Lat scientist at the far side of the room.

"No."

Sorbatchin did not allow this to go without explanation. Neither did the others in the room, including Walden.

"What happened to their computer?" he asked.

"A complete destruct program had been initiated before our probes entered the *Prolum*. We had only hints of the data remaining before it vanished. Their block circuits are similar to ours—and are quite devoid of all information. They erased their data to prevent us from learning the location of their home world."

"Just like us," muttered Walden. Once more he was struck by the similarities between Frinn and human, rather than the differences.

Others with a more technical instrumentation and power bent demanded to see the physical machinery, the engines and controls and sensors used by the Frinn. Something that Nakamura had neglected so far caused Walden to stand.

All eyes turned to him in the faint illumination cast by the hologram of the alien control room.

"What happened to the *Prolum*'s crew?" he asked. "None of these pictures shows the Frinn."

"They died," Nakamura said simply.

"How?"

Major Zacharias rose and stepped in front of Miko Nakamura. He cleared his throat, motioned for the lights to come up, and then said, "We have reason to believe that they killed themselves. When confronted with a superior force, they committed suicide rather than surrender."

Walden tried to keep from laughing. The Frinn robot tanks ravaged Schwann. The *Prolum* had landed enough fighting machines to destroy a world—and they had almost destroyed two of the NAA's most powerful warships.

"This is a logical response," said Sorbatchin. "Is there any chance that we might examine these fine holograms at our leisure?"

"They are available under code name Frinn in the ship's computer. You may access them through the computers in your quarters."

Walden watched Sorbatchin and O'Higgins leave. He waited for the door to slide shut behind them before he spoke. "What is this nonsense? They didn't kill themselves. They were crushing us like bugs under boot heels!"

"Dr. Walden, your skepticism is misdirected," said Nakamura. "We had no desire to reveal everything we know—or suspect—in front of our unwanted visitors."

"We're all in this together. It's not a civil war among humans any longer. We're fighting for the survival of our species!"

"We still have to deal with old allegiances and ideals," said Zacharias. "The Sov-Lats may not be enemies any longer, but they're not our friends, either."

"There is another consideration in this matter," said Nakamura. She cleared her voice. Walden sucked in his breath and waited. The subtle change in the woman's expression told him something of her fears. "The aliens died slowly. They continued to fight well, even after critical positions were taken over by their robots."

"What killed them?"

"They died slowly from a disease contracted on the planet."

"The Infinity Plague?"

Nakamura nodded. "The Sov-Lats fought back with every weapon at their disposal, as we did. Their bioweapon turned the tide against the Frinn."

"And we don't know what it did or how it worked on the Frinn," finished Walden. "Why not admit it and ask the Sov-Lats? We can work together on this. O'Higgins sounds as if he is more willing to cooperate than Sorbatchin."

"We cannot be held hostage by the Sov-Lats," said Zacharias. "We have to find out the nature of their Infinity Plague ourselves. Otherwise, they can deal with the Frinn to eradicate the NAA, using the plague as a lever."

"Absurd." Even as Walden uttered the word, he saw that Zacharias believed firmly in such an unholy alliance. The expression on Nakamura's face confirmed it. The two had agreed on this point. They had to know the details of the Infinity Plague before trusting the Sov-Lats any further.

Paranoia ran deep. And Walden felt the green rot of it begin to destroy the trust he had experienced with the Sov-Lats.

"Did you recover any of the alien corpses?"

"We have fourteen in a vacuum freezer," said Nakamura. "We ask that you begin the autopsies immediately to learn the cause of their death—and the nature of the plague."

"And how to reproduce it?"

"Of course," said Zacharias, angry at Walden's apparent denseness.

"How did you remove the bodies?"

"Cargo loader robots," said Nakamura. "We disposed of the mechanisms and have done all in our power to prevent contamination among our ranks."

Walden heaved a sigh. He'd have to go into the vacuum chamber and perform the autopsies there. He lacked the automated equipment to take the samples he needed without personal exposure. He hoped the biohazard suit would be enough.

"Let's take a look."

Walden, Anita, and Nakamura went to the cargo bay holding the vacuum freezer. Walden stared at the vidscreen and wondered what he had gotten himself into. The camera mounted inside the chamber panned slowly along the rows of Dewar bottles holding the alien corpses.

"Bring one out. It doesn't matter which one. I'm going to try to get my samples without going in."

"There are fully automated hands inside," said Nakamura. "Will they be sensitive enough for your work?"

"Let's hope so. The Infinity Plague might not stop at the surface of a hazard suit."

"Such a virus can be gengineered?"

Walden looked at the woman and nodded. He had worked on such a project himself.

"Too clumsy, Jerome," said Anita, working with the mechanical hands. "Even with finer controls, it's not going to work. We need the equipment in the lab down on Schwann."

Walden didn't need to see Nakamura shaking her head to know the impossibility of that excursion and retrieval. The Frinn computer-driven tanks scourged the planet's surface. Getting anything off-planet would be a miracle.

"I'm going in to do the work directly." He closed his eyes and prayed that God would grant him a single wish: to suspend the laws of the universe for him. "Get me a hazard suit that's been checked out fully."

He quickly donned the suit and stood in front of the airlock door leading to the death chamber. Walden thought his heart would explode when Nakamura closed the second heavy Ultimate Strength Steel door behind him and left him exposed and alone inside.

CHAPTER

Walden took deep breaths to keep from shaking too much. He knew the hazard suit had been checked out twice—once by Anita and the final time he had checked the suit's integrity himself. Doubts still nagged him. A small hole, a tiny pinprick in size, and he would be dead.

He wished the distrust of the Sov-Lats didn't run so deep. He needed to know more about their Infinity Plague. Did it eat hazard suits? What might he expect if he became infected? Was it a virus, virtually undetectable and quick-acting or had the Sov-Lats come up with a disease that worked more insidiously?

"Specimen fourteen," he said. "I'm taking over from the robot." He pushed past the machinery and stood beside the Frinn. The alien's body in death had taken on a faint purple pallor, perversely reminding him of boiled red cabbage. Walden kept four holocameras running to record every movement as he drew out blood samples and took necrotic tissue samples for biopsy.

"What about the eyes?" asked Anita Tarleton. "Some types of their viral weapons rupture the blood vessels."

"Don't see any indication of that," said Walden, peering into the sightless catlike eye. The slit had opened in death and formed an almost perfect circle. He did a quick study of the internal

171

capillaries in the eye. None had been damaged. The Frinn had not died of a concussion or stroke.

"Nasal cavity is clear of mucosa. In fact, it is very dry." Walden twisted around and peered into the alien's nose, using a magnifying lens on his helmet. He switched to the IR goggles and studied the decomposition in the nose, then worked through a series of spectral filters, taking pictures using some and simply observing with others.

"I got back the first readouts on the blood. Something's wrong with the structure. The hemoglobin equivalent is screwed up."

"How scientific," Walden said. "Can you put that into simpler terms for me?"

"Quit being such a stickler for accuracy," Anita said. "There's no way the blood could carry enough oxygen. He might have suffocated to death."

"This one's a she," he said. "What was the oxygen content in the *Prolum*?" he asked Nakamura.

"Slightly lower than ours, but it checked with present levels. We had no reason to believe anything was amiss with their life support systems."

"Suffocation," mused Walden. "It's possible that's why she looks purple. Cyanosis."

"Checking the tissue samples now. These are all sex cells, I see," said Anita, working at the computer console. Walden continued to study the body, wondering about the last minutes of life. Breathless? Choking? Or had it been a swift end, too fast to react to?

"Got the DNA structure worked out. Just about like ours. Same number of chromosomes and—"

"What's wrong?" Walden went to the small window and peered through. Anita had moved the computer console so that he could look over her shoulder to see the readouts.

"I don't know. Things don't check right. The number of genes is off, but the number of chromosomes is identical to ours."

"No, it's not. I've got a haploid number of twenty-three—just as we have. Here is a diploid of fifty!"

Walden and Anita worked for almost an hour on the samples before the idea came to him. "The haploid is damaged. The diploid isn't."

"What are you saying?" asked Nakamura.

"Their chromosomes pair up with twenty-five instead of twenty-three, as ours do. For some reason, the gamete is damaged and the somatic cell isn't. It's as if something interfered with cellular reproduction.

"Run the nerve cells through the analyzer," requested Walden. "This might be the key to the Infinity Plague. It might be a virus that unravels the DNA a bit, bringing it down to look like our structure."

"You win first prize," said Anita. "The Infinity Plague worked on unraveling the top two pairs of chromosomes. This prevented accurate cell reproduction and began to work on the nerve endings. It wasn't inadequate oxygen uptake or gas transport in the blood that killed them, it was the death of the automatic nervous system. The body just forgot how to breathe!"

"The longer the exposure, the more the plague worked," said Walden. "But I don't understand. It would take some time before the nerve cells would be affected."

"Weeks," said Anita. "Checked it on the computer. Make that almost two months. This is one hell of a *slow* death."

"They didn't die from anything released by the first Sov-Lat lab," said Walden, his head beginning to ache. "There hasn't been enough time for it to have interfered with cell reproduction to this extent."

"The *Prolum* became increasingly easy to fight almost twenty hours ago," said Nakamura. "The change was progressive and rapid."

"The crew became infected months ago. The results didn't show up until then."

"That doesn't make sense," said Anita. "This implies all the Frinn caught the Infinity Plague at the same time."

"It might have spread incredibly fast. They didn't have any resistance against it, so it swept through them like a laser through rotted ice."

Nakamura fell silent. Walden ignored Anita's musing as she continued to massage the data in the computer, turning it inside out, trying to find new combinations and better answers. He sat down in the chamber and stared at the bodies. It struck him as incredible that a vicious war-loving race would allow every member of their crew to be infected simultaneously. It was as if most of the *Prolum*'s crew had landed on Schwann and become infected, then took it back to the ship and those who had remained in orbit.

If they had come to wage war, why parlay? Why not take elementary precautions against naturally occurring diseases, much less those conjured in a gengineering laboratory for biowarfare?

The Frinn must have known what type of research was being conducted on Delta Cygnus 4. They were vicious killers; didn't they have any worry about their enemy? Or did they feel so vastly superior to humans that they believed themselves invincible?

Walden's headache turned into a splitting migraine. He heaved himself to his feet and gave the alien woman's body one last cursory examination. So much more information lay locked within those infected cells that he wanted to cry out.

Only hard work and long hours would give him the answers. Genius might have helped, but Walden was so tired, he couldn't muster anything more than soft moans as he walked. Brilliance lay light-years beyond his reach.

"I'm coming out. Get the decontamination equipment ready."

"We'll put you in a chamber and hose you down," said Anita.

The acids, UV, and heat lasted for an hour. Simple disinfectants were followed by harder radiation that pushed him perilously close to his exposure limits for the year. He didn't worry about that. If he carried the Infinity Plague out of the chamber, he'd be dead from its treacherous effects long before his cells revolted against ionizing radiations.

"Get out of the suit and leave it inside," ordered Anita. "I'm not taking any chances." To Walden's surprise he didn't step out into the ship. He found himself in a second decon chamber, going through an abbreviated version of what he had already endured.

He was bone-tired by the time he stumbled out of the chamber.

"You have done well, both of you," said Nakamura. "I will study the implications of these data."

"Good," said Walden. "I'm going to get some sleep. The stimulant Burch gave me is wearing off."

Thoughts of rogue elephants raced through his mind, or had Burch said rogue bulls? Walden couldn't concentrate long enough to remember. Anita helped him back to their room. He fell face forward and slept almost instantly, his dreams of Frinn war machines and the Infinity Plague haunting him.

Walden awoke with a start when a cold, wet nose pressed against his ear.

"Egad, leave me alone. Haven't you ever heard the expression, 'Let sleeping dogs lie'? Let me get some rest." He rolled over and tried to get comfortable. A heavy weight pinned him to the bed.

"Talk. Now. Dangerous not to."

Walden opened one eye and stared into a big brown one. He rolled onto his back and let Egad hold him down.

"What's wrong? Anything with Anita?"

"Anita is nice bitch. Nothing wrong with her."

"What do you want?" Walden was in no mood to bandy words with the dog.

"Overheard Sorbatchin and O'Higgins plotting. Have question, too."

Walden heaved and got the dog off his chest. He lay with the dog beside him on the bed, trying to decide which question to ask first. "What's your question?" Walden knew that Egad might go off to ponder the answer if the question was sufficiently complex. This would let him go back to sleep, possibly for hours.

"What happened to other pig ship?"

"What other *Frinn* ship?" he repeated, correcting Egad. He didn't want him getting into the habit of calling the aliens by a derogatory name.

"The one exploring system. We saw it when we entered."

Walden sat upright so fast the dog tumbled off the bed and onto the deck. Egad scrambled to get his feet under him, growling fiercely.

"I forgot about them. So did everyone else. We've got to tell Captain Belford."

"Want to hear Sov-Lats' plotting?"

"What is it?" Walden had to speak to the captain soon. In

the battle to rescue Sorbatchin and the others, he had completely forgotten that they had detected two Frinn vessels. The second had been at the far fringes of the solar system, possibly exploring the Oort Cloud. What would they do when they discovered their sister ship had been destroyed?

"They want to use spy to poison us all and take over."

"How?" Thoughts of the Infinity Plague flashed through his mind.

"Nerve gas. Sorbatchin has nerve gas with him. Tiny canisters. Look like buttons on his coat."

Walden remembered the big gold buttons on the Soviet uniform. With the aid of the spy onboard the *Hippocrates*, the colonel might be successful in taking over. But the *Hippocrates* was no war vessel and the *Winston* had been undergoing repair since defeating the *Prolum*. After all, the *Tannhauser* provided a ready supply of spare parts. The *Winston* might not be returned to full fighting capability but it wouldn't find the *Hippocrates* any threat if Sorbatchin were successful.

Walden pushed such a crazy plan out of his mind. The Frinn ship posed immense danger to them, however.

He vaulted out of bed and went to the computer console. He typed in an access code and said, "Walden requesting a meeting with Captain Belford. Priority red." The computer beeped and flashed a time across the screen. His request had been granted. For the first time, Walden felt grateful for his position. He commanded the captain's attention above most others on the ship when he demanded it.

He and Egad made their way along the winding ship's corridors and got to the bridge a few minutes before the scheduled meeting. Captain Belford and his first officer huddled over the com unit. From the crackles and pops, Walden guessed they had problems talking with the *Winston* because of solar activity.

"Captain," he said without preamble, "what about the other Frinn ship? Where is it?"

"What other ship?" For a few seconds, Captain Belford looked ancient. His eyes had turned to hollowed, dark pits and he had lost a considerable amount of weight. If anything, he looked like Walden felt.

"When we shifted into the system, two Frinn ships were

picked up. One orbited Schwann. The other was on the outer edge of the system.''

''Play back all the records,'' Captain Belford ordered his exec. ''Put it through the computer and filter for the ship. I'd forgotten about it until Dr. Walden mentioned it.''

Walden glanced at Egad and smiled. The dog bobbed his head as if saying Walden would be nothing without him. The scientist wasn't about to dispute that claim right now, either.

''We've isolated it. While we were engaged with the *Prolum*, the other ship started spiraling sunward,'' the first officer reported. ''It hasn't made any hostile moves, though.''

''Where is it now?'' asked Walden.

''Can't say.'' The officer shrugged. ''We tracked it into the asteroid belt between planets six and seven and then lost it.''

''Why haven't you been trying to find it?'' asked Walden.

''Doctor,'' the captain said in a voice infinitely old and tired, ''we put the ship on full combat status. The sensors warn us of immediate danger. The *Prolum* provided that and more. If we had failed to stop that ship, it wouldn't matter if the entire Frinn home world waited for us. After the *Prolum* was no longer a danger, our sensors sought other threats.''

''And found none,'' Walden finished, ''because the other ship is hiding in the asteroid belt.''

''So it seems.''

''Captain Belford, are they waiting for us to starlift home so they can get a bearing on Earth?''

''Dr. Walden, I had no idea the other Frinn ship still existed until you brought up the matter. How the hell should I know what they intend to do? Ask Zacharias. That's his field.''

Walden left, Egad at his heels. He had no intention of going to Major Zacharias with this. Better to find Miko Nakamura. The woman had more authority than anyone else on the ship— or at least exerted more command.

He rapped on her door. It took several minutes for her to open. She was dressed in a flowing red silk kimono with blue-green and yellow flower patterns on it. In one corner of her room burned a scented candle. Walden saw a pad in front of the candle. She had been kneeling; indentations still remained.

Had she been praying? Or meditating? Or did it even matter?

"We need to talk," he said, pushing past her. "Is the room cleaned of spy devices?"

"Yes."

She sat tailor-fashion and looked at Walden. The dog cocked his head to one side and let out a sharp bark. Then he dropped to the deck and put his head on his crossed paws.

"Do *we* need to talk or should I address . . . Egad?"

"What do you know of him?" asked Walden.

"He is very bright, for a human. For a dog he rivals genius. The computer voice box hidden in his collar allows him to speak."

"I was afraid you'd figured that out."

"He is a valuable asset."

"Of course I am," spoke up Egad. "I reminded him of the other pig ship."

"Frinn ship," Walden corrected automatically. Walden quickly explained. Nakamura's face remained impassive as he spoke. When he came to the part about Egad overhearing the Sov-Lat plot, she became more animated.

"This is a serious matter. I have deduced the identity of the spy and have observed carefully."

"You know!"

"The spy is responsible for the assassination attempt at the Japanese ambassador's party. Knowing the identity has allowed me to observe and learn their communications techniques."

Walden heaved a sigh of relief. "You can eliminate the spy whenever you want?"

"Yes."

"What about the Frinn ship lurking in the asteroid belt? We can't shift for Earth knowing they're watching."

"The *Winston* is once more at full strength. Repairs are completed. The *Tannhauser* has been gutted and its few crew transferred to the *Winston*. We can find the Frinn vessel and destroy it."

"What about the other ship?" asked Egad.

"What other ship?" asked Walden and Nakamura simultaneously.

"The third pig ship. The one Sorbatchin thinks left the system."

Walden and Nakamura looked at each other, bleakness in their eyes. The Frinn had already launched a third ship for their home world. If they didn't destroy the hidden ship and launch for Earth they might never be able to go home without revealing Earth's position to a fierce enemy.

CHAPTER
21

No one in the room sat without fidgeting. Captain Belford stood and sat repeatedly, saying nothing. The haggard look on his face aged him a decade. His once neatly groomed white hair now went off in all directions, greasy spikes pointing outward like an ancient morningstar. Even his unflappable executive officer had dark circles under his eyes and looked as if he hadn't slept in a month.

Walden had trouble sleeping even in quick catnaps. Nightmares of the Infinity Plague haunted him. Computer work continued to give them a better idea what the plague did and how it might be countered—but results were months in the future. No one could expect duplication of what might have taken the Sov-Lats years to accomplish.

No one expected it except Jerome Walden.

Not for the first time he wanted to go to Pedro O'Higgins and ask directly about the plague. He hated the notion, in spite of the threat presented by the Frinn, that the Sov-Lats were still the enemy. Nagging at an even deeper level, he wondered who the traitor in his ranks was. Nakamura knew. She claimed the spy was neutralized after the Japanese ambassador's New Year's party.

Memory of the cargo launch explosion kept coming back. Had

the spy turned saboteur for that? Was his misadventure in the cargo bay the result of an assassination attempt or had it been bad luck on his part? Walden wanted to know, just for his own peace of mind.

He kept detailing all the foibles of his staff, trying to find the single clue that would betray the spy. Was it Chin or Burnowski? Paul Preston? Klugel? Doris Yerrow? Marni Donelli or even Claudette Wyse? Nakamura hadn't said it was one of the senior staff. It might be a lab tech.

Walden's head throbbed and threatened to explode at any instant.

Beside him Anita Tarleton stirred. He jumped when she touched his arm, pulling him away from his uneasy musings. For a fleeting instant he doubted even her.

"We've got to make some headway, or we'll sit till the sun goes nova," she said in disgust. "Captain Belford is losing control. Just look at him."

Walden nodded. The pressure had mounted on the *Hippocrates'* captain until the cracks appeared in his once solid façade. Zacharias gained increasing power over decisions that ought to be made by the captain—and Miko Nakamura controlled Zacharias. Walden wasn't sure if that was good or not. The woman knew about Egad and hadn't revealed his abilities to anyone else over the past two weeks of apprehensive waiting.

He reluctantly decided her silence was in Nakamura's self-interest. The dog gave her a new source of intelligence gathering.

"We've tried contacting the Frinn ship several times," Captain Belford said unexpectedly.

"What?" blurted Walden. "They can home in on us!"

"We considered that," cut in the executive officer. Walden tried to remember the man's name and failed. He was too weak a personality to be memorable—and Walden sensed that the XO had instigated the attempts at contact.

"What happened?" To his surprise, the question came from Nakamura. She seemed as startled as the others. This worried Walden even more. Captain Belford had either tried to hang on to a semblance of command by sneaking around—or the exec saw this as a chance to gain more power. Neither was fit for command now.

"We saw this as our only chance to get away from this system," explained the executive officer. He stood while Captain Belford squirmed in his chair. "The Frinn ship is hiding somewhere in the asteroids. We sent out peace messages for almost a week."

"You were not testing damaged equipment," accused Nakamura. She glared at Edouard Zacharias. The major started to protest this betrayal of his trust but only incoherent noises came out. Walden didn't have to ask who had authorized the "tests."

"We did not get a reply," said the XO. "We tried to solve our problem and nothing came of it. We are no worse off than before."

"We still can't lift for Earth," said Anita. "They know we're still here. How many are out there? Sorbatchin says two left orbit. We only destroyed one-third of their fleet. One's in the asteroids and the other may have starlifted for their home world."

"We are sure that one left the system," Sorbatchin said. "Dr. O'Higgins has analyzed our data further and finds definite starlift patterns in the spatial geodesics."

"Can you get a line on their home world?" asked Nakamura.

"No." The Sov-Lat colonel's answer came too quickly for Walden's liking. Sorbatchin lied behind his bland, friendly smile.

"Perhaps we are mistaken and all the vessels have left," said the executive officer. "Our failure to reach them points to this. They would want to parlay if they were still in the system."

"Why?" asked Anita. "We blew the hell out of the *Prolum* or so it must look. And their ship was aggressively reducing our planet to igneous rock before the others left orbit. It looks as if they have every right to believe hostilities still exist."

"And not everyone is stupid enough to reveal their position," muttered Sorbatchin. Walden smiled at this. It was the first sign that the Sov-Lats were not entirely happy with the revelation. He wondered how it put a damper on their plans to take over the *Hippocrates*—if those plans were real.

Walden's headache became a full-fledged migraine that sent blinding waves of pain through his skull. He tried too hard to unravel the plots and counterplots.

The merest thought of unraveling made his headache unbearable. Images of DNA ribbons unraveling and preventing vital cells from properly replicating danced in his brain. The Infinity Plague had worked well against the Frinn. How well did it work against humans?

Walden worried that he had become infected, in spite of the extreme precautions they had taken to prevent it. Unconsciously, he moved a little farther from Anita, as he had been doing for the past two weeks. This was futile and only put an emotional barrier between them, but he couldn't stop himself. The pain in his head and the fear working at his insides proved too real.

"Excuse us," said Nakamura, rising. "Major Zacharias and I must consult with the captain of the *Winston* about possible adverse responses from this abortive attempt at communication." She did not wait to see if the officer followed her. Zacharias glared once more at Captain Belford and then raced after the small military advisor.

"We've got work to do, too," said Walden. Anita kept her distance. He didn't try to get any closer to her.

"A moment, Dr. Walden," called out Sorbatchin.

The headache brought waves of pain across Walden's field of vision. He saw the Sov-Lat colonel through a veil of blood-red mist.

"What?" Walden spoke too loudly. His head split apart and his brain was exposed to the oxidizing effect of the air.

"Dr. O'Higgins has requested access to the bodies of the Frinn ever since we discovered they had been brought aboard. We have asked. Now we *demand* to perform our own tests on them."

"Fine," Walden said. "Your demand is noted, as your requests have been." He turned to leave and find Leo Burch. The medical doctor had to give him a painkiller or he would be driven crazy by the migraine.

"This is not good enough!"

"Later, Colonel. I'm not feeling well." Walden stopped, cold fear clutching at his heart. Was this never-ending headache the first symptom of the Infinity Plague? Had the Finn experienced it before their DNA unwound, their autonomic systems rebelled, and all involuntary functions of their nervous systems failed? He wished he could ask, but he knew better.

"You'll probably see the results of my examination before I do," Walden said tiredly. He rubbed his throbbing temples and peered at Sorbatchin.

"What does that mean?"

"Your spy is keeping you informed." Walden spun and stalked off. Every footfall on the hard deck sent a shock wave of pain roaring up his spine. He ignored it as much as he could as he made his way to Burch's surgery.

The past two weeks since Egad had pointed out the obvious to him had been hell. He looked around, expecting to see the dog. Egad was nowhere to be seen. He sighed and rubbed his temples again. He had driven off even this good friend. He had to know if he had been infected by the Infinity Plague. Not knowing was making him crazy and driving off those around him who cared.

"What are the lab results, Leo?" he asked, seeing the doctor sitting behind his desk, working quietly at his console.

Burch looked up. "Except for the headache and your miserable attitude, you're disgustingly healthy. *Now* will you let me prescribe something for the headache?"

Walden nodded and hated himself for it. His head tried to come loose from his neck and tumble to the doctor's desk.

"I could have run the blood tests you asked and screened out the drugs. That's what computer analysis is for."

"I couldn't take the chance. No problem with neuron-neuron connectors? Dendrites? Axon firings?"

"You've got nerves on the brain, old son. Here." Burch passed a small vial across the desk to Walden. "A pentagan derivative. If you want the chemical formula, I'll punch it up direct for your computer banks."

"I'm familiar with it. I used it a few years ago in an experiment." Walden bit off the rest of the explanation. He had no reason to divulge classified material to Burch.

The medical doctor heaved a deep sigh. "Feeling any better yet? Pentagan takes only a few seconds to work."

"Twenty seconds to a minute," Walden corrected mechanically. He smiled weakly. "The migraine is easing. Thanks."

"Want to tell me what this is all about? I know you clamped

a full security blackout on the autopsy. I tried to look at it. What killed the Frinn?''

"Anita and I are still running correlations and making guesses. We're not even up to the theory stage.''

"Did I tell you that pentagan makes it impossible to lie? If you try, your tongue turns bright orange and grows fuzz. Want to look at it in the mirror?''

Walden moved to hide his mouth with one hand, then laughed. "When the data is crunched into shape, I'll let you know.''

"My educated guess is that the virus that killed the Frinn did something to their autonomic system. Right?''

Walden had to be sure he wasn't dying of the Infinity Plague and had given Burch too much information.

"Something like that. Thanks, Leo.''

"Anytime you've got secrets to tell, think of me.'' Burch turned back to his work at the console.

In the corridor outside the doctor's office Walden ran into Miko Nakamura. The small woman shifted her weight slightly, and Walden found himself pinned in a corner.

"A word, Dr. Walden.''

He noticed she had touched her lapel to check the telltale sensor hidden there. No one listened to them using any detectable spy equipment.

"I'm very busy,'' he said, still not feeling good. The drug dulled the pain rather than making it go away. Walden knew the pentagan increased the electrical potential at certain nerve receptors, making it more difficult for the axon to fire. Taken over a long enough period, the drug affected the myelin sheath surrounding the axons and permanently inhibited all pain.

"Schwann cells,'' he said to himself, marveling at the irony of it. Schwann cells insulated human nerve fibers and the Infinity Plague had been developed on the planet they called Schwann and—

"Doctor,'' Nakamura said sharply. "Are you all right?''

"Yes, what is it?''

"Information. I need information about the Frinn.''

"You have full access to our autopsy data and the biopsy samples. I can't give you much more than that at the moment. We're not even getting good guesses yet.''

"I monitor your work and note your progress. This is a difficult analysis, isn't it?"

"Yes." He wanted to lie down. The dull throbbing was more tolerable than the migraine, but only by a small bit.

"I need information about their psychology, their physical makeup and how it affects thought patterns. You specialize in neurological research. What can you tell me about *how* they think?"

"Not much. I never had a chance to talk with the prisoner more than a few minutes. I'm not sure there is a correlation between physical structure and mental or emotional development."

"I need to know why their warship has not responded in some fashion to Captain Belford's ill-considered communication attempt."

"They're waiting for something. How should I know?"

"Their nervous system," pressed Nakamura. "It is identical to ours?"

"Not quite. Their DNA is different and this makes them different. How, I can't say without studying live specimens." His head began to hurt again. He spoke of an alien and intelligent race as "specimens." He was getting to be as bad as Zacharias.

"They would respond as a human might?"

"How can I say? They're the first alien race we've ever come across. Their reactions parallel ours. They wiped out an entire planet, didn't they? Aside from the fact that we've been trying to perform racial suicide for a couple of centuries and haven't made it yet, I'd say we're no different."

"They are more efficient?"

"There doesn't seem to be division in their ranks, as in ours, but who can really say? This might be only a small part of their culture. Others may snipe at them constantly like the Sov-Lats do at us and we do at them."

"Cohesion of culture," murmured Nakamura. "Taken with physiologic responses like ours. Given a mild correlation of internal . . ." Nakamura walked off muttering to herself.

She bothered him more than fear of the Infinity Plague now that Burch had given him a clean bill of health after the autopsies. With the drug coursing through his system, he found it easier to concentrate—and to worry.

What in the hell *were* the Frinn waiting for out in the asteroid belt?

CHAPTER

Jerome Walden still moved away from Anita whenever she came close. Try as he might, he couldn't shake the gut-level, irrational fear he had somehow become infected with the Infinity Plague. He forced himself to stand behind her, hands on her shoulders, as she worked at the computer analysis. The long weeks had given them few clues to the nature of the plague. Walden's first guesses had been augmented by some solid facts, but they were too few for his liking.

"Why is it so difficult getting a handle on this?" he asked aloud, not expecting an answer.

"We're not trained for this," she answered. She pushed both hands through the thick shock of her flame-red hair and looked up at him, her green eyes brighter than the cosmetic dyes she had applied to her cheeks. He saw the fatigue there—and more.

Her eyes were a mirror to his own alienation and fear.

He hugged her close. "It's been too damned hard on us. We weren't supposed to do this type of work."

"All we're supposed to do is *breed* the viruses that will kill billions, not stop them," she said bitterly. He had seen how she had hardened since coming to Schwann. What had been a once-in-a-lifetime opportunity for research had turned into a nightmare of galactic proportion.

"We're going to have to crack this one," he said.

"What's the difference? I talked to Leo and he said your physical came back clean as a whistle."

Walden said nothing.

"Jerome, I know you're still worried, but the Frinn died sooner than you think. They *had* to show symptoms within days. You're fine. You're not infected."

He held her tighter. "Knowing something intellectually and accepting it emotionally are worlds apart. I'm keeping a close check on my reaction time." He turned his hands over several times, worrying that he was slowing down.

"Looks good to me," Anita said, returning the squeeze he had given her.

Walden heard Egad whine. He turned to see Miko Nakamura coming down the corridor.

"Just what we need. Another dose of spy business."

"Has she ever told you who the spy is?" Anita clung to him, a portion of the closeness they had before returning.

"She says the spy is neutralized, whatever that means."

"She knows who spy is and watches," spoke up Egad. The dog settled down, mismatched eyes watching as Nakamura hurried into the room.

"I need your support with Captain Belford," she said without preamble. "Time is critical. We must leave orbit. His first officer is blocking me. I have demanded a meeting."

"Wait, slow down," said Walden. His headache had never gone away. The dull throb made thinking difficult at times and Nakamura presented him with too many questions. "Why is the first officer cutting off your access to the captain?"

"He has de facto control of the Schwann."

"So?" asked Anita. "You and Zacharias—"

"We have been increasingly shunted to the side," Nakamura said. "My computer analysis cannot be ignored. We must leave orbit, and the first officer refuses to listen."

Walden frowned. None of this made any sense. "Explain what's going on. We might be able to back your play, if we know."

"There is no time to waste."

"A trade," said Anita. She squeezed Walden's hand. "We'll

go along with whatever you tell Captain Belford if you give us the name of the spy on the staff.''

Nakamura opened her mouth, then clamped it firmly shut. "This is not possible now. Soon, yes, I will tell you soon. The matter progresses along paths closed to me.''

"You're lying through your teeth," Walden said, disgusted with the petty intrigue.

"Peril comes from the Frinn, not from within. We must leave Schwann immediately. We and the *Winston* are in terrible danger.''

The woman's agitation after so many months of presenting a cool exterior convinced Walden of her sincerity. He looked to Anita. She shrugged. She had tried to pry the information that burrowed at the heart of the research team and had failed. Getting the spy's name would have been a round won for openness. Such gains over secrecy were not easily accomplished.

"It is important," Nakamura said, uncharacteristically repeating herself. "Vital to our survival.''

"Enough," said Walden. "We'll back you in this.''

Nakamura nodded sharply, spun, and hurried from the laboratory. Walden signaled to Egad to accompany them. If Nakamura went to do battle with the *Hippocrates'* executive officer, she needed as many allies as she could get.

"What's eating at her?" asked Anita.

"We'll find out." Walden stopped and stared. Blocking the corridor were two of the *Hippocrates'* crewmen. They were armed with their ponderous oxygen-iodine chemical laserifles. They nervously shifted from foot to foot, making Walden edgy. Either of the young men might accidentally discharge the powerful rifles and do considerable damage to the bulkheads, overhead—or innocent bystanders.

"Sorry, you can't go on into the captain's quarters," one young ensign said. He cleared his throat. "Mr. Brittain says no one's allowed in, except those on the list. Neither of you is.''

"Brittain. The first officer. Why can't I remember his name?" Walden loudly swatted the palm of his hand against his forehead. Both of the men on guard looked at him. This gave Egad the chance to slip past. Neither noticed.

"Mr. Brittain said only *Hippocrates'* crew was allowed onto the bridge."

"Nakamura invited us to a meeting with Captain Belford."

"Sorry, ma'am," said the ensign, blocking Anita's way with his rifle. "All civilians are barred. Fact is, Major Zacharias' EPCTs aren't welcome, either."

"What is this? A mutiny?"

"We're obeying Mr. Brittain's orders. That can't be a mutiny. That's following orders," spoke up the other crewman. His uneasiness showed neither man thought following the officer's orders was the smartest course in the universe, yet they were doing what the regulations demanded of them.

A sharp crack followed by a wave of heat boiling down the corridor knocked the four of them flat. Walden got to his feet first and helped Anita stand. Parts of the composite walls had blistered and boiled away to leave a familiar starfish pattern of destruction.

"A bomb," Walden guessed.

"A laserifle inside the briefing room," was Anita's contribution.

The two guards shook off the effects of the concussion and pushed past them to race down the corridor. The ensign ordered the other guard to the bridge. He stopped in front of the door leading to the briefing room. Walden and Anita approached cautiously, watching the young officer. The strain showed on his face. He kicked at the door. It fell to pieces.

Face pale with fear, the ensign jumped into the room, his laserifle ready for action.

When Walden heard the young man vomiting, he sidled closer and peered around the ruined door. The ensign retched in a corner. The far end of the room gave mute evidence to the cause of his condition. A charred skeleton showed where one man— and Walden guessed at this—had stood. A curiously untouched human hand rested on the edge of the conference table. The body was no where to be seen.

"Out of the way." Strong hands shoved Walden back. Two of Zacharias' EPCTs forced their way into the room. One took charge of the sick ensign and began a quiet, firm interrogation.

The other slung his rifle and substituted a camera on his shoulder, making a permanent record of the evidence.

"Who was in there?" asked Walden, seeing Zacharias stride up. The man had four marines acting as bodyguard.

"Commander Brittain requested that I meet with him. I do not know who else was present."

Walden backed away and let the EPCT major conduct his own investigation. Nakamura gestured to him from the open door of the bridge. Beside her stood Egad. Walden and Anita stepped onto the bridge.

"What happened?" Walden asked.

"We have no time for such matters," said Nakamura. "I am trying to persuade the captain of the danger presented to us by the Frinn."

"You said that before. There's nothing they can do to us that they wouldn't have done earlier. Explain."

Nakamura ignored him. Walden knelt and pulled Egad close. "Tell me about it, boy. What's going on?"

"First officer dead. Killed by spy."

"The spy tried to blow up the first officer with a bomb?" Anita frowned.

"Did," insisted Egad. "Zacharias too late for meeting or he'd be dog food, too."

"Is this part of the plot hatched by Sorbatchin?"

Egad shook his head. The dog looked over his shoulder at Nakamura, who spoke earnestly with Captain Belford.

"*She* arranged it? She used the spy to kill Brittain and tried to include Zacharias?" To this Egad bobbed his head vigorously.

"Who was the spy? Who was in the room?" Walden shuddered. The solitary hand belonged to the spy-turned-assassin.

"Bad smell," said Egad. "Not her," the dog said when Walden looked toward Nakamura. "The one with plastic smell. Her and her plastic cat."

"Who?" Walden and Anita looked at each other. Then Walden remembered how the woman's odor had disagreed with the dog's sensitive nose. "Doris Yerrow?"

"Yes," said Egad. "That bitch."

"Why her?"

"She might have been a ringer," Anita said slowly, her mind

racing. "Why does she smell like plastic? Maybe she isn't—wasn't—Doris but someone surgically altered to look like her. The silicon rubbers needed for facial and body reconstruction might be the odor Egad was smelling. Doris never did any real work during the trip. You commented on it. And who better to replace than someone who is reclusive?"

"It's possible, but—"

"Doctors, come here, please. I will give my evidence of our danger." Nakamura's strained face convinced the two to join the advisor.

They went over, Egad eagerly rubbing against their legs. The dog jumped up, resting his paws on the back of Captain Belford's chair. The officer never noticed.

"My computer analysis of the situation took into account all factors of known Frinn behavior. Those that remain unknown, I extrapolated as being essentially human."

"Reasonable assumption," said Anita.

"They destroyed our bases on Delta Cygnus 4 for reasons still unknown. The Sov-Lats retaliated by releasing the Infinity Plague."

"We know that already," said Walden. "What conclusion did you reach about the Frinn ship in the asteroids? Why hasn't it shown itself?"

"What would *you* do if our positions were reversed?" asked Nakamura.

"I'd look for an opening and either make us commit ourselves on a course for our home world or try to destroy us."

"I have found thousands of starlift detectors scattered throughout the system," said Captain Belford. The man's voice sounded ancient. "There's no way we can ever find and destroy them all. They have us pinned down."

"We either destroy them or we reveal Earth."

"We could always lift for some other destination."

"Some *unexplored* destination? Starlifting is routine because of difficult exploratory mapping. How many scouts were lost mapping the lift route to Delta Cygnus 4?"

Anita shrugged, not knowing.

"Fourteen," supplied Captain Belford. "We can't starlift for an unknown destination. We might never arrive, and if we did, we might never find our way back to Earth."

"I didn't know it was that hard," muttered Anita.

"So we find the Frinn and blow him out of space. The *Winston* is back to full fighting power, isn't it?" asked Walden.

"It is," said Nakamura. "However, what else would *you* do if you were the Frinn?"

"Detectors to get us to expose our home," said Walden. "I'd try like hell to get rid of us, though. I'm vindictive, and I'd want to avenge the deaths of those aboard the *Prolum*."

"They've come up with a weapon that poses a threat to us?" scoffed Anita. "They're out in the asteroids, a hundred A.U. from us. They can't do a damned thing to us!"

"Their compact toroid weapon can't reach that far," Walden said, supporting Anita. In his gut, though, he felt he'd missed something—and Nakamura hadn't.

"They have had adequate time to find an asteroid and equip it with a propulsion system. If their computer abilities are on par with ours, the elapsed time has been enough to calculate a trajectory for the asteroid to impact with Schwann."

"They're going to drop a rock on the planet? So what?" asked Anita.

Nakamura reached past Captain Belford and touched the keyboard. A new set of figures appeared on the screen. "A small asteroid, one massing out at a few thousand metric tons will crack open the planet if it hits squarely."

"The Sov-Lats' crust-buster didn't do that kind of damage," pointed out Walden.

"We are talking different orders of magnitude, bigger, more potent. Such weapons were banned by treaty on Earth scores of years ago. We had no desire to destroy our world totally."

"We can't turn tail and run," said Captain Belford, voice shaky.

"We must. Order the *Hippocrates* from orbit immediately. Find sanctuary in free space. The *Winston* must join us. *Give the order!*"

An older officer manning the external sensors turned and called out, "Incoming projectile."

"Mass," snapped Nakamura.

"Very low. Not more than ten grams, rest mass."

"What do you mean?" Nakamura punched up the officer's display on the captain's console. Her quick fingers worked out the answer. "The Frinn have sent us a particle traveling at half the speed of light."

"Blue doppler on it confirms speed," came the officer's precise words. "Impact on Schwann in less than one hour."

"Get out of orbit," urged Nakamura.

"It's only ten grams. Why worry?"

"It is coming at half the speed of light. That will cause damage equivalent to a one-megaton bomb."

Walden didn't argue. Mass and energy became esoteric principles at near-light speeds. He was a biologist, not a physicist.

"Even so, that's not too much. We just endured a bomb eight hundred times more powerful."

"Not so," said Nakamura. "There are more incoming particle bombs. Thousands of them."

"Big one on doppler," confirmed the sensors officer. "Ten-kilo mass."

"Is the increase in energy linear?" asked Walden. He saw that it was. This rock would detonate with the ferocity of a thirteen-hundred-megaton bomb. From the data creeping across the captain's console, each particle bomb would release one-eighth of the total amount it would during a complete matter-antimatter conversion.

"How many particles incoming?" asked Nakamura.

"Too many to count. They must have used a shotgun to get so many on their way this fast."

"Mass drivers," said Nakamura. "They have been building mass drivers and have now begun to launch."

"Captain, we must leave orbit *now*!" Nakamura shook the man violently. He hardly stirred. The pressure of command had robbed him of all decision-making powers.

Unless the order was given within minutes for the ships to leave orbit around Delta Cygnus 4, they were doomed. No one survived blasts measuring in the thousands of megatons, not on the planet or in orbit around it.

CHAPTER
23

"What do we do?" cried Walden. He shoved Captain Belford away from the command console and slid into the seat. For a fleeting instant, he experienced the fear and pressure that had paralyzed the *Hippocrates'* captain. Then the deluge of information overwhelmed him. All he could do was try to keep up and respond the best he could.

"*Winston*, this is Nakamura. We have a critical condition onboard. Repeat, a Code Nebula condition. Do you read?"

"What's going on?" Walden saw the console go crazy. Colors flashed and the speaker beeped loudly. Everyone on the bridge turned to stare at him. One officer at another console rose and started over.

Nakamura pulled out a small diode laser pistol and shot the officer. He clutched at his burned-out throat and sank soundlessly to the deck. She paid no attention to those remaining. Walden wondered if she had run psych profiles on everyone or if she merely guessed that one death would keep the others in line.

These men and women weren't military officers; they were the officers of a hospital ship.

"Anita, bar the hatch from the bridge. I don't want to be disturbed—by anyone," Walden ordered. The woman jumped to obey. Walden had the vision of Edouard Zacharias barging in at the wrong instant to question them about the bomb that had almost taken his life.

"Dorris Yerrow," Walden muttered to himself. "She was the spy."

"Bitch smelled bad. Deserves to die," said Egad. "Only people with good smells deserve to live." He glared at Nakamura, who busied herself at the communications console.

"Walden, start the engine sequence. I'll have the navigational data before ignition."

Walden stared at the panel, saw an INFORMATION key and pressed it. A menu of options popped onto the screen. He found the engine sequencer and typed in the command string. From deep within the *Hippocrates* came a vibration he felt through his bones and bounced his internal organs against each other.

"The *Winston* is altered to the danger. They are flaring off now," came the com officer's crisp voice. His alertness and seeming calm gave Walden a model to pattern his own behavior after.

"Wait, wait, wait," cautioned Nakamura. "We must not leave too soon."

"That's one hell of a big particle coming at us," gasped Anita. "It masses out at ten thousand kilos!"

"But it is traveling only a fraction of the speed of light. The others will reach Schwann first," pointed out Walden. He couldn't keep his eyes off the vidscreen focused on Schwann. Tiny pinpoints of brilliance rose on the surface, each the equivalent of a small atomic device.

More and more blossomed—and they grew in size until the charge coupled device for the vidscreen dropped magnification by an order of magnitude. Even so, the brightness grew. Walden tried to imagine what those deadly ten-gram and one-kilogram particles did to the surface. The Frinn microwave weapon had scoured clean the surface of all vegetation.

These planetary bombs wiped out the outer crust and turned it to molten rock. Soon it would be indistinguishable from the magma core a hundred kilometers beneath it.

"Jerome." Anita shook his gently. "There's something on the console screen."

Walden jerked his attention away from the hypnotic symmetry of the destruction below them. Warnings popped up on the screen and on the control board. More and more lights flashed amber and red.

"External temperature is rising. The planet's atmosphere is heating and expanding past us. We can't maintain orbit," came the frightening word from the navigation officer.

"Let's get out of here," Walden said.

"A moment. Wait a moment longer," said Nakamura. She watched as they swung around the planet. Only when they were hidden by Schwann's bulk did the woman give the command. "Now! Apply the engines *now*!"

Walden's finger stabbed down onto the proper button. The entire process could have been automated but men still distrusted computers—work done by hand carried more satisfaction, the psychologists said. Walden knew that adrenaline surged when he ignited the engines. He had *done* something.

"In the groove," came the navigation officer's appraisal. "Computer's got us riding in high line to perfection."

Walden leaned back, soaked in sweat. The time between shoving Captain Belford from the chair and this instant amounted to less than two minutes. It had stretched for an eternity.

"We had to leave when the planet shielded our rocket flare," said Nakamura. "The Frinn will think we were destroyed by their planetary barrage."

"What about the *Winston*?" asked Anita. "They would have seen it leaving."

"We must risk it. They have seeded the entire system with starlift detectors. We cannot leave before them—and we must be sure they are destroyed. The *Winston* will have its work ahead when we engage."

Walden turned back to the vidscreen. Schwann's destruction looked fake. He had seen better special effects in the hologs. Tiny parcels of the world arched into space, slowed, and tumbled lazily back down. All the while huge chunks of the surface erupted into space, new explosions peppered the surface.

"The CCD has dropped the magnification by five orders of magnitude," said Anita. "And the radiation counters are showing dangerous levels. We're going to be in real trouble soon."

"Radiation? With our shielding?" Walden hardly believed it. The *Hippocrates* was equipped to go through near-star proton storms unscathed. He worried the console controls and found the proper display. He went cold inside. It was worse than Anita made it out to be. They were nearing critical levels caused by Compton neutrons from the planetside explosions. Radioactives aboard ship might be in danger of exploding from the heavy X-ray bombardment.

"Everyone into hazard suits," he ordered. No one stirred until Nakamura reached past and touched a button marked COM-MAND. His voice echoed throughout the ship then and purple radiation danger lights began flashing ominously.

"The suits will do little against these levels," said Nakamura. "We will be safe if we continue along this vector."

The words were hardly out of her mouth when Walden saw the danger levels begin to fade. In three minutes they were back in the green and in ten the only radiation they detected came from the distant planet of Schwann.

"There's nothing left," he marveled. "The entire planet is gone."

"What now?" came Egad's voice. The dog jumped into the man's lap and curled up, head resting on Walden's forearm.

"I don't know. The Frinn's detectors are scattered throughout the system. If just one gets a reading on us, they can find Earth. Is there any way of destroying all their detectors?"

"None," came the com officer's appraisal. "They're too small and are passive electronics. They don't activate until we starlift. The lift field is so potent it can turn on the sensors from anywhere in the system."

"Is there any way we can send out a burst of radiation and fuse their circuits?"

"No," said Nakamura. "We have no means of generating such an intense X-ray burst. Even if we did, it would destroy us along with the detectors."

"Can't we get the Frinn ship and destroy it? Won't that be good enough?" asked another of the bridge officers.

"Think with your brains and not your butt," snapped the com officer. "The pigs can return at any time, send out an activating signal, and read our starlift vector. That might be in months or even years. Destroying the single ship in-system doesn't mean a damned thing.''

Walden sighed. The communications officer was right. The Delta Cygnus system had become a trap not only for the *Hippocrates* and the *Winston* but for all humanity. If they returned to any human-inhabited world they left a trail for a Frinn invasion fleet.

"Pig ship flare in sector nine," barked a sensors officer. Walden transferred the man's screen to the captain's console.

"They're blasting out of the asteroid belt," he said, checking the small parade of numbers across the bottom of the display. "They're leaving!"

"All detectors!" Nakamura flew into motion, fluttering from one console to the next. "Get the flight vector. Get the readings on the Pierce pinholes formed by their starlift engines. Full analysis! Do it now! We need a fix on their home world!"

"Got it!" cried the com officer. The navigation and sensors officers were only fractions of a second later with their recordings.

Walden watched as Nakamura put the data into the ship's computer. Within a minute the vector to the Frinn home world popped onto the console. They knew the distance and direction taken by the fleeing ship.

"They thought we were destroyed," mused Nakamura, "or did they? Their detectors remain to watch over the system. Does it matter to them if we know their destination? They want only to destroy Earth."

Bleakness assailed Walden. Everything Nakamura said was true. They were trapped. Returning to Earth started an interstellar war that meant only genocide. He hadn't believed it possible that an entire planet could be wrecked in the span of an hour. The Frinn's sublight particle bombardment had devastated Schwann and left it uninhabitable for eons.

He didn't want that to happen to Earth.

"What are we going to do?" he asked. "We're still in the middle of quite a dilemma."

Miko Nakamura stood to one side, eyes hooded and breathing deeply, regularly, almost in a trance as she thought. Walden wasn't sure he wanted to know the thoughts raging inside that devious mind. She had eliminated Doris Yerrow along with the mutinous executive officer—and had almost gotten rid of Major Zacharias, too.

Turned against the Frinn, she might prevail. But were a destroyer and a hospital ship enough of a fleet for her?

They had to be—and that worried Walden.

"We follow immediately. We find their home world. Only by doing so can we ever insure Earth's survival."

"How do you figure that?" demanded Anita. She brushed back her flame-red hair and almost angrily snorted. "We're not up to a battle with them. Look what they did to Schwann!"

"We must find their home world," insisted Nakamura. "We find their world, then return to Earth immediately. This gives each side the knowledge of the other's planet. We can bargain then. Now we can only die."

Walden considered this. Another point niggled at his mind. The Infinity Plague had destroyed the *Prolum*'s crew in short order. Did Nakamura believe he could discover the secret of the plague before they arrived at the Frinn's world? Would she use it on billions of sentient beings?

One look at her impassive face gave the answer. She would. Within her mind she carried the seeds of the greatest mass killer in history. Walden cursed himself for agreeing with her. Earth wasn't equipped to carry on a lengthy war. The Soviet-Latino Pact Countries and the North American Alliance spent all their time, money, and energy fighting each other. To battle an alien foe would require cooperation never even imagined.

Earth could only lose.

Unless the first retaliatory blow came from the *Hippocrates* using the Infinity Plague.

Walden frowned as he worried another thread of thought. Three ships had orbited Schwann for some time. One departed directly for . . . where? Those on-planet hadn't tracked it, or if they had they were far beyond revealing their data. The second ship had hidden in the asteroids. The third had been destroyed in orbit around Schwann.

Had all three become infected with the Infinity Plague? Walden had no way to know if the Sov-Lats had released it after the Frinn attack or before.

The Infinity Plague might already be winging its way toward a world peopled by billions and billions of sentient beings.

"Course locked on. Transmission to the *Winston* complete."

"What's going on?" Walden snapped back to what went on around him.

"We're going after them. That way it won't matter if they track us. They'll only get a recording of the vector to their own system. We dip in and get the hell out and have something to bargain with. That's the way Nakamura sees it."

"And?" pressed Walden. "What do you think?" He looked steadily at Anita Tarleton.

"I agree."

"Me, too. Kill the pigs," spoke up Egad.

Walden scratched the dog's head. The *Hippocrates* prepared to starlift for an alien world, possibly to eradicate all life on it. And he agreed with the others. They had to go.

Either the Frinn died for their unprovoked attack on Delta Cygnus 4 or Earth eventually perished.

Walden knew what side he was on.

"Someone is going to have to warn Zacharias and his EPCTs," he said.

"He's figured it out already," Nakamura assured him.

That worried Jerome Walden even more. He leaned back in the captain's chair and watched as the ships prepared to pursue. Whatever lay ahead, it wouldn't be dull.

The *Hippocrates* quivered as the starlift engines kicked in and hurled them toward an unknown sun.